DRIFT

M. K. HUTCHINS

TU BOOKS
an imprint of Lee & Low Books, Inc.
New York

For my brother, Matt

Copyright © 2014 by M. K. Hutchins
Jacket photograph © 2014 by Thinkstock—Turtle: George Bailey/Island: Soft_Light

TU BOOKS, an imprint of LEE & LOW BOOKS Inc.,
95 Madison Avenue, New York, NY 10016
leeandlow.com

Manufactured in the United States of America by Worzalla Publishing Company, May 2014

Book design by Sammy Yuen
Book production by The Kids at Our House
The text is set in Cochin

10 9 8 7 6 5 4 3 2 1
First Edition

This book has been manufactured using environmentally friendly materials: the paper is certified as responsibly sourced, the hardcover boards are made from recycled materials, and the inks are vegetable based.

Library of Congress Cataloging-in-Publication Data

Hutchins, M. K.
Drift / M.K. Hutchins. — First edition.
    pages cm
Summary: To raise his family out of poverty, seventeen-year-old Tenjat joins a dangerous defense against the naga monsters that gnaw at his drifting island's foundation.
ISBN 978-1-62014-145-8 (hardcover : alk. paper) — ISBN 978-1-62014-146-5 (e-book)
[1. Fantasy. 2. Monsters—Fiction.] I. Title.
PZ7.H96164Dr 2014
[Fic]—dc23
2014002568

CHAPTER
1

I REMEMBER PERFECTLY the last night I saw my father.

My family huddled on the shore, the sky a patchwork of clouds and stars above us. The surf and cool breeze muffled our whispers—all the better for us. We couldn't afford to be caught. I felt numb, shocked.

"I'll stay with Ven. They won't hurt Ven," Mother told Father. "You take Tenjat and Eflet and get on the raft."

Father gave her a crooked, sad smile. "You're trying to be brave, aren't you? Do you really think the Ita Handlers are kinder than the water monsters? The nagas, you might avoid. The Handlers, though . . ."

Mother pursed her lips. "We could wait—build a second raft."

"There's no time. The Handlers will come soon, and you'll miss the current if you wait any longer."

I glanced at my sister, Eflet, and then my little brother, Ven. His six-year-old hands clutched Eflet's hem, his face buried in the fabric. She stroked his messy black hair and whispered comforting things I couldn't hear. I didn't know what to say or do—we'd never been fugitives before.

"I could stay. Take care of Ven," I offered, my voice cracking. Then, at least, my parents would be together.

Father shook his head. "No. The Handlers will probably leave Ven alone because he's so young, but not you, Tenjat. I'll stay. If they try to take Ven, I'll throw a few punches and he can run to Old Man Tul's. He'll hide Ven."

Tul wouldn't sell Ven into slavery, either. I bit my lip. What would the Handlers do to Father, if they caught him?

The wind tugged Mother's long dark hair away from her face, streaming it behind her. "You can't hide from them forever."

Father laughed—the saddest sound I'd ever heard—and kissed her on the forehead. "I know. But I couldn't live with myself if I got on that raft and left you here."

Mother nodded. I could barely see her face in the bluish-black starlight, but I knew the expression she'd be making: lips pursed, eyes down, muscles tight around her chin.

Ven looked up at Eflet. "You're really going?"

She knelt next to him. "I'm afraid so. The Handlers are mad at us."

"Why?" he demanded, his chubby lower lip sticking out in a pout.

"It's better if we don't tell you."

He cried in earnest.

"Shh, shh," Eflet cooed, holding him close.

I stood and watched, arms limp, wishing I knew what to do.

Mother pulled Ven away from Eflet. "Kiss your mama good-bye?"

He gave her a wet six-year-old kiss with a loud smack. Then he bawled. Mother scooped him up and rubbed his back. "Hush, hush, you'll be all right, my little one."

Would any of us be all right?

Ven kept crying. While Mother comforted him, Eflet and I said good-bye to Father. Eflet just hugged him, silent. She was one of those people that didn't often need words. Then she backed away.

My chest felt too tight to speak. With the faint starlight casting him in blue and black, my father already looked like a stranger. I wanted to see his warm brown face, exactly the same shade as mine, under the noon sun as we planted cassava together. I wanted to hear his laugh ringing out over green fields. "I'll . . . miss you."

Father pulled me into a rib-crushing hug. "Take care of your mother and sister for me, all right?"

"I will."

He held me a step away from him, both hands on my shoulders, and slowly shook his head. "My son, all grown up. I'll come find you sometime, all right?"

"All right."

We shared a smile, both knowing it was a lie. Father couldn't follow us. We were setting out at random with only the hope of finding another island. We wouldn't see him or Ven again, even if we survived this risky journey.

Eflet and I collected our wet, tear-sticky kisses from Ven.

"Time to go." Mother ushered us onto the raft, a small crisscross of split logs. It barely floated once Mother, Eflet, and I were aboard with our pair of crude paddles and bag of provisions. There was no room for Father, or even little Ven.

Mother knelt on the edge, facing Father as he slowly shoved the raft off the shore. The tip pulled free of the sand with a soft grating and the back splashed against the outgoing waves. Our island, Ita, rested on the back of a massive Turtle. The creature was partway through a long, even backward stroke — the current it created would carry us smoothly out to sea.

Father continued pushing until he stood up to his waist in water. He stopped, but didn't let go of the raft.

"You should get out of the water," Mother said, hand

lovingly touching the side of his face. "The nagas could come."

"There aren't any nearby right now," Eflet whispered. I peered at her. Could she see through the water in the dark? Her eyes were sharper than mine—I saw only black waves that could hide any number of sharp teeth and fangs.

"Thank you, Eflet," Mother said softly, as if she didn't want me to hear. Then she turned back to Father.

"I'll miss you," she said. Father didn't smile this time. Mother bent over to kiss him; he stretched on tiptoe to meet her. I turned away. I didn't want to invade their last moment together.

I didn't look back until the waves taking us out to sea smoothed to a gentle rock. Father stood on the shore, holding Ven, silently waving. I wanted to shout, to say something, *anything*, but swallowed against the lump in my throat. The Handlers could be anywhere in the dark hills above the shore, and nagas anywhere in the water below. We mustn't be heard.

"Why do we have to go like this?" I asked Mother quietly. "Why are the Handlers mad at us?"

I'd always admired Handlers. They ruled the island and fought the nagas, protecting everyone. I couldn't imagine why they'd want to hurt us.

Mother dipped her paddle into the water and pulled it through the rippling blackness. "We committed high treason, dearest."

"High treason? What did we do?" We were only tenant farmers.

Mother glanced at Eflet, whose dark hair draped around her like a curtain. "It's safer if you don't know for now. Help me paddle, Tenjat."

I bit back my protests. A loud argument would bring the nagas. Stroke after paddle stroke, my family drifted apart.

An hour later we were far enough away that the shore looked as round as the Turtle's back that supported it. The details of the jungles and hills blurred together, giving the impression of a gently domed shell. From the center of the island, the massive Tree rose. I couldn't make out the top of it—its branches pierced the Heavens and its roots penetrated the foundations of Hell. Between the shore and our raft, uncounted waves glittered like liquid obsidian in the starlight. My heart pounded. The nagas lived under those waves. People weren't meant to drift on rafts. That's why the gods created Turtles long ago. They kept us safe, elevated from the shimmering surface of Hell and the monsters beneath. I hoped the nagas wouldn't find us.

I can't say the exact moment I last saw my father. I glanced over my shoulder as I paddled, squinting against the cold blues and blacks that outlined the Turtle and her massive Tree. I told myself I could still see him there, even when Island Ita was nothing more than the line of its Tree blocking starlight.

Five years had passed since that night, but the coolness of dawn always made me relive it. My tattered rush mat was almost as dank and cold as the earthen floor, but I didn't want to get up.

I'll come find you sometime, all right?

I breathed out slowly. It was probably best Father couldn't keep his promise. Mother never made it to the shore of our new island. The secret of our treason died with her. Father could dream we were all safe, and Eflet and I could dream the same about him and Ven. I wondered if they'd recognize me — I was seventeen now, taller and thinner, though I could never decide if I'd grown to look like my father or not.

"Do you want breakfast?" Eflet asked. Grudgingly, I rubbed my eyes and sat up. Outside, the world was dark, but inside our hut, the coals glowed orange. Eflet flipped the sizzling cassava cakes on the clay griddle with her fingers.

"Thanks."

"Sleepyhead," she said with a fond shake of her head. Eflet slapped a piece of dough back and forth in her hands, shaping another cake.

"I had a hard day of planting yesterday. I've every right to be tired."

She raised an eyebrow, giving me a look she must have learned from Mother. I sighed. "I wasn't trying to say you don't work hard, but at least it's in the shade, and . . ."

The eyebrow arched higher.

I sighed. "You're right, I'm sorry. I'm just lazy."

She handed me the pair of starchy cassava cakes hot from the griddle with a smug sparkle in her eyes. "Better eat up, Tenjat. You've got another hard day of planting."

We ate quietly. Eflet never talked much, and for me mornings were well suited to listening: the crackling of the fire, the wind in the thatch, birds rustling outside.

I thanked Eflet for breakfast, and she smiled in return. I went to work.

The only land I'd been able to claim on this little island— Island Gunaji—was a swath on the shore, between the forks of a muddy river. With the glittering surface of Hell not a dozen paces from the edge of my fields, nagas occasionally swam upstream here. I crossed the split-log bridge carefully.

I planted a cassava stem, patting the soil around the foot-long cutting. The ground smelled musty, but I'd heard farmers complain it was like this all over the island. I planted the next stem two paces down, leaving room in between for squash. Sprawling squash leaves kept moisture in the soil and discouraged weeds. Later I'd plant beans to trail up

M. K. HUTCHINS

the cassava stems. Beans helped offset poor soil, but with how weak our half-starved Turtle was, I doubted I'd get a good harvest. I only needed a half-decent one, though. I planted another cutting, careful to put the root side in the soil. Cassava doesn't grow if you plant it upside down.

By midday, pale, sun-cracked mud caked my feet and hands. My loose tunic and knee-length trousers reeked of sweat and subpar soil. But a stubble of knobby stems covered a full fourth of my land.

When I'd claimed this land, it was unusable. I'd cleared the rocks, built the soil up, and dug the drainage channels. I gathered a basket of turkey droppings from the forest twice a year and cut it into the soil to ensure a decent crop even when the Turtle was hungry and the harvest promised to be sparse, like this season.

That's what brought the trouble, I think. I made it too well.

When I turned to plant the next row, I spotted Eflet, standing just upriver of the fork — boxed in against the bank by three men. Eflet wasn't even supposed to fetch water alone. Water was dangerous, but doubly so for her.

I left my bag of stems and strode back across the field. Eflet, chin up, tried to calmly walk past the men. They chortled and shoved her toward the river.

I broke into a jog. "Hello!" I called. "Hello! Who's there?"

The tallest turned. It was Rud, Shant's son. "Just who I wanted to see!" He grinned, displaying a hole where his top two teeth should have been. He'd lost those last summer in a fight with a man from across the island. "We were having a nice chat with your sister."

While Rud was distracted Eflet tried to duck out, but one of the men — Rud's cousin, Dorul — pushed her back. The last culprit was Rud's brother, Ajan. He was younger than me, but thanks to a stocky build, still bigger.

I crossed the split-log bridge. "How about you come inside, away from the river, and we can talk."

Rud chortled. "But it's so nice out!"

"What do you want, Rud?" I stopped two strides away from him.

"You sound annoyed!" A stupid, mocking grin covered his face. "I'm hurt!"

"What do you want?" There were a lot of other things I wanted to say, but I didn't quite dare.

"We've already planted our fields, so we'll help with yours. We're being neighborly."

"Neighborly!" Ajan chuckled to himself.

Idiots, all of them.

"I'm afraid I don't need your help." Or the extortion of cassava certain to come with it.

"Oh, that's too bad," Rud replied. He took a step backward,

bumping into Eflet and nearly knocking her into the river. "With all four of us, we'd do a quick job of planting. Then when harvest comes in, we'll help with that, too."

I gritted my teeth. I wanted to tell them that just because they were too lazy to keep a field producing during a bad season didn't mean they could have mine, but I bit my tongue. Taunting them would only provoke them further. "I don't have enough work for any of you."

"But you've harvested extra for two years now," Rud said. "You can spare some."

Some would turn to *all*, as soon as harvest hit.

"I'm saving it," I said flatly.

"We'd be good help. We'd make sure no accidents happen."

Ajan laughed again, and Rud shot him a sharp glare. He shut up. Rud turned back to me, all gap-toothed smiles. "You should consider it."

He edged backward again. Eflet's heel scraped the edge of the bank, sending pebbles skittering into the water. Downriver, I caught a flash of silver. Naga. Rud and his cronies hadn't seen. It moved fast — toward us.

I did the only thing I could think of.

Rud still grinned. "We really are — "

My fist connected with his jaw. Then I sprang back. Rud wiped his mouth, eyes widening with shock. "You ungrateful little . . ."

Ajan and Dorul eagerly watched Rud stomp toward me, fists clenched. Eflet used my distraction to quietly, quickly slip away.

Rud's knee cut up into my gut. Then he slammed me backward with a punch to the nose. I tried to block and I tried to hit him, but three heartbeats and several kicks to the ribs later, I lay flat on my back, blood trickling from both nostrils. I turned my head and saw Eflet, standing safely behind some thin trees. I didn't bother getting up.

"We'll be back tomorrow." Rud spat on my face. "Filthy hub."

They headed upstream to their fields. The silver fin flicked, leaving a splash and an eddy, then the water smoothed. No prey for that naga today, thankfully. I closed my eyes and breathed slowly against the throbbing pain in my ribs.

Eflet's feet hardly made a noise in the grass. She knelt next to me. "Is anything broken?"

"Don't think so."

"I'm sorry. You didn't have to do that."

"No?" I squinted up at her with one eye open. "There was a naga in the water. If they'd pushed you in—"

"Rud would have seen the naga before then. He's a bully, not a murderer."

"Really? Because he hadn't noticed and I'm sure he was ready to shove you."

Eflet pursed her lips, eyes downturned.

"You're not supposed to come out by the river," I said sternly.

"Let's get you cleaned up, all right?"

Eflet filled her jug with clean water from the river. I rolled onto my good side, sat slowly, and stood. Eflet waited for me, then we walked back to our house together. I leaned against a boulder while she fetched a rag.

"The river's not safe."

She dipped the rag into the jug, then wrung it out. "When I went to fetch water, there weren't any nagas."

"That doesn't mean," I said as Eflet cleaned my mouth, "—that doesn't mean one won't swim up, or that there's not one hiding on the river bottom. They do that sometimes."

"There *wasn't*." She rubbed the last of the blood off a little too vigorously and I winced.

"You can't know that."

She turned her back to me, picked up the jug, and watered her garden of chilies and herbs that grew on this side of the hut.

"They always show up when you're near," I continued.

Eflet kept watering, her loam-brown eyes tracing the glittering light of the falling water.

"I think they follow you."

"You're paranoid. Overprotective."

I picked up the cloth and used it to wipe the rest of my grimy face, hands, and arms. It was mercifully cold. "Nagas aren't bored bullies and they aren't going to just push you around. They'll devour you!"

She screwed her eyes shut, breathing slowly through her nose. Her knuckles tightened on the rim of her jug.

I set the cloth down. "I know you haven't forgotten what happened to Mother. Do you think I want to see that again?"

"I was perfectly safe until those boys showed up!"

"And they'll show up again!"

She glared at me.

"Promise me," I said, "that you won't go to the river alone."

She held firm.

"Promise me! Eflet, you're the only family I have left and whether you like it or not, that means I'm taking care of you." I'd promised Father and I'd promised Mother. It was the last thing Mother asked of me, right before calmly diving into waves glittering with naga scales. I still couldn't get the sounds of her death out of my head.

"I've already told you I'll be safe."

"And not go near the water," I prompted. Eflet looked away. "Being safe *means* not going there! The nagas follow you, I swear they do."

She returned to watering the last of her chili plants.

"The river might look clear, but—"

M. K. HUTCHINS

"I was safe," she stated firmly.

I snorted, and instantly regretted it. Pain shot through my tender nose.

Eflet turned her back to me and disappeared into our hut, leaving the jug outside. I pushed myself to my feet and followed.

Our home was small—little more than lashed-together sapling sticks on a hard-packed earthen mound with a palm-thatched roof. The hearth, Eflet's backstrap loom, our basket of cotton, and the tight-lidded pots for dried beans and cassava flour barely fit inside. But it still felt empty and hollow compared to the hut I lived in until I was twelve. Two people don't make as much laughter as five.

Eflet had brought some of this harvest's cassava from the pit outside. She snatched up a chunk of pink chert and started skinning a root.

"Rud said they'd be back. Will you at least promise to stay away from the water tomorrow?" I asked.

Scrape, scrape. The brown wisps of cassava skin littered the ground by her feet.

Was I being too harsh? Not harsh enough? I didn't know how to do this. "Eflet . . ."

She was intent on her work, as if her silence could mandate mine. She wouldn't look at me.

I trudged back to the field, picked up my bag, and

stabbed cassava stems into the ground with unnecessary force, despite my tender ribs. Even if Eflet couldn't see it, I could. Nagas flocked to her like children to sweets, almost like they wanted more of Mother's blood.

I wiped the sweat out of my eyes. It was a stupid thought. The nagas didn't stalk me, after all.

CHAPTER

2

I ONLY STOPPED planting when night leeched the last bit of sunlight from the high eastern sky. The stars appeared one by one: bits of white twisted through dark blue. I walked toward my hut. I couldn't see the giant Tree at the center of our Turtle-island, only the solid darkness where stars should have been.

When I was little, when we still lived on the massive Island Ita, Father would set me on his lap and point up at the Tree.

"There," he'd say, "live the Handlers. They keep us safe from the nagas. I was one of them once."

I'd rub his crippled hand with my tiny, whole ones.

"They don't go hungry there. They spend their days doing

more than farming. I want that for you, Tenjat. I want better for you than this."

Even that young, I ached to be a Handler. A warrior, a ruler, a hero. Now, if I could make it through the tests and training, Eflet and I wouldn't live poor for the rest of our lives. But Eflet needed cassava to live off while I trained. I couldn't abandon her to scrape by, alone—planting and processing the cassava, tending the garden, doing all the spinning. It was too much for one person.

I headed home, crossing the bridge slowly, thinking. Somehow, I had to deal with Rud.

A gray haze of cooking smoke lingered above our hut. Eflet had left the fire burning against the chill of evening. I pulled aside the lashed-together sticks that served as our door and ducked inside. Eflet lay curled near the hearth. She shivered in her sleep and tucked up her feet—soot-blackened soles against her thatch-brown legs.

We'd both grown in the last year. Her dress was sewn in the usual way with loose short sleeves, but the ragged garment only reached her knees now, instead of her midcalves. I'd grown enough cotton last season for a new dress, but it'd be months before she finished spinning enough thread to start weaving.

The firelight cast gold and purple highlights through her dark hair, especially where it spilled over her musty rush mat onto the earthen floor. Eflet deserved better than dirty, bare feet and a dress of rags.

I laid our only blanket over her, then looked to the clay pot near the fire, which held a sluggish, lukewarm stew of cassava and beans. I ate it all.

Then I checked our storage jars. They were half my height, round and sturdy, but barely half-full of flour and dried beans. It was a good store, but not enough.

I slumped to the ground, curled up on my side, and closed my eyes. It usually took three years of training to become a Handler. If I left now, Eflet was only guaranteed food for two.

The coldness of the ground seeped into my battered side, stiffening it. With my injuries, I actually felt the pitch of the Turtle's strokes. Weakened Turtles—Turtles that need to feed—swim less smoothly. I groaned and rolled over.

Sleep wouldn't come. One more decent harvest and I could make a better life for us—if Rud would leave us alone. I couldn't ask the Handlers to intervene because Rud hadn't done anything yet. My stomach knotted. By the time he had, would it be my sister or the field that paid?

I only had one idea that might permanently scare away Rud and his kin.

Any plan that required my sister's blood was a bad idea.

~ ~ ~

When I woke, Eflet was patting out cassava cakes.

"You came home late." She dropped the first cake onto the sizzling clay griddle.

I rubbed my aching side. "I was thinking."

"About?"

"How to keep Rud away. He's not leaving on his own." Rud enjoyed tormenting us, but his family also didn't maintain their fields. They'd have to ration their stores to make it to harvest—if they managed a harvest at all in this poor season.

Eflet carefully avoided my eyes. "We can't go to the Handlers yet, we can't force Rud and the others away ourselves, and that only leaves one thing, Tenjat."

"I am *not* asking Jesso for help."

She shook her head, her long braid swinging behind her. "I like Jesso."

"I don't." When we first reached Island Gunaji, I convinced the Handlers and Tenders that we were refugees from one of Island Ita's recent conquests, braving the ocean rather than face slavery on Ita. They allowed us to stay, but fearing we might be Ita spies, they required us to stay with a local. We lived with Jesso for three years, until the Handlers' suspicions finally evaporated. Time living in his house had not made me any fonder of him and his backward ways.

Eflet patted out another cake. "You're thick, Tenjat."

"We've been self-sufficient for two years. Do you think I want to give that up?"

"When you pass the Handlers' test," — Eflet always said it that way: *when*, never *if* — "do you think I'll stay here, alone? I'll go back there."

"But you won't have to depend on him."

"Why take the test at all?" she pleaded. "Stay. Farm. Get married one day, Tenae. Would that be so horrible?" *Tenae* — that's what she'd called me when we were little, before she could pronounce Tenjat.

Using the baby-name felt like a slap. Become a husband, a hub? Only the poor who couldn't care for themselves in their old age married and had children. I'd promised Father I'd take care of us. If he and Ven were alive, they'd be living in poverty. But Eflet and I didn't have to, not when I could provide for both of us as a Handler.

"I'm no hub. And our island needs Handlers," I said. Other farmers always complained that the island didn't have as many Handlers now as it did even ten years ago. High Handler Banoh might have legendary skills, but even he couldn't protect the Turtle by himself.

"More than farmers? Whose taxes do you think keep the Handlers fed?" Eflet slapped another cake on the griddle.

Now she was just being obstinate. "Have you smelled the soil? Island Gunaji is weakening, with nagas gnawing on our roots and the Turtle half-starved. Without Handlers and Tenders to fight the nagas and see us safely to coral reefs for the Turtle to feed, the soil couldn't grow anything. Farmers need *them* to survive."

"I don't understand why you're so set on joining them. Handlers drove us from Island Ita, remember?" Eflet's words were heavy with Mother's death and the likely fates of Ven and Father. She expertly flipped the cakes with her fingers.

I sighed. "This is about Ceibak again, isn't it? That island's a fable, Eflet. A fable to make hubs feel better."

Eflet's face hardened. She muttered something. The only words I caught were "stupid" and "Tenjat." But she still tossed me a few cakes when they finished.

I popped one in my mouth, working the chewy, starchy bread between my teeth before swallowing. "I came up with an idea to keep Rud away. One that doesn't involve Jesso."

Her whole body seemed to sigh, shoulders, eyes, and mouth, without making a sound. I explained while we ate.

"Do you think it will work?" I asked.

She frowned. "I don't like drawing attention to myself."

"That's a yes, then." I fought the grin pulling on my mouth. "Yesterday you said nagas don't follow you."

Eflet shrugged. Her voice was tight—her lying voice. "Maybe it won't work."

So she had noticed the way they trailed her. I swallowed

the part of me that wanted to berate her for yesterday. "Rud won't know it was you. He'll decide this land's infested and not worth his efforts."

"I hope you're right."

I handed Eflet a potsherd—a remnant of a former water jug. It had a good cupped shape to it.

Eflet picked up a piece of sharp chert and pressed it to her thumb. I turned my head. The stone whispered against her flesh and Eflet stifled a grunt. When I looked, bright blood had pooled in the shard. Eflet wrapped her thumb in the dirty sash of her dress.

I winced. "Thank you. Are you all right?"

"Of course." She blinked at me, as if it were a stupid question, but her arm, from thumb to shoulder, tensed with pain.

I carefully took the shard from her. "You'll stay inside today, away from the river?"

For once, she agreed. "I have plenty of peeling to do."

She stared at the shard with pursed lips and a line between her brows. "Be careful, Tenjat."

"I will." I ruffled her hair on my way out. She glared at me—she hated it when I did that—but I smiled back. "Thanks, Eflet."

She snorted and we both went to work.

～ ～ ～

I kept a close eye on the riverbank as I planted. Sure enough, around midday, three figures walked through the stand of stunted trees. I left my bag of cassava stems, crossed the bridge, and jogged upriver with the half-dried bloody potsherd cupped in one hand.

I reached the bank before Rud and his two companions were out of the wispy trees. Checking for nagas first, I carefully bent over and wedged the shard between two rocks under the surface of the water. Blood attracted nagas. If any showed up, Rud would leave. If he came tomorrow, I'd have another shard waiting—for as many days as it took Rud to decide my land was too dangerous to farm.

Rud, his brother, and his cousin had reached me when I saw a silvery flash downstream. I couldn't help but smile. Eflet's blood was working.

"How kind of you to come talk to us," Rud folded his arms. "Decided to take us up on our offer?"

"I came to tell you to go away."

"Yeah, I can tell your mind's been muddled by Jesso." Rud oozed confidence and condescension. "How many years did you live with that hub? I guess a day would be enough to ruin you."

I hated that even lazy thugs like these could insult me so easily—I couldn't deny a long association with Jesso, the island's most notorious hub.

M. K. HUTCHINS

Rud glanced back at his cousin and brother, with that stupid grin plastered on his face. Then his little brother, Ajan, pointed downriver, eyes wide.

"R-Rud?"

They followed the line of his finger, and Rud swore—the rapid, colorful swearing of someone who'd heard a lot of it in his life.

I glanced downriver again. The nearest fork looked like thick, roiling coils of silver. Among the snakelike bodies, I glimpsed a few of their misshapen, humanesque heads and clawed forearms. I stumbled away from the bank and fell on my backside. I couldn't count them. I couldn't tell where the bodies started and ended.

Rud and his relatives fled. I picked myself up off the ground and sprinted home.

"Eflet?" I panted, one hand clutching the door frame.

She blinked up at me from the grinding stone.

"You are *not* going near the water again, understand?"

"You lied to a Handler?" I asked, shocked. It was evening; I was already exhausted from another long day of planting.

Eflet remained as serene as always. She handed me my clay bowl filled with soup hot from the hearth. "He asked if there was a problem. One of the Tree's Tenders felt a gathering of nagas and he came to check on it. I told him we didn't have a problem. The nagas were gone by then, so it wasn't lying."

"There were *dozens* of them! That's not a problem?"

"They're just sensitive to blood, Tenjat." Some dusty evening light streaked through our patchy walls, and warm hearthlight illuminated Eflet's face. She didn't flinch as she lied to me, too. Nagas weren't that sensitive.

I shook my head. "Three years ago, remember when Emju went naga fishing on a bet?" Emju was one of Jesso's children, and not the brightest one at that.

Eflet nodded as she ladled herself a bowl of squash and bean soup from the pot.

"He smeared a cassava cake with his blood and used that to bait his fishing hook. Only four nagas came."

She swallowed her soup. "They ate the bait, so the blood was gone. That's why more didn't come."

I waved a finger at her. "The nagas bit through his line again and again, so he kept baiting hooks—ten, I think, before he managed to drag one to shore."

"Idiot," Eflet muttered.

The point of naga fishing was to haul a naga far enough up the beach that it couldn't do much more than flail about and try to crawl with its forelimbs. Then you could harpoon it with a sharpened planting stick. It was the kind of stupid stunt that only a would-be hub trying to impress a girl would try.

"After he was bit, there was lots blood," I said. "Twenty times what your potsherd held."

"On the beach, not in the water."

"There was plenty in the water." Emju had stood too close to the shore. A clever naga had jerked his line—and him—forward, then bit off most of his calf. "And the tide was incoming. Emju said he never counted more than six nagas."

"I think that demonstrates his prowess at counting more than anything else. Or he didn't stay long enough to watch them gather."

I stirred the clay soup pot with my spoon, then refilled my bowl. "Emju couldn't walk. His friend pulled him up the beach, then fetched Jesso. But Jesso's place is nowhere near the shore. That took half the night."

She pursed her lips, frustrated. "Then most of the nagas were on the other side of the Turtle that night, and there just happened to be a lot around today."

"'Just *happened*?'" I raised an eyebrow. "Do you think I'm as dumb as Emju?"

"You're paranoid."

"I haven't resorted to name-calling yet. I think that means I'm winning this argument."

Eflet didn't have a retort for that. I slurped my soup— pretty good tonight with plenty of squash and diced chili peppers. "Even if Shant's boys aren't around, it's not safe for you to go near the water, especially not alone. I don't know how you could say otherwise after what happened today."

"Today was different. You put blood in the water." Eflet's hands clenched around her spoon. "Fetching water is perfectly safe."

"Safe?" I spluttered my soup. "Even if the nagas didn't love you, *safe* and *water* don't mix. Sometimes I wonder if that was our treason—that at least you, maybe Mother, too, attracted nagas."

"Seeing as I *don't* attract nagas, that couldn't be it. We'll never know why we had to leave Island Ita. There's no point dwelling on it."

How easily Eflet brushed the past aside. "You're not blind. Surely you've noticed the nagas' strange behavior."

Eflet turned her back to me, then settled herself for sleep.

I sighed and likewise curled up on my rush mat, my insides leaden despite the hot soup. I didn't spare Rud more than a passing thought—surely he'd leave us alone now. I rubbed the tight pain between my eyes, trying to figure out how to convince Eflet to do something she didn't want to. Jesso used to say the answer was easy: you didn't. Not helpful advice. How could I leave my little sister for three years if she stubbornly insisted on being as reckless as Emju?

I should have worried about Rud. I thought the splashes I heard that night were parts of my dreams—dreams filled

M. K. HUTCHINS

with rivers of nagas. I thought the creaks and rustlings were the wild imaginings of my drowsy mind, or the ocean wind playing with our stick-and-thatch hut.

The bright light of dawn showed me otherwise.

CHAPTER
3

SOMEONE HAD LODGED several stout green poles across the right fork of the river. Against the poles rested boulders—I could see the lines of ripped-up grass where they were rolled. Lesser rocks crammed the gaps. Half the river still squeezed through this crude dam and continued on its merry way, meandering over a pebbly beach to the ocean— the surface of Hell.

The rest of the water, unable to breach the far bank, washed back upriver, across my land. I sank to my knees. My field was nothing more than a low, muddy flat, crisscrossed with hundreds of sparkling rivulets, littered with upturned cassava stems. The morning sun had only just appeared, high in the western sky, illuminating every detail.

I stared, numb. I don't know for how long. I didn't hear Eflet walk up behind me, but I felt her hand on my shoulder and the thick silence that accompanied it. I knew what she was thinking: we'd have to go to Jesso now. But she was kind enough not to say it.

I walked to the dam. Rud must have fetched the Garums, their cousins from farther inland, then started work with the whole family not long after I left my fields, to finish this in one night. I leaned over the water and tried to yank one of the two dozen poles out. They wouldn't budge, not with the boulders wedged against them, and I doubted even ten men could pry those rocks out of the muddy river bottom.

I leaned a little farther and my foot slipped on the dewy bank, tipping me forward.

"Tenjat!" Eflet ran toward me.

I pushed hard against the pole and fell backward onto the bank.

"Don't you come near the water!" I shouted, glaring at her. "Understand?"

She stopped dead, lower lip trembling. I never yelled. Eflet opened her mouth as if to say something, stopped, then whipped around and ran into the hut.

I sat up and pressed the heels of my hands into my eyes. How could I protect her if she didn't listen to me? I just wanted to keep us both safe and fed. Not that I could do the latter with ruined land.

I looked for any evidence that I could bring to the Handlers to hold Shant's family responsible for this—a button, a bit of cloth, a distinctive trail of footprints leading to their homes—and found nothing.

After finding a stick sturdy enough to serve as a lever, I wasted half the morning trying to break the dam down. I knocked free some of the smaller rocks, but that didn't change much. Water still trickled over my field. I had to stop when I skinned my knee against a boulder, sending a few drops of blood into the water. Time would eventually destroy this makeshift dam, but human hands couldn't. That meant no harvest this season or the next. Not from this field. For the rest of the morning and into the afternoon, I wandered down the shore looking for an unoccupied plot of land I could wrestle a crop from with my remaining stems. Some areas might eventually give a harvest, but I couldn't get anything ready fast enough to take advantage of the rainy season. I laughed bitterly at my optimism. If there was prime land waiting to be had, why would Rud want mine?

I collapsed against a thin tree and stared over the sparkling ocean waves: the surface of Hell, a pretty facade to hide nagas. Father once told me that stranger creatures dwelled deeper in the water. Eflet and I lived so close to them.

M. K. HUTCHINS

If I'd been able to get us a field a little farther from Hell, closer to the Heavens, near the Tree where the soil was best, perhaps I could have done better for us. As it was, the two years' worth of flour I'd saved for Eflet might not keep both of us fed until I managed another harvest. Even if we survived, I'd be too old to take the Handler tests by the time I'd saved enough cassava to support Eflet for three years.

Jesso was my only choice. Jesso, or live poor on the shores of Hell for the rest of our lives.

I stood and straightened my muddied tunic, my pride hurting more than any of the dull, aching bruises Rud gave me two days ago.

After Father crippled his hand and couldn't be a Handler anymore, he married and had me. I didn't blame him for that. Farmers needed children to support them when age clouded their eyes and hollowed their arms. On massive Island Ita, my birth hadn't hurt anyone. One child wasn't much extra weight on that Turtle.

But my new home, Island Gunaji, wasn't a tenth of Ita's size. The Handlers and Tenders relied on our small island's speed to avoid would-be conquerors. The poor reluctantly had a few kids — maybe three or four — to ensure there'd be strong, young people to care for them when they couldn't farm. It was shameful, but understandable. No one wants to starve, even if more children weakened and endangered the island.

Jesso knew no shame. He had fourteen children and the gall to be proud of it. The whole island would be greener and better-fed without men like him unnecessarily burdening the Turtle. Worse, he'd always treated me like one of his own. Even scum like Rud could sneer and look down on me for that.

His first wife died after birthing their eighth child. Everyone told him it was punishments from the gods for slowing the Turtle with enough children for two men. That didn't stop him. He remarried, to a girl who was nearly as young as Eflet, and pressed onward. Jesso never tried to become an artisan or a Handler. He just bred.

Unfortunately, that meant he was the only farmer I knew with any kind of wealth. Fourteen children can plant a lot of cassava. No one else could feed Eflet while I was gone, even if they'd be willing to help out someone so closely associated with Jesso.

I trudged toward his farm. It lay inland, midway around the Turtle. My fields were nearer the tail, leaving a walk of several hours between us — a buffer I cherished.

I passed plenty of small farms, all half-planted. The musty smell of weak, dying soil lingered in the air. A handful of the farmers waved at me — those who didn't blame me for the years I'd spent at Jesso's.

Halfway to his house, rain drizzled down on me. As the mud sucked my toes, I realized I hadn't told Eflet where I was going. I sighed. She'd probably guess anyway, and assume I'd been too ashamed to tell her. Which was true.

Just past midday, I reached Jesso's fields, a patchwork of flat land broken up by swaths of ferns, saplings, and greater trees. The rain lightened to a pleasant misting, but despite the greenery, the faint, rotted smell of dying soil lingered here, too. The fields currently held only cassava cuttings. This land grew cotton even better than it did cassava, but cotton-planting wasn't until the end of the wet season.

One of Jesso's brood, six-year-old Fesi, spotted me and shouted, "Gyr! Gyr!"

The young man working alongside Fesi, my friend Gyr, jogged over with a grin. "Tenjat! Did someone die?"

I shrugged guiltily. "I know, I don't come by much. Any. Ever."

"The last time I saw you was, what? Four months ago when I came to see you?" Gyr asked.

"Probably. You could come more often, you know."

He wiped his muddy hands on his rain-damp tunic. "I take it that means you're not here to visit?"

I nodded glumly. "I need to talk to Jesso."

"So someone did die!" he joked, a bright smile in his eye.

"Not quite."

Little Fesi, not understanding, screwed up his face for crying. He tugged on Gyr's tunic. "Eflet? Eflet's dead?"

He looked so much like Ven had, that night we left him and Father behind, complete with messy black hair.

Gyr patted him on the head. "She's fine. Keep planting cassava. I'm taking Tenjat up to the house."

"Can I come?" he asked.

"No. Keep working."

Fesi kicked at a stick and tried to curse. He didn't do the latter very well.

Gyr and I meandered up toward the house, skirting the fields. "You still practicing pottery?" I asked.

"Hoping to be apprenticed soon."

"Good for you."

Gyr had already failed the Handler tests. The weaver, dye-maker, and beekeeper had all rejected him as possible apprentices. Pottery was one of the few crafts left for him to try. But that's why I liked Gyr. Unlike most of Jesso's offspring, he strove to abandon his father's legacy of breeding.

Gyr brought me to the front door. Their home had three rooms, each bigger than my house. Both side rooms were for sleeping, the middle chamber for cooking and other chores.

"You can wait inside," Gyr said, setting aside the door of lashed sticks. "I'll fetch Father."

I sat on a low stool near the door. A pair of Jesso's girls, not much younger than Eflet, spread thick cassava paste over baskets. After drying the paste in the shade all afternoon, they could grind it to flour. They giggled at me. I tried not to look at them.

Jesso's wife, Arja, sat in the corner spinning cotton, her sleeping baby in a sling around her shoulders.

"We haven't seen you in a long time," Arja said. She caught the spindle whorl before it reached the floor, reeled in the length of string, and with an expert flick of the wrist, sent it spinning again. Her thin fingers regulated the thread weight with practiced ease.

"I've been busy."

She gave me a smile that resembled a sneer. Then she ignored me and focused on spinning. Jesso arrived soon after.

"Tenjat, Tenjat!" He pulled me to my feet, and wrapped me in a tight hug against his barrel chest. "We've missed seeing you, boy!"

"Um, thanks," I fumbled. Jesso might be cheerful, but he was still a disgraceful hub.

"Did you bring Eflet to visit too?"

Eflet, admittedly, would have liked that. She liked Jesso, Jesso's house, and being with Jesso's daughters. That's the only reason I could go through with this.

"I didn't come for a visit."

"Oh?" His jovial mouth dropped a fraction.

Arja's ears pricked up and the girls stopped their work to listen. I frowned. "Perhaps we could discuss this privately?"

His forehead crinkled like old brown mahogany bark, but he nodded. "Come, then." He gestured with a broad, meaty hand. I followed.

Jesso led me to the forest. Here, two miles away from shore, the trees soared over our heads and shaded the ground. The shores only grew wispy, sapling-like trees. We twisted between trunks until we reached a clearing ringed with split-log benches. Jesso's family usually ate here. They didn't all fit comfortably inside their main room.

"Tell me what's wrong." His gray eyes filled with fatherly concern and compassion. I suppose when you have fourteen children, it's hard not to act fatherly toward anyone younger than yourself. I wish he wouldn't. I couldn't think of anyone I'd be more ashamed to call Father.

"My field is gone."

Jesso blinked at my bluntness. "I know the Turtle hasn't fed in some time, but—"

"It's not rotted. It's *gone.* Shant's boys tried to bully the land off me. Last night, they made a dam and flooded the whole thing."

"Are they idiots? Destroying a perfectly good field because they couldn't have it?"

I didn't bother to enlighten Jesso as to the finer details

M. K. HUTCHINS

of the situation. Rud didn't want my naga-cursed field; he wanted to stop the nagas from swimming upriver to his land.

"We should report this to the Tree," Jesso said.

"I have no proof. I didn't even see them do it."

His thick brows knitted together. "I'll go have a talk with Shant, then. Let him know what his foolish boys have done — and what he owes you."

"You think Rud, Ajan, and Dorul could have moved that many boulders by themselves in one night? Shant and the Garums were part of this." Shant had a decent mind for construction — I wouldn't be surprised if he'd suggested a dam in the first place.

Jesso slowly shook his head. "This is bad, Tenjat."

"I know." I wouldn't have come otherwise. "I'll give you the land and all my stored flour if you'll take care of Eflet. It'll be good land once it drains. You could sell it, or give it to one of your sons when he marries. I've already paid the Tree this season's taxes."

That was one of the good points of the field: in such a poor location, the Tree only required one sack of cassava flour.

"Tenjat, you don't have to buy my help. I'd take you both in, for any reason, or none at all." He looked wounded. "You know that, don't you?"

"Yes. I do."

Jesso genuinely liked having droves of children around — I

think that's why he took us in. He'd cried the day the Handlers permitted me to farm on my own, far away from him and his shamelessly huge family. But I hadn't cried. I wasn't his son. I wasn't *anything* like him, even if we'd had to live at his home for three years. If I could soften the shame of asking Jesso for help by phrasing it as a business agreement, I would.

"We've missed having you here, both of you," he said, his eyes sad above a melancholy smile. "I hurt for your land, Tenjat, but the girls will be so happy, and Gyr, too. He's been restless lately. Keeps sneaking off to practice pottery—I can't get him to settle down. Won't even talk about marriage."

Good for Gyr. I wanted to tell Jesso that if everyone single-handedly tried to sink the Turtle with a horde of children, we'd be supper for another island, but I swallowed the insult. "I'm not coming."

Jesso's smile dropped.

"I'm going to the Tree, for the Handlers' tests. If I pass, I'll be gone for three years. That's why I need you to watch Eflet. After that, she can live in luxury in the House of Kin."

"And if you fail?"

"I won't." I said it more sternly than I felt.

"Gyr tried the tests. He . . . doesn't recommend it," Jesso said softly, still fathering me. I bristled. I didn't need—or want—his concern.

"I remember." Gyr hadn't spoken for two days afterwards.

He still had the scars all over his back. "And I'm going."

"I wish you'd stay with us."

Jesso had his way of ensuring his future and looking after his family—and I had mine. "You'll take Eflet in, then, for the land and my cassava flour?"

"I'd do it for *free*." The corners of his eyes turned down in hurt.

Eflet would be well cared for, then. Jesso might be the filthiest hub on the island, but he'd cut off his left arm before he let one of his children go hungry.

I swallowed my revulsion to clasp the man's hand and seal our agreement. "Thank you. Eflet will be happy here."

Jesso's smile hung crooked on his face, a little sad, as if he doubted Eflet would be pleased with the arrangement. At least he didn't try to lecture me again. I wasn't his son.

Gyr sat on the edge of Jesso's house-platform waiting for me. He jogged over. "Now can you tell me what's going on?"

"Eflet's coming to live with you."

His eyebrows jumped, along with the corners of his mouth. "That's excellent! You're coming too, right?"

I shook my head.

"Oh."

I walked with him toward the edge of Jesso's land, the way I'd come in. "My field's destroyed, Gyr."

He gaped. "How?"

"Flood." I didn't have the energy to explain again.

"But . . . but . . . weren't you close? To having enough flour stored for Eflet so you could take the tests?"

I nodded. "I was. Now that my land's . . . well."

I stopped at the edge of Jesso's field. All rain had stopped; mist rolled off the ground in white curls.

"I'm sorry, Tenjat."

"Me too."

We stood there for a long moment, neither knowing what to say. I rubbed the back of my neck. "I offered Jesso my stored flour and my land to take care of Eflet."

"You didn't have to offer him anything."

"I know."

"You're going to go take the tests, then?" Gyr's voice tightened on the word *tests*, the old fear in his eyes. He scratched his back—and the scars under his tunic.

"Yes." I knew the tests were dangerous. Gyr didn't like to talk about it, but he told me once that the tests happen far below the surface of Hell, below where even nagas will go. It didn't matter—I'd try anything to give Eflet and myself a better life. I wasn't going to be a hub and she wasn't going to sleep on a musty mat forever.

"Good luck, then," Gyr said. "You'll be serving under High Handler Banoh soon. I'm sure of it. You'll have to tell me if those legendary arms of his really can throw a javelin a hundred feet underwater."

We used to spend hours repeating the stories about High Handler Banoh's victories for Island Gunaji—dodging invaders and fighting off nagas—but now didn't seem like the time. Again the conversation settled into silence.

I tried to think of something to cheer him, but I'd never been good at small talk. I could only come up with something depressing. At least it changed the topic. "Jesso sounded like he's trying to get you married."

"Trying, yes." Gyr shrugged. "I'm not that old yet. I know I'm *almost* hopeless, but not quite. The potter could still accept me as her apprentice."

"Who's Jesso got in mind?" The old man loved playing matchmaker.

Gyr wrinkled his nose. "That Leki girl three farms over."

"You should practice your pottery more." Leki was a flirt who'd never bothered to take the Tenders' test or apply for an apprenticeship.

He showed me his hands—clay stained the outline of his fingernails. "Trust me, I do. As much as I can, every day."

Gyr, unlike his father, was one of the best men I knew. "You'll make it. I'm sure."

He chuckled halfheartedly. "I hope so. There aren't any other apprentice openings right now. If I don't make it into the artisans' village with this . . ."

"You'll make it," I repeated, as firmly as I could. Gyr worked hard. He deserved the life of an artisan—not the shame of a poor farmer, forced to marry and have children that could support him when he aged.

"Thanks." Gyr shook his head. "It's too bad there aren't more openings, or you could be an apprentice with me."

"Yeah, it is." I said it, but I didn't mean it. Artisans made stuff; Handlers protected everyone. Artisans could help support their kin while in their prime, but they relied on their adopted apprentices for support when they aged. The Tree took care of all its Handlers and Tenders in old age, as well as one of their kin.

I tried to joke with Gyr a bit more before leaving, but the silences crept back in. I told him I'd come see him as soon as my training ended, but sadness lingered in his eyes. Three years was a long time.

I told myself as I said good-bye that soon Gyr wouldn't lack for sane company. The potter would surely adopt him. He worked too hard not to make apprentice. I smiled. When he was a potter and I was a Handler, Eflet and I would visit him in the artisans' village.

I walked toward the Tree to arrange my test.

CHAPTER
4

AT THE SHORE, trees are as small as saplings. By Jesso's, they're twice as thick as a man. As I walked to the center Tree, they turned to titans. I passed a lot of cleared area with typical farms: a hub and a son or two working the fields, a mother and a daughter peeling cassava or spinning cotton with drop spindles. The families were small, only able to farm a humble swath. This far inland, most of them didn't know me or my connection to Jesso, so most gave me a friendly nod or wave.

Everyone's soil smelled like decay—it would be a lean season all over the island. But their modest lands and houses filled me with respect. These people were nothing like Jesso, willing to put the pressure of fourteen additional lives on the

Turtle so he could have his bounteous fields.

The path hit a swath of forest and I started to sweat. The trees blocked any cool breezes and left the ground damp. I emerged on the other side, sticky and footsore, into a flock of turkeys. The males flashed their brilliant tail feathers at me and hopped up into the lower branches of the trees.

I stopped to see if they'd left any feathers on the ground, white and brown or green and glittering, either way, it would make a nice present for Eflet. I didn't find any, though. They hadn't been here long. I glanced up at the flock, perched on all different levels, and considered throwing a few stones. Not to kill one. The Handlers had decreed strict regulations on turkey hunting. But if I could spook them, scatter them, they might drop some feathers for Eflet.

Wesha, one of the prettiest young women I knew on the island, headed down the path in my direction. Not wise to throw rocks at turkeys with someone watching. I kept walking. She tripped just as we passed.

Skeins of red thread from the artisans' village tumbled from the basket she carried. Red—the color of shame. Maybe she'd weave it into a cloth for her brother to give to his intended wife. I didn't ask. Not polite. But I did pick up the skeins with her, trying to brush the mud off as I did.

Once everything was clean, she flashed me a dazzling smile— mahogany-red lips against limestone-white teeth. Wesha's deep brown eyes shone with gratitude. "Thank you so much, Tenjat. What are you doing out here? I thought you lived on the other side of the island now. Are you visiting Jesso?"

She asked that last question without disdain—she should be glaring scornfully at me for knowing Jesso so well.

"No. I'm headed to the Tree."

"Oh. What for?" She tilted her head quizzically and fidgeted with the end of her braid.

Was she flirting with me? Standing alone in the forest with a pretty girl, my cheeks burned with shame. If I were a hub, I'd flirt back and offer to walk her to her farm. I jerked my gaze down at the mud, gave a polite nod, and said good-bye. I hurried on my way. I wasn't a hub. I didn't let pretty girls distract me. I had a future in the Tree.

I climbed the ridge. Soon the ground leveled to a flat plain of grass stretching up to the base of the Tree—that, and the artisans. Their broad homes rested on whitewashed platforms, the bases painted to indicate their profession: potter, thread dyer, turkey trapper and butcher, flintknapper of fine knives, weaver of delicate things. There were less than a dozen homes in all, each beautiful.

Many of their goods were destined for the Tree or other artisans, but better-off farmers bought too. A special vase for a wife. Thread for weaving the sash of a married woman. Honey mead from the beekeeper for a feast.

The path took me between the houses. The stucco still smelled of fresh-ground limestone and newly-mixed paint. It was better than the breeze off the sea. Pride rested in every corner of their dwellings. Here lived those who had risen above their beginnings—the best the island had to offer. Here, no one needed to father living support for their old age. I prayed Gyr would be part of it soon.

I skirted the House of Kin, where a Handler or Tender could bring one—only one—relative to live. The Tree didn't want their trained Handlers and Tenders abandoning their work to take care of a relative with no other kin, a relative who needed them. Usually, these situations didn't arise for many years, perhaps when a sibling might die, leaving an aged parent no support.

The dozen or so who lived in the House of Kin weren't exactly artisans, but they lived in comfort as they prepared food and cleaned clothes for those who dwelt in the Tree. They, too, never needed to marry. It would be a good place for Eflet.

I reached the dull gray bark of the Tree and laid my hand against it. It was smoother than cassava roots. The lowest branches—thicker than any tree on the island—started so far above my head that the afternoon sun, high in the east, gave enough light for grass to flourish under the Tree. Its branches continued upward until my vision failed me. Even out to sea on the raft, I'd never been able to make out the top of a Tree. Soft, leaf-green light fell on my face.

I ached to live inside. I told myself not to worry about the tests.

I walked around the base of the Tree, to the front door. The door stood twice as tall as me, carved and inlaid with beaten copper, with copper hinges. That was nearly all the copper on the island—beautifully twisted, dancing in the greenish light. I knocked twice and waited.

A girl my own age answered. She didn't wear the belted, loose-sleeved dress of common women. A netted skirt fell to her calves, and a tight shirt gleaming like fish scales covered the rest of the essentials, leaving her midriff bare. Farmers' daughters wore their hair long, braided for working, let down for impressing people. Hers was cropped short. Practical. She was a Tender, one of the women who cared for the Tree. She didn't need hair to impress anyone.

"I'd like to take the Handlers' test," I croaked. Despite the humid afternoon air, my throat was dry as sand.

She closed her eyes briefly, running through a mental list, I suppose. "We can arrange a trial for tomorrow evening. Come here before sundown. Your name?"

"Tenjat."

"Are you on the tax record as a landowner?"

I nodded—I paid my taxes every year, pitiful as they were.

"If you succeed, who do you declare as heir to the land?"

"Jesso."

She arched a slim eyebrow with cool condescension—apparently Jesso's infamy reached inside the Tree. "Tomorrow evening, then."

She stepped back and closed the door.

My hands shook. I wiped them on my tunic and started home. I could be a Handler *tomorrow*. Just like Father once did, I could protect our island from invasions while the Tenders steered the Turtle toward coral reefs to feed on the jellyfish and octopus gathered there. I'd fight the nagas that gnawed on the Tree's roots—roots that Tenders used to draw up clean water and fertile silt to replace what the streams washed out to sea. Handlers and Tenders gave this island life.

Maybe the legendary High Handler Banoh would even teach me the secrets of javelin throwing.

Despite being filled with excited, nervous energy, it was still long dark by the time I arrived home. Inside, Eflet sat against the back wall, patiently spinning her drop spindle in the dying hearthlight. She didn't look up to greet me.

"I'm sorry I'm late."

No reply. The fast walking I'd done over the past several hours hit my legs with aches and cramps as the thrill of finally taking the tests drained away. I slumped onto the floor next to Eflet. "I'm sorry. I was working on things."

She barely blinked. Cotton spun between her practiced fingers.

"I talked to Jesso. You can live with him," I said in my most cheerful tones.

"Gyr came by."

"Oh." My ribs twisted. "So you already know."

"When Jesso heard you were headed to the Tree first, he sent Gyr to let me know you were fine and would be home late." She stared into the fire, long hair shadowing her eyes from my view. "Jesso's thoughtful like that."

I should have talked with her before I left. "It's for the best, I think."

An itching, echoing silence followed. The wind touched the thatching of the roof. A stick in the fire cracked. Sparks danced lazily over dying coals.

"My tests start tomorrow evening," I offered. "I promised Jesso our flour."

"Gyr said he'd be over in the morning to help haul it if you're determined to go."

"I'm making a life for us." I sat next to her, exhausted. Why was she upset when I was doing this just as much for her as for me?

"I don't need you to take care of me."

I sighed. "You want to live like this for the rest of your life?" I gestured broadly at our hut—the dirt floor, the walls made of poles. "Or do you have some apprenticeship offer I haven't heard of?"

"Jesso's not poor. You could stay. Help him expand his fields, build your own little home and—"

"This island doesn't need another hub slowing us down." Island Gunaji was small. We had to stay fast to flee the stronger metropolis Turtles that could conquer us. That's why, despite how much our Turtle needed to eat, the Tenders had pulled away from the last four reefs they found—bigger islands were already there. "I'm going to be a Handler, Eflet, and keep this island strong. I'm not going to be some filthy breeder."

She stared at me, face cold and rigid. "And without husbands, where would we get Handlers?"

My ears burned. "I'm not going to spend my life wallowing in poverty."

"You think Jesso's impoverished?"

"You know what I mean."

"Mother wouldn't." She grabbed more cotton from the basket and kept spinning, her fingers as deft as ever despite the frustration lining her face.

I frowned. Mother had believed in Ceibak, a mythical island where people had as many children as they liked and, impossibly, the Tree and Turtle thrived despite it. "Ceibak is rubbish to make hubs feel better about themselves."

Eflet pursed her lips into a thin line.

"Mother told me to take care of you," I continued. "Do you think she wanted me to leave you living on the shores of Hell forever?"

Eflet and Mother were the only people I'd ever met who thought Ceibak was real—everyone else recognized it as a fable. Well, and Ven. He'd been too little to know better.

"You think she'd want you to leave me for three years?" Eflet asked. "Get yourself killed fighting nagas? I know everyone likes to think Handlers are invincible, but they're not. Not even High Handler Banoh. Do you think Handlers' lives are just like the stories farmers tell on Market days? What do farmers know of being a Handler?"

"By that reasoning, I shouldn't listen to you, either."

Eflet shook her head. "I'm not dull enough to only imagine glorious battles. No one tells stories of the Tenders' work in the infirmary, patching up what's left of everyone. Father's lucky he only crippled one hand. You should stay and farm."

"Why are you being like this?" I couldn't keep my voice from tightening. Of course I knew being a Handler was dangerous. "I'm on the brink of making a good life for both of us. Let Ceibak go. You should know better by now."

Eflet bristled. She lowered her voice, but that only made her words sound sharper. "And you should know better than to speak so foolishly."

I exhaled, steadying myself. "Any Turtle burdened with lots of kids would be conquered—everyone slaughtered or enslaved, if famine didn't kill them first. Ceibak is wishful thinking."

Father crippled his hand just before Island Ita stripped a too-slow island bare and left their Turtle to wander, deserted of all human life.

"At least I am capable of thought." With that, Eflet shifted her back to me and continued to spin, her movements as sure as ever.

My shoulders sagged. "Eflet."

She didn't respond, effectively ending this bout of our argument. I frowned and glanced around for a half-full pot of soup or some cold cassava cakes. There was no food left out for me, and our sparse pottery was clean—freshly scrubbed if the light didn't deceive me. Which also meant Eflet had fetched water, and plenty of it. I sighed, but didn't comment.

"I'm sorry you're upset. Good night, Eflet."

Again, no response. I curled up on the far side of our house, my stomach gurgling in protest. I wished I'd taken Jesso up on his offer of lunch.

Eflet sat and spun. For how long, I'm not sure. When sunlight bleached the high western sky in the morning, she lay on the floor, her black hair a tangle around her, the fire dead and cold.

CHAPTER
5

I STARTED THE fire for Eflet. I tried to be quiet about it, but as I settled the griddle onto the hearthstones, she stirred. She'd always been a light sleeper.

"Good morning," I said.

She quickly braided her hair and tied it up into a bun with a cotton string. Then she kneaded cassava flour and water together for cakes without speaking. Apparently, I wasn't forgiven yet.

"How early is Gyr coming by?" I asked.

"Early, if I know Jesso."

Jesso liked hard work, early morning, and the two of us. I wasn't sure which Eflet meant regarding Gyr's arrival, and I didn't ask. "His daughters will be happy to see you, especially Afela."

"Afela married and moved to the other side of the Turtle six months ago."

"Oh." I paused. "But you get along with everyone else, right?"

Eflet nodded. "Gano's wife Lechat is very nice. They're all nice, Tenjat."

I stood and stretched my legs. "It'll be fine, then. Just the other day you said we ought to go back to Jesso's."

"I thought you'd be coming with me, Tenae." Bags hung under her eyes; she hadn't slept well.

I didn't reply. She'd get upset again, and I didn't want to spend our last full day together arguing. We sat in awkward silence while I uselessly watched her make breakfast. I'd always imagined my whole family cheering when I finally arranged to take the tests—Father, Mother, Ven, and Eflet. Families usually celebrated. Eflet's disappointed gaze made my insides squirm.

There was a knock on the door frame, followed by Gyr's voice. "Hello? Can I come in?"

"Please do," I said.

Gyr set aside our door of lashed sticks. His bloodshot eyes suggested that he'd slept about as well as Eflet.

"How early did Jesso wake you?" I asked. It took hours to walk here. He must have left before the sun appeared in the west.

"Oh, you know." Gyr flipped me a crooked, wry smile. "He woke up in the middle of the night, decided it was bright enough to get to work, and sent me on my way."

"Would you like breakfast?" Eflet asked.

"I ate some cassava cakes on the way."

"Old and cold, I bet. I already made extra, so you might as well eat." She pulled several cakes off the griddle and offered them to him.

Gyr breathed in the steam and practically drooled. "That looks wonderful."

Eflet handed them to him with a smile I hadn't seen all morning. Gyr sat, sticking his feet near the fire, and devoured the cakes at an alarming rate.

"So," he said through a mouthful of crumbs, "how much do we have to move?"

I nodded at our storage jars. Gyr crossed the room and lifted the lids. "Not bad, Tenjat, not at all."

"Plenty bad if you look at the field."

Gyr winced. "I saw it on the way here. I think you'd soon have enough, otherwise." He took one last look before closing the lid.

"What else is coming besides the flour, Eflet?" I asked.

She raised an incredulous eyebrow, not deigning to ask aloud if I was stupid. We didn't own much, and apparently it was all coming.

"We'll have to make a few trips to get all the jars, anyway," Gyr said. "Tenjat and I can get whatever you can't carry in one trip when we come back."

"Thank you," Eflet said, "But I'm afraid Tenjat is only helping with this first load. He's abandoning us to take his test at sundown." Her tone dripped with cold accusation.

Gyr gave a low whistle. "So soon? I had to wait—what was it? Four days?"

"Something like that," I mumbled. Was Eflet going to insist on being upset all day—our last day together?

We talked briefly while finishing up breakfast, then Eflet put out the fire, and we loaded up. I helped get the jar situated on Gyr's back, the carrying sling snug around his forehead. Eflet helped me with my own sling for the second jar.

"Go ahead," she said. "I'll gather some things and catch up with you."

I would have nodded, but the sling encircling the bottom of the jar and my forehead made that difficult. "All right."

Gyr and I started upriver, keeping our distance from the banks.

"Nasty dam—that's a big mess," Gyr said.

"I know."

We hiked in silence after that, saving our energy for the long trek. Eflet didn't catch up with us until we were halfway to Jesso's fields. She wasn't carrying that much, but her feet dragged

M. K. HUTCHINS

and caught on every root, it seemed. Had she slept at all?

Jesso's girls would help her transition. In a few days she'd be laughing, with a soft mat under her and a thick roof above. Then, in no time at all, I'd be a Handler and she could move to the House of Kin, where she'd never lack for anything. I hoped by then she'd realize this was exactly what our parents wanted for us.

The grain jar tugged my head from side to side as we walked. I sweated freely, especially as we passed through a muggy swath of dense forest. Eflet didn't say anything. I told myself it was because we had so much to carry, but I still felt awful.

Midday hadn't quite come when we reached Jesso's fields. Four of the girls, aged nine to nineteen, poured out of the house and ran to us. Or, as it turned out, ran to Eflet. They quickly relieved her of all her burdens and pulled her inside with a flurry of questions, hugs, and laughs. She smiled weakly and tried to chuckle, but her eyes were too tired for any of it to seem sincere—at least to me. The girls didn't notice.

"Guess we're not important," Gyr said as the five of them disappeared inside without a word to us.

"Guess not."

We followed them into the house. Jesso's wife, Arja, spared our jars a glance and a brief wave of her hand to the far wall. "Those can go over there."

Then she continued fussing over Eflet, bombarding her with questions like the other girls. I don't know how they always had so much to say. Eflet had just visited them recently, maybe a month ago. Reshla jabbered about a tunic she'd made, Tama about the boy three farms over, Oja about making flour. Even Lechat's infant squalled for attention.

"You're overwhelming the poor dear!" Arja shooed the girls back from Eflet. "Tama, cassava peeling. Reshla, Oja, Lechat, go work on lunch."

They whined, but dragged themselves off to their chores. Arja settled down next to Eflet and nursed her child. "You look exhausted."

"It's a long walk."

Arja glared at me. "I know, dear."

My tunic suddenly felt itchy. "I should head to the Tree," I said to Gyr. I didn't need to leave yet, but I didn't want to stay at Jesso's. "Thanks for helping."

"You can't leave," Arja snapped. "Jesso's planned you a special farewell lunch. Before you disappear into the Tree forever." As the stepmother of eight with six children of her own, Arja had perfected the stare of matronly disdain.

"That's . . . kind of him." I managed not to grimace.

"It was, wasn't it?" From the forced smile I'm pretty sure she thought the crumbs of burnt cassava cakes would be too generous a send-off for me. Then she turned back to Eflet. "The girls have made you something. It's not quite finished, but they've been working nonstop since yesterday. They're so excited."

Eflet nodded politely. "It's good to see them again."

I turned to Gyr. "Can I see the pottery you're working on?"

"Good idea."

We slipped away and Arja, gratefully, didn't stop us.

"I think Arja hates me."

Gyr shrugged. "She doesn't like me, either."

He led me to a small lean-to he'd constructed, not far from Jesso's most port-side field.

"Sorry it's cramped," Gyr said as we ducked inside. There was barely enough room for us, a small pit of wet clay, and four crude, sun-dried bowls.

"Are those yours?"

"Yeah." He picked one up and handed it to me. "They're not fired or anything, but I think I'm getting better. That's my latest one."

"Lots better." I swallowed once to steady my voice. Poorly tempered clay and unsteady hands had produced a knobby body and wobbled rim. Eflet made better for our house. The artisan made only the thinnest of bowls and smoothest of platters.

"I know, not the best, but I don't have anyone to teach me the finer points. I bet there's lots I'll only learn as an apprentice." His voice had a hopeful, pleading tone. He knew he wasn't any good.

"Yeah. Lots." I almost told him *I* could teach him plenty, and I hardly knew anything, but I bit my tongue. He deserved his pride, at least. "I'm sure you'll make it."

He hugged his knees to his chest. "Jesso mostly buys our pottery from the neighbors or the artisans. My sisters aren't any good at it, but Eflet made your things, right?"

I nodded.

"I'm glad Eflet's here now. I'm hoping she'll give me some suggestions. Any extra help . . ."

"I'm sure she'll help," I reassured him. "She's always gotten along with you. You'll just have to pry her away from your sisters."

Gyr managed to chuckle. "They certainly like her more than us."

Under the lean-to, the earth was damp. We sat in silence, soaking up the coolness into our tired feet until Jesso bellowed from across the field that lunch was ready.

I sighed as I pulled myself back outside. "How hard do you think it would be to run away right now?"

"Eflet would never forgive you if you didn't say good-bye."

"I know. I'm not exactly excited about attending a farewell

lunch planned by Jesso, though. He's probably trying to convince me to stay instead of wishing me luck."

"Father's only had a day to plan," Gyr said. "How bad could it be?"

Gyr and I entered the clearing with the split-log benches after everyone else had already arrived. The men splashed water on their faces from rainwater jugs and drank it down in equally liberal amounts. Reshla sliced papaya with a large chert knife while Lechat tended the food on the fire— honeyed wafers, spiced squash stew, and toasted pumpkin seeds. A feast. The scents tumbled together in the air, tugging at my tongue and reminding me that I was ravenous from a hard morning's work. I hoped that sometime in the past five years, Father and Ven had enjoyed food like this. Guilt twinged through me, knowing they probably hadn't.

Arja dished up platters and the girls handed them out, each one big enough for two people. Six-year-old Fesi ran up to Gyr, barely balancing his platter in his small arms. "Gyr! Share with me!"

Gyr took one glance at the plate, brimming with enough food for three men, let alone himself and a small boy. "Of course!"

"Don't eat all the wafers this time!" Fesi pouted, but Gyr laughed and ruffled his unruly black hair. They sat together on one of the benches, balancing the platter between their knees. I glanced around for Eflet, but she already shared with Lechat.

I was looking for someone else to share with when Lyna approached me with a platter—extra wafers, chili sprinkled liberally over the squash, and a mountain of pumpkin seeds.

"Jesso said I'm supposed to share this with you."

She shuffled her feet, eyes modestly downturned. She was the only daughter of Jesso's I got along with, probably because she was Gyr's favorite sibling and she never giggled or talked about boys. Gyr and I used to keep her company while she practiced weaving, but the weaver took a different apprentice.

"Thanks." I'd have someone pleasant to eat with after all.

She gestured at an empty bench and I followed. As she turned, her long, loose hair swished around her hips. Water still sparkled on the tips and on the lattice of delicate braids that crowned her head. My heart sank into my stomach. Had she changed so much since I saw her last? She'd never cared about looking elegant before.

We sat, resting the plate across our laps. Lyna shifted uncomfortably, not eating. Her dress, fresh-scrubbed and fairly new, draped elegantly down to her midcalves.

"How have you been?" I asked.

"W-well." She glanced at me, then turned quickly away. Strange. She was usually as cheerful as Gyr.

Jesso cleared his throat. "It is my pleasure to have you all here for lunch with our special guests. This is a time of great joy, as we welcome Eflet and Tenjat back to us! My only regret is that we didn't manage to snare a rabbit or an iguana for the occasion."

One of Lyna's younger sisters shot her a pitying look.

"I think later there will be more speeches and a presentation," Jesso continued with a knowing wink to his daughters. I supposed that referred to whatever they'd been working on for Eflet. "But for now, eat! Enjoy yourselves! Be merry! Enjoy the pleasurable company of friends long missed."

When he looked at Lyna and me, smugness danced in his eyes. That was the plan, then. Snare me with his daughter to keep me here.

"W-wafer?" Lyna asked, offering one up to me. Her hands, calloused worker's hands, were scrubbed raw. They shook.

"Thank you." Sick to my stomach, I took it.

Lyna bit her lower lip, but it still trembled. I'd only seen her actually cry once; a little brother had tangled the weaving sample she'd planned to present to the artisan. I'd sat and helped her carefully unknot it, though she'd been better at it with her thin, graceful fingers.

"I'm supposed to tell you I've missed you," Lyna said. "I . . . I suppose I have. You weren't unkind to me."

I crammed the wafer in my mouth so I wouldn't have to answer. I wanted to run.

"Am I saying too much?" She glanced up and immediately away again—but I could still see that someone had rubbed her eyelashes with charcoal. They fluttered, thick and heavy, above doe-brown eyes.

"No."

"I'm sorry I'm not good at conversation."

"Then eat." I followed my own advice, hoping we could pass the rest of the meal like that, but she left her spoon on the platter. "Not hungry?"

"The food's meant for you, anyway," she said.

I blinked twice at that and reconsidered the dishes—honeyed wafers, hot peppers, bright colors. This was *wedding* food. Food to lighten the heart, flame desire, and distract the mind from the guilt and shame of being too poor to live without marriage and children. My ears went hot first, then my face, and down my neck.

Arja came around with a pitcher of honey mead. She smiled pleasantly. "Would you like some, Tenjat?"

"No."

She glanced at Lyna. "You've hardly eaten, Tenjat. Is something not to your liking?"

"Everything's wonderful." I gave her a broad, fake grin. Arja nudged Lyna with her foot as she continued, asking the next pair if they'd like some. The rest of the family sat in clumps, four or six together, chatting. No one sat near us. I supposed Jesso had told everyone to give us time alone. Filthy hub.

Lyna, as if in obedience to Arja's nudge, shifted closer to me. Her hair fell against my shoulder. They'd perfumed it with something floral—orchids? I wasn't sure.

I turned to her. "Arja didn't even ask if you wanted some mead. Did you?"

"No." She paused. "Did you want me to?"

"Why would I want you tipsy?" I stabbed a spoonful of stewed squash.

She clasped her trembling hands over her trembling knees. "I . . . I don't know."

"Would you like some pumpkin seeds?"

Lyna shook her head. It would be better if we both just ate. I polished off more than half of the food and got Lyna to eat some wafers. She'd always had a sweet tooth.

One of her youngest sisters came and cleared our platter.

"I hope everyone enjoyed their meal!" Jesso stood near the cooking fire. He beamed at me, with Lyna sitting so close. I bit my teeth together in frustration. What did Eflet see in this man?

"I believe someone has a presentation to make?" Jesso continued.

Several of his daughters sprang up. Oja, the nine-year-old, ran to fetch something from the house. She returned with a half-finished dress, neatly embroidered on the bottom with blue.

"We haven't done the sash yet, but we thought you'd like it—something new and pretty!" Tama babbled. Eflet only had one dress—the ragged, too-short thing on her back.

"The boys will all think you look rather handsome in it." That was Reshla, who couldn't shut up about boys.

I jumped to my feet, indignant. "My sister—"

Eflet glared at me. I swallowed the next words: *isn't a hub-maker.* I coughed. "My sister loves blue. That was very considerate."

"Yes, it was." Eflet graciously accepted the garment from the younger girl. "Thank you all."

The girls beamed. Jesso then rambled about how happy they were to have Eflet back and how sad they were to see me go—three years was a long time. I wanted to tell him eternity was longer, because other than picking up my sister, I was never coming back.

"Eflet, Gyr, myself, Arja, Lyna . . . we grieve to see you go," Jesso said, wrapping up. "We hope that you won't miss us too dearly, Tenjat, as we will miss you."

I smiled politely. Gyr, I could miss. Lyna, too. I hated leaving Eflet behind. But the rest? Never.

"I want you to know you're always welcome here. If you don't pass the tests"—here he sounded cheerful—"come back to us! If you decide the lonely life of a Handler is not the one you want, you'll have a home. I recently acquired a small span of land from a neighbor I'd grant you if you return. I know how you like your independence."

"That's very kind." And unnecessary. I'd never take him up on it.

"I think the rest of us will get back to work, but Lyna can show you the land. Take your time to survey it, walk around. But do come say good-bye before you leave."

"I will."

The men and boys drifted back to the fields, and the women and girls flocked around Eflet before Arja shooed them away to their work. Lyna and I stood. Her hand twitched. Jesso nodded encouragingly. Lyna hesitated, then interlaced her clammy fingers with mine.

I wanted to jerk away, but I didn't know how without offending Lyna. The burning in my ears penetrated my chest, twisting down into my lungs. As we left the clearing, I silently cursed Jesso.

Filthy, filthy hub.

CHAPTER
6

ROCKS AS BIG as my head dotted the small span Lyna brought me to, but no trees or fronds touched it. Lyna dropped my hand as soon as we stepped onto the field. Clean air moved between my fingers again. My mouth was dry. We were alone. My innards screamed to run, but my legs wouldn't move. Running would be an accusation against Lyna. I wanted to think her above trying to make me her hub.

"How'd Jesso come by this?" I asked, trying to distract myself. I forced my eyes over the field, away from Lyna. It had the same musty smell as the rest of the island's farms, and it needed some work before it could be planted—but it wasn't a bad stretch of land, up on a small rise, not close to the shore. Rainwater would drain well here.

"Old Man Ruvant bought it some time ago from the Handlers, so each of his sons would have a field to inherit. You probably heard how his oldest boy, Pum, lost his leg felling a tree last season. Now the family doesn't have enough manpower to work this field, too."

"And Ruvant needed the cassava-price of the sale more than the field."

"I hope they'll be all right," Lyna said. "Esun is a hard worker, and Pum is good at repairing tools. He hopes to become the flintknapper's apprentice."

"It's a pretty piece of land."

"Y-yes. It is." She sniffled.

I was so set on not looking at her, I hadn't noticed she'd started to cry. "What's wrong?"

Sooty lines ran down Lyna's cheeks and splashed gray onto her fresh-scrubbed dress. I wasn't sure if I should step forward or back.

"Arja's going to marry me to Panti. He's taken a fancy to me."

"Panti?" He was one of Rud's cousins from this part of the island, and the only man I knew who was a worse hub than Jesso. He'd gotten a young woman named Nashi pregnant, then refused to admit his hubbish actions, take responsibility for them, and marry her. After that, a respectable farmer married Nashi—he was happy to start his family with an adopted child instead of weighing down the island further by fathering

his own—but that didn't make me loathe Panti any less.

Lyna closed her eyes and nodded. "Arja said it was him or you. She told me how to make you want to . . . to dull the pain of shame with me. She said you'd want to stay and be my hub if I did. But I . . . I can't do that to you."

Dull the pain of shame—a euphemism for what happened between a husband and wife. The consolation for being poor was having a spouse to share your suffering with. The empty dirt under my feet felt less stable than sand. How could anyone ask Lyna to seduce me?

"I don't want to get married. Not at all." Lyna wiped her eyes, spreading sooty tears all over her face. "But the only thing I'm good at is tending little children. You can't be an artisan doing that."

"I know, Lyna. You're not like your father." I almost laid a reassuring hand on her shoulder, but thought better of it.

"Pass the tests, Tenjat. For all of us who didn't. Father hopes you'll fail or drop out."

I felt like I'd be sick there on the field. "Jesso wants me to stay badly enough that he'd tell you to . . . to do this?"

"Father? No." She wrinkled her nose. "He hates anything lewd—he's always getting after Reshla for chasing boys."

"Then . . . ?"

"Father came up with the plan to dress me nice, have us talk, but I told him you wouldn't be tricked into staying so easily. Father dismissed my complaint, but Arja took it to heart—in the wrong direction."

I paused. "Will Jesso make you marry Panti?"

"I don't know." She'd stopped crying, but her hands shook. So did mine. "Arja's good at convincing Father, and he does want me to marry. But I hate Panti. He always tells me I'm more beautiful than the Tree itself. That he'd rather be with me than be a Handler, as if that's romantic instead of horrible."

For a brief moment, I wanted to stay and marry her, to save her from Panti. But I wasn't a hub, and Eflet came first.

"I know you'll have to marry and have children eventually," I said, "but you deserve better than Panti. Far better, Lyna."

She smiled shyly up at me with her puffy eyes. "Thanks."

Awkward silence hung between us. I should have been thanking her.

"Should . . . should we head back, then?" I asked. My face felt as hot as if I'd worked all day in the fields.

Lyna nodded. We started toward Jesso's. The trees shading the path rocked in the wind, throwing ever-changing dappled patterns over the forest floor.

"Will you watch Eflet for me while I'm gone?" I asked. "Make sure Arja doesn't marry her off too?"

Lyna grinned. "Of course."

Until that moment, I thought becoming a Handler would make life perfect. It would keep Eflet and me out of the poverty and shame of marriage. Now it seemed woefully inadequate. I could do nothing for Lyna or Gyr.

We walked slowly. I'd visit Lyna and Gyr after my training. I'd help with anything I could, but I knew what their futures held. I couldn't save them from that.

Lyna flashed me a shy smile in the green-dappled light under the trees: a thank-you kind of smile. I returned it with a sad one of my own.

When we returned to Jesso's fields, something was wrong. The girls still puttered around the clearing, washing platters and glancing at the house. The boys clumped together in the first field, barely making an effort at farming, whispering among themselves. Gyr jogged up as soon as he saw us.

"What's going on?" I asked.

"I don't know." He jutted his chin at the house. "You probably shouldn't interrupt them right now."

"Them?"

"Father and Arja," Gyr said, voice low. "I've never seen Father so upset before."

Lyna hid behind me. My palms already itched. "Explain, Gyr."

His eyes glittered with excitement, unlike the younger children. Some of them looked ready to cry. "Not long after you two left, they started fighting—really fighting. Father

M. K. HUTCHINS

hasn't yelled like this since Emju lost half his leg naga fishing."

"And?" I demanded, motioning for him to speed up. I wasn't in the mood for a dramatic retelling.

"Well, Father called me. Told me to go fetch you and Lyna right away. Then Arja hissed something into his ear and he got flustered and told me to wait. They kicked everyone out of the house, told us to stay away. That was just a moment ago. Then you showed up. I'd stay back for a bit."

I shook my head and quietly walked up the steps of the house. Lyna followed, but Gyr stayed behind, brow scrunched and puzzled.

Inside, whispers rose and fell like the sound of swarming hornets, but I couldn't make out the words. I knocked on the doorpost. Jesso shoved the door of lashed sticks aside. His face was slack, his eyes pleading. Arja stood in the back of the house, arms folded across her chest, one smug eyebrow raised.

"Can . . . we come in?" I asked. My back felt hot with the stares of Jesso's children. Jesso nodded and stepped back. It was blessedly cool and dim inside.

"We . . ." I stuttered with both of them staring at me. I wished I hadn't had so much spicy food. I swallowed the heat back down. "The field was nice, Jesso, but I'm afraid I can't take it. I'm going to be late for my tests if I don't leave soon."

Arja's fists clenched. "Lyna, child . . ."

Lyna shook her head, not looking at her stepmother. She

spoke softly enough that I'm not sure Arja could hear her. "I wouldn't do that to him."

Arja took a step forward, as if to shake Lyna or slap her, but Jesso was quicker. He caught his daughter in his arms and buried his face in her hair. "I was so worried about you—"

Lyna pulled back, embarrassed. "I'm fine, Father."

She looked horrible, of course, soot smeared on her face, dress mussed by tears. Jesso sighed, then turned to me.

"Tenjat, you are welcome on my land anytime, understand?" His earnest eyes drilled into mine.

"Yes, sir."

Arja retreated into the corner, shoulders bunched as she sulked.

"I'd be happy to see you married to one of my own," Jesso said, "but not like that."

I shifted uncomfortably. "I need to be going. Tests to take and all."

Jesso nodded. "Is there anything I can send with you? More food? Something to drink?"

"Don't think so." What I'd eaten kept threatening to come back up.

He pursed his lips. "I wish I could do something for you."

"Take care of my sister," I said. "And don't let anyone bully Lyna into marrying someone she hates."

Jesso blinked. "I only intended a pleasant meal. It's not easy to find honest spouses for my children. Some only see our wealth in cassava, and come seeking us. Others only see that I have more children than they think I ought, and avoid us." Jesso gave me a sad smile, as if painfully aware that I fell into the latter category. "But you should know me better than that, Tenjat. I wouldn't make Lyna marry anyone she didn't want to. I only asked her to sit by you because I thought you would be happy together. My apologies, to both of you."

"I don't hate Tenjat," Lyna said, hugging her arms to her chest.

Jesso peered at both of us, confusion plain in the broad lines of his face. He didn't know about Panti.

Lyna could explain later. "Thank you for your help, Jesso," I said. "For watching Eflet." I hoped he understood that I could be grateful, even if I couldn't like him.

"You're still going, then?"

I nodded. He embraced me. "Good luck."

As I left, Jesso turned to his wife, lips pursed. The anger was already gone: Jesso didn't really know how to be angry. Only the disappointment, the sadness lingered. Almost the same look he'd given me when I told him I was leaving Eflet here to take the tests. Lyna gave me a stiff, respectful nod good-bye. I returned it.

I'd barely made it off the platform when Gyr ran up. "Tenjat? You don't look so good."

"Maybe I ate too much."

He frowned at me. "What was that all about?"

"Have Lyna explain." My face still burned and I didn't want to talk about it. Lyna was Gyr's favorite sister, and if he misunderstood, well, I'd hate for our parting words to involve Gyr's fist and my face. "Steer clear of Arja for now too. She's rather unhappy."

"More than the time we ruined her best griddle?"

"Definitely."

"Ouch." He peered at me. "What did you *do*?"

"More like what I didn't." I wiped my hands on the front of my tunic. "Ask Lyna. Maybe later. She's had a bad day. Be nice to her, all right?"

Gyr nodded and didn't prod anymore. He understood. I liked that about him. I wished we could have been Handlers together.

"I should go," I said. "But I'll come find you the moment I'm allowed out, okay?"

"Check the potter's house in the artisans' village first!"

He grinned, I grinned, and we chuckled together—but our laughter drooped at the edges. In three years, he'd be a hub on some farm, maybe have a child. Poor Gyr. I clapped him hard on the back and told him I'd buy Eflet a whole new set of crockery from him when I visited.

CHAPTER

7

EFLET WALKED WITH me to the Tree. Farmsteads flanked our path, where men and boys planted cassava fields that looked less vibrant than they should. Occasionally we passed through a patch of forest with flocks of turkeys whose feathers turned sunlight into the color of jewels. A deer crossed our path once as well. An hour later, as we passed the conglomerated fields of some ten houses, Eflet spoke. "Lyna was upset."

"I know."

"Reshla said that Jesso wanted Lyna to convince you to stay," Eflet said, "but that can't be all. Not with how he and Arja fought."

I let my eyes wander over the cassava stubs and musty, dying soil. No point in trying to hide anything from Eflet.

"Arja wanted her to dull the pain of shame with me. Keep me here."

"And?"

"Nothing. Lyna just wished me luck tonight."

"Good." She patted my shoulder and offered me a small smile.

"Eflet, please be careful around Arja," I said. "She's more backward than Jesso."

We passed a tidy field the size of the one Lyna had shown me. The farmer—not anyone I knew—paused to wipe his brow and wave. We waved back.

"Arja actually likes me." Eflet clasped her hands behind her back.

"I think that might be worse."

"You worry too much."

The wind stirred, bringing with it the smell of dry dust and pending rain. We didn't talk about me leaving—but the undercurrent was there. This felt like trying to warn her away from the river all over again. Except I wouldn't be there to tell Arja off. "You don't think what Arja did was wrong?"

"Of course it was." Rain—more of a fine mist—began to fall, though the sun stayed bright. "It just doesn't surprise me."

I blinked at her.

"We lived there with her for three years, Tenae. You didn't notice?"

"Notice what?"

She raised an eyebrow at me, as if I were dense. "Did you think a normal girl would marry Jesso, a man who already had eight children? Someone without some kind of past?"

"I . . . never thought about it."

"You always spend too much time avoiding people to understand them."

"Only people like Jesso."

She shook her head at me. The mist built to a drizzle, turning the ground to mud under our feet. We crested a ridge and continued down the path, now flanked by freshly-planted, well-maintained cassava fields. Even so, a whiff of decay clung to the soil, just like everywhere else.

"Explain, then."

She raised a critical eyebrow.

"Please explain? Would you like me to apologize for being an idiot as well, or is *please* enough?"

Eflet rolled her eyes. "So dramatic today."

I'd hauled a huge jar of cassava flour halfway across the island and spent a tense afternoon with Lyna—it had been a dramatic day. I sighed and wished my shoulders didn't hurt. "*Please,* then."

Maybe Eflet empathized with my long day; she began without further ridicule. "Arja was one of two children. Her parents were too proud to have more. Then her father broke his leg. Always had a limp afterward. It became harder to keep the farm up."

I nodded in sympathy.

"They would have been all right, but Arja's brother decided to take the Handler's test. He actually made it."

"Leaving mother, crippled father, and sister all alone."

Eflet nodded. The rain turned back to mere mist. "He promised he'd put the father up in the House of Kin, but the family couldn't survive three years without the son's labor. They were destitute."

Only full Handlers, men who had been through three years of training, had the right to put one of their relatives in the House of Kin. "And Jesso's wealthy."

"That's how they made the match. Jesso took good care of her parents until they passed, but Arja . . . Arja never forgave her brother. He visited once and never came back."

I bit my lip. "And so she doesn't like anyone who tries to be a Handler?"

"Or artisan. And you're abandoning a sister too. Are you surprised she hates you?"

"I'm not abandoning you," I said firmly. "I'm taking care of you. And you won't starve while I'm gone."

Eflet's mouth tightened. "I doubt Arja sees it that way."

"That doesn't make what Arja did today right."

"Oh, what Arja did was horrid." A small smile crept onto

her face. "Still, I would have liked to watch Lyna try to seduce you. She wouldn't be any good at it."

"Eflet!"

She laughed, clear and happy. "The look on your face, Tenae — I wish you could see it."

We started into the swath of trees just before the artisans' village. Rain trickled down onto our heads from the leaves. A howler monkey jumped overhead and scurried farther up a branch. I wished we were at the Tree already — I wanted to leave with Eflet smiling.

Maybe she fretted for nothing. Most people failed the tests. She could be tending gouges on my back before the sun rose and disappeared into the east tonight.

"Arja is right about you leaving me." Eflet's normal solemn face returned. "Three years is a long time."

I kept my eyes on the ground, partly to watch for snakes, but mostly to avoid looking at Eflet. "It's not that long."

"We've only been away from Jesso's for two, but I bet you don't know what Sora, Bohn, Wesha, or Duneh are doing," Eflet said, naming some of Jesso's neighbors our age.

Despite my run-in with Wesha yesterday, I couldn't answer. "You're my sister. It wouldn't be like that."

Eflet brushed past the rain-wet fronds of a young palm tree. "Bohn's getting married, Wesha's taken over caring for her mother's beehives, Sora's obsessed with becoming the next weaving apprentice, and Duneh's half a foot taller and managing his own field."

"You've just been back to Jesso's more than me. That's all," I said.

"You could come to Jesso's now. Come and stay."

We'd barely started this tired old argument, and I already felt exhausted. "Who would give up being a Handler for a life of shame?"

"Tender Sosani and Ohn did."

When we first arrived on Island Gunaji, people could talk of little else, how a Tender and a man from the House of Kin had been caught sleeping together. Disgraceful. They'd escaped poverty—they didn't need a spouse's companionship to endure this life. Both were expelled. Gyr had dubbed that scandal "mocking the poor."

"Being expelled is hardly the same as *choosing* to be a farmer."

"Isn't it? They knew they'd be thrown out for their actions," Eflet said.

"I doubt they planned on getting caught. They were both idiots."

Eflet pursed her lips with some other comment, but held it back. We walked in silence for a few moments. The rain stopped entirely and curling white mist rose from the ground.

Eventually, Eflet sighed. "Is it so impossible to imagine you could be happier outside the Tree than in it? Because

I remember parents who adored each other and took joy in raising their children. You wouldn't be the first man to chose a wife over the Tree."

Marriage, children, farming. All the trappings of poverty. "Those parents wanted a better life for us. I'm no hub."

Eflet scowled. "Do you have to say it that way?"

"Hub?"

"Would you ever call Father that?"

I gave Eflet a hand over a log that had fallen across the path. "Father was a Handler first."

"And that makes all the difference?"

"He *tried*. I won't call Gyr a hub when he's married, either. Or Ven, for that matter." I doubted it would be safe for Ven to take the tests, given our family history. If he still lived.

She shook her head in disgust and wouldn't talk to me until we'd passed through the artisans' village and stood at the doors to the Tree. The copper work glimmered with beads of rain. So beautiful. And I was about to step inside.

Eflet hugged me tight. "You can still come back to Jesso's with me. Do it. Turn around."

"Eflet, I can't."

"Is this about Mother? Wanting to hurt the nagas because they took her?" She pulled back, loam-brown eyes intent on mine.

"How can someone seek revenge against dumb monsters?" I asked, confused.

"Fighting them doesn't change anything." Eflet's voice was earnest and low. "They don't dwindle. You could kill them all, and they'd come back."

I frowned, my stomach twisting. "Can't you just wish me luck?"

Eflet's eyes pinched—she looked ready to cry.

My shoulders dropped. "Is this about Ceibak again? Eflet, if Ceibak ever existed, it was conquered long ago by stronger, faster Turtles not bogged down by breeding."

"Trust me. Stay, Tenae. Everything will be fine."

"Fine *how*?"

Eflet didn't answer. I peered at her. "You ask me to trust you, but you won't explain yourself—you won't trust *me*."

"If you refuse to become a Handler, I'll tell you everything I know. Why the nagas follow me. Why we had to flee Island Ita."

My throat dried out. I felt like she'd punched the wind from my lungs. "Only Mother knew what our treason was."

"I *am* the treason. I know everything."

I stepped back. Mother's screams echoed in my head. "Leaving Father and Ven . . . Mother's death . . . you didn't think I deserved to know *why*?"

"You're still set on being a Handler." She held her chin up. "*Handlers* forced us to flee Island Ita. You think Island Gunaji would be different?"

I didn't know what to say. I wanted a *life* for her. For both of us. Why did she think that entitled her to hide secrets? "Tell me how you're the treason. Tell me what you did."

"Are you still taking the tests?"

"Of course!" I burst. "I made promises, Eflet. Neither of us has to stay poor if I succeed today. Why won't you answer me?"

Eflet sighed through her nose. "You've always been stubborn. Dedicated. That's why you'll make a great Handler. I'd hoped, even now, that you'd choose to be my brother instead."

The door opened behind us. The same Tender I'd talked to earlier stood there in her glimmering fishskin shirt and netted skirt. "Hmph. I thought I heard something," she said. "Are you coming in for your test?"

Eflet hugged her arms to her chest, and turned her face from me. It felt like an accusation of betrayal.

But Handlers weren't evil. Father had been one. High Handler Banoh was a hero. Handlers fought nagas—they kept the island safe. And to become one would allow me to provide for myself and my sister for the rest of our lives.

"Good-bye, Eflet." My voice rasped dry against my throat. "See you in three years."

She didn't say anything. Just stared at me, her eyes pleading.

I bit my lip, then turned and stepped inside.

CHAPTER

8

I FOLLOWED THE Tender through the corridors, trying to think of anything but Eflet's words. *I am* the treason. *I know everything.* Oceans, why hadn't she told me? I'd fled Island Ita, just like her. Left Father and Ven behind. Watched Mother die. I didn't deserve to know *why*?

What could Eflet have even done to earn the ire of Ita's Handlers? We were only children then.

I brushed my fingers against the wall, feeling its grain, trying to think of anything but Eflet. I wouldn't fail because I was too frustrated to focus. For five years I'd lived without knowing. In three years, when I could leave the Tree, I'd convince Eflet to tell me everything.

The walls looked hewed from the Tree's living wood—

pale, honey-colored, with a few knots. The wood gave me no splinters, but it wasn't polished hard, either. It was . . . vaguely warm.

When the hall forked, the Tender took a sharp right. A Handler stood in front of an arched door. His bare feet were freshly scrubbed and his uniform immaculate: loose breeches that cinched around the knee and a darkly gleaming fishskin-tight shirt like the Tender's that left his stomach bare. I self-consciously brushed my tattered cotton tunic. He wore the simple markings of a man of power. I wore the garb of peasants who only existed because of the Handlers' protection.

"You will take the test now." The Handler opened the door.

Awe and dread bubbled in my gut. Gyr came out of these tests with forty-three gashes. Forty-three gashes and a pinched face whenever anyone talked about the tests. Eflet had prevented the wounds from festering. Eflet, who kept secrets.

I pushed her from my mind and stepped into the room.

I'd expected darkness, or a monster, or a torture chamber full of cunningly flintknapped daggers. Instead, light filled the room. The wood here glowed softly, the color grayer than the corridor. The opposite wall held twisted gold veins that reminded me of the copper work on the door of the Tree. These veins reached, spiderweb thin, over the ceiling as well, but on one wall they gathered together in spots as thick as my hand, coiling around each other in a mesmerizing spiral pattern. I stepped closer.

The veins were more than gold—they were liquid light with floating flakes of burnished gold and dark yellow gold drifting up and down, as if caught in a gentle breeze. Light washed through the flakes, casting watery patterns on the wall.

I gingerly touched the golden vein. My mind spun.

I was *in* the vein, spiraling upward toward the Heavens, up past the island, up into the brightest part of the sky. Suddenly, as if I had broken through a ceiling or plunged in the wrong direction, I hung in a world of black smoke. I must have turned the wrong way. I floated weightless in a never-ending mist.

I swallowed and looked around. An impish monster, only twenty feet away, dived at me. Not a naga—this creature had four limbs, each with claws as long as its forearms. Right behind him, a glowing Handler drifted, calmly watching us.

"Help!" I screamed, feebly flailing my arms. I didn't know how to swim, let alone swim through mists. "Help!"

The imp swiped at my head. I managed to duck. I felt slow, like I was suspended in honey. The imp curled back its lips and hissed at me, dark smoke trickling from its mouth. It coiled its body to spring.

M. K. HUTCHINS

The Handler smiled and dived forward with a superhuman grace. The outline was a young woman's, with a chert-tipped javelin in her glowing arm. She looked like a plunging arrow. I feared she'd run me through as well, but she stopped as smoothly as she'd dived. The remains of the imp slid off her javelin and dispersed into the mists.

"Is it dead?"

She laughed—a shimmering sound like rain falling on a brook. "They can't die. But he'll take many days to recover from that."

"Where are we?"

She was young, about my age, and she kept glowing—like polished palm wood under a noon sun.

"You're used to seeing the surface of Hell, the ocean, where the nagas live. We're far below that, in Deephell. Here we rob the gods of the underworld to outfit ourselves for fighting the nagas and protecting the Turtle and Tree."

So I had turned the wrong way—I hadn't been flying up to the Heavens after all. I felt the fool: I should have waited in the room for whatever the Handlers were sending.

"Th-thank you," I stammered at last, remembering my manners. "For saving me. I'm lucky you were here."

She raised an eyebrow. "Luck? Luck had nothing to do with it. That, my friend, was the test. You passed."

"Passed?"

Excitement exploded in my gut. It made me feel nauseous as my panic faded. Eflet had been right about this, at least.

"You could see the imp, couldn't you? Now, look between your toes."

A patch of mist, not far away, swirled with pale gold.

"That's the deepest Tree root—what you came through. Swim to it, touch it, and you'll travel back to the Tree."

"I don't know how to swim." I hated admitting that to her.

She didn't laugh at my ignorance, though. "You'll get the hang of it. Just kick your legs and move your arms. You'll get there soon enough."

I nodded and thrashed in the direction of the Tree. I glanced back once. She floated there, appraising me with eyes that seemed too serious for her young face. I tried to swim straighter, faster, but I knew I looked like an idiot.

But what did looking like an idiot matter? I had actually *passed*.

Just like Eflet predicted.

The gold glow caught me. I spun . . . downward? I supposed it must be upward, and the motion and mists confused me.

I stood in the silvery room again, the mass of golden veins in front of me. Black dots swarmed my vision and the room spun. I promptly fell to the floor. This wasn't like the pleasant weightlessness of the mists—gravity wrenched on me one direction, while my eyes said otherwise and my feet put in a third vote.

Later, the Handler girl told me I threw up. I only remembered waking up on a soft mattress, laid in a recess in the floor. A real mattress. In a few years, Eflet would sleep on a luxurious bed like this.

The Handler girl sat cross-legged on a clean rush mat next to me, her eyes crinkled in a smile, her skin the rich color of Gyr's unfired pottery. "The mucks are still trying to clean up the insides of your stomach, splattered all over the Hellroom. The half-Handler in charge thinks what you did was art, pure art. What did you eat?"

"A cassava cake?" I mumbled, trying to remember where my lips were and how to make them go up and down.

"Ah, that would explain the bright shades of yellow, then, but not the orange. Or really the red."

"That many colors?"

"Like I said, the half-Handler thinks it's art: 'Variation on a Grotesque Sunset,' I believe is what he wants to name it."

"Ah. So are you here to pity me before whoever's in charge reprimands me?"

Her smile only widened. She had unnervingly straight teeth. "Oh no. My name's Avi. I'm the one in charge — at least of you, my dear little muck."

~ ~ ~

She fetched me something cool to drink. I sipped as we talked, letting my stomach settle. "What's a muck?"

"You. It's slang for novice."

Novice. I hadn't heard her wrong. I'd passed. "I don't understand the test. I didn't do anything."

She sat cross-legged in her Handler's breeches, elbows on knees, playful face cupped in her hands. "There's not much *doing* with the test, Tenjat."

The small cell was empty, other than the bed, the girl, and myself. The walls were of living wood—this time mahogany red. A thin lattice of gold veins pulsed on the ceiling, giving us soft light. "My friend was slashed up. I thought it would be harder."

She winced. "Sometimes, the testing coordinator, Handler Odev, makes an error, forgets to have Handlers watching. And if no one stops the imp . . ." She shook her head. "No, the test is if you can *see* imps."

I took another sip and peered at her. This still didn't make sense.

"I'll explain from the beginning." She held a fist up at the level of her head. "Here are the Heavens, high above the branches of the Tree." She dropped her fist to her sternum. "Here's us, floating along the surface of Hell. Got that?"

I nodded.

"Good." She dropped her hand slightly and wiggled her

fingers. "Here is what we call Nearhell, the watery ocean. Nagas live here and attack the roots of the tree. Far below *that*"—she dropped her fist to the floor—"is Deephell. That's where we were—misty, inhabited by imps. Not everyone can see in Deephell, but if you can, you're fit to be a Handler."

Even with the drink, my head ached. "If there aren't any nagas to fight in Deephell, why is it important?"

"Treasure." Her eyes glittered. "When you finish your muck training, you'll rob Hell."

"This is about wealth?" They'd endangered my life, scarred Gyr. Maybe Handlers, as Eflet said, weren't to be trusted.

Avi laughed, a clear, ringing sound. "Hell doesn't have *ordinary* treasures. Each of us has a cache that glows only for us—these are the treasures we can use. Most of them you have to claim in Hell first, but a few always work—like the pair of gold coins that lets you see in Deephell. Anyone without that treasure is blind."

"What else do these treasures do?"

"Men almost always get the ability to breathe underwater, allowing them to fight the nagas."

"And women?"

"We test them differently—see if they can pull themselves through a Tree vein that doesn't have a sucking current like the one that took you to Deephell. If she can do that, she almost always has treasures that allow her to manipulate the veins. It's not as showy as fighting, but those veins *are* responsible for pulling up clean water for the island's rivers and replenishing the silt."

I'd always thought the gender division between Handlers and Tenders was to discourage any hub-like thoughts. But here Avi was.

She read the question on my face. "When I robbed Hell, I had a wide variety of treasures." She shrugged. "I can do any job in the Tree, but right now, we're short on Handlers. Tenders don't die in battle as often. I mean, the nagas *do* go after Tenders first, but Tenders can drop off Handlers and disappear into the veins until the Handlers have won or need to retreat."

I stared. She must be the most important person in the Tree, and she sat with me, explaining what must be rote to her.

Embarrassed, she mumbled, "It's not like I could pick what my treasures were. Caches like mine almost never happen."

The *almost* snagged my mind. "You said anyone who passes the test *almost* always finds a treasure. My cache could be empty?"

"That hasn't happened in decades. I wouldn't worry about it. You might only have the knife that allows you to breathe underwater—or you could have something to turn you into a Seer, something so rare we only know of it from other islands."

"A Seer?"

"Someone who can See everything," Avi said with a

M. K. HUTCHINS

disarming smile. The golden light from the veins danced in her cassava-brown eyes. "Don't worry, I'm not one."

I could get the hang of this. "The test wasn't so bad."

"It's plenty bad if you're blind. Suddenly floating in mists, then a Handler drags you back?"

"That's worse than seeing the monster?"

She smiled again. "I *like* the imps. What fun would it be if they didn't come play with us?"

I laughed. "You really love being a Handler."

The door opened. A tall gray-haired woman stood there. "I heard you talking to the new muck and figured I should feed him while he's up."

"This is Lilit," Avi said, "the Tender in charge of our infirmary. Mucks are always dizzy after their first trip, so we keep you here overnight. You'll move to the barracks tomorrow."

Lilit knelt and pressed a hand to my forehead. "Do you still feel dizzy?"

I sat up to prove I didn't, but the room spun and I fell back on my bed.

Lilit tsked, then handed me a bowl of lukewarm cassava gruel. "Eat all of this, or I'll lecture you." She stood. "Avi, better let him get some rest."

Avi smiled, waved, and left with Lilit.

I sat alone, eating my gruel. Unspiced. Eflet made better.

Maybe treachery and cooking skills went together. I only managed a few bites before I set it on the floor next to my recessed bed. My stomach churned. I closed my eyes.

So much to learn. I'd always thought Eflet would be proud of me, but right now she was probably sulking or spewing Ceibak nonsense to whichever one of Jesso's daughters would listen. Maybe the Handlers on Island Ita couldn't be trusted, but Avi? There was nothing evil about her.

I thought of Father instead. Father would be proud to see me in the Tree, ready to train. Ven would have clapped his chubby hands . . . except if he'd survived, he wouldn't be a little boy now. Thoughts of where Father and Ven might be carried me to sleep.

I dreamed memories. I dreamed of glancing back at Island Ita, squinting through shadowy starlight to see Father and Ven one last time. I dreamed of waves licking at our raft, day after day. I dreamed of Mother. We had used all our rations when we saw this small island—Island Gunaji. We paddled toward it. We would all be safe.

Uncounted nagas buffeted our raft with their thick bodies. Eflet nearly fell off. All three of us were going to die. Mother knew that blood distracts nagas, though. She kissed us both and, before we knew what had happened, dived calmly into the water. The nagas forgot about our little raft. Eflet and I made it to shore. Mother didn't.

M. K. HUTCHINS

Eflet knew why Mother died. And she wouldn't tell me.

I woke screaming with Lilit's freezing hand on my forehead. Her face blurred in and out of focus. My skin burned like someone had rubbed me down with chili peppers.

"Oceans," Lilit swore.

"What's happening?" My words sounded slurred.

"Imp poison." Lilit didn't explain further. She ran in and out of the room, every motion blurring together. I tried to sit up, but couldn't manage. A distant-sounding voice admonished me to stay still.

Someone spooned bitter gruel into my mouth. I saw Eflet, except that must have been a dream because we sat on Ita, the island where I was born.

Then Avi knelt over me, delicate eyebrows pinched together. Spoonful by spoonful, she fed me a bowl of herbed broth. Half of it trickled down my chin, soaking my tunic. Eventually, she set the bowl down and took my hand. "Are you feeling any better?"

"Yes?" My skin prickled as if swarmed by hot ants.

Avi frowned. I didn't like that. "Why do you look so sad?"

Her image flickered, but I heard her ever-so-soft words perfectly: "Because you're dying, Tenjat."

CHAPTER
9

"I DON'T THINK that's a good idea," I protested. My lips felt leaded. Maybe the herbs in the broth weren't strictly culinary. "I'd like to *not* die."

Avi folded my burning hands into her slender, cold ones. "Lilit's been trying to look up this fever in her records. She thinks an imp poisoned you—a rare number of them can shoot it from their mouth. Do you remember anything like that?"

"During my test!" I gestured wildly and giggled. No, those hadn't been ordinary herbs. "He hissed at me!" I curled back my lips and demonstrated, clawing the air for extra effect.

Avi gently brought my hands down to my sides.

Lilit turned to Avi. "Poison imps tend to be shy. They're

only that bold if they find a potential poison shroud."

"Poison shroud?" I closed one of my eyes and squinted at Avi.

"A treasure that grants immunity to poison," Lilit said. "You must have one, unclaimed, in Deephell. Avi's one as well."

"You can heal me!" I giggled at Avi.

Avi's voice wavered like it came through a waterfall. "No, Tenjat. It only makes *me* immune. I can't save you. It's not as useful as it sounds."

"Hell, Hell, Hell." I giggled. Avi swayed in different directions. It was a good game, trying to watch both her faces at once, but I got dizzy and stopped.

Lilit turned toward the door. "This is no poison I know, but I'll keep checking the infirmary codices. I'm not sure what else to do for him."

Lilit disappeared.

"You poor thing," Avi whispered. More broth trickled down my throat. "And I thought I had it bad."

"You got poisoned?"

Avi nodded. "I threw up for a day straight, but Lilit found a cure in her records. Once Master Tender Manoet Called it, I recovered right away. You, though . . ."

"So you're a poison shroud and I'm *going* to be!" How nice to have something in common. "Is everyone a poison shroud?"

"I'm the only one in the Tree."

I beamed at her. Then it *meant* something that we were both poison shrouds. "I'm glad."

"Glad you're poisoned?"

"Yes!" Avi was blurry, but I could still find her face, a swath of warmth circled by the black of her hair.

"You need to rest. Close your eyes, Tenjat."

I did, then frowned. "But now I can't see you."

"That's right." Avi patted my face with a damp cloth. "Try to sleep now, my little muck."

"It's that rare?"

"Looks like the nastiest poison an imp can carry—at least, the nastiest that won't kill you outright."

I felt a soft bed under me. Infirmary. My eyes were too heavy to open, my body burned, but I heard Avi and Lilit's voices.

"What's the cure?" Avi asked, voice cool and clear.

"I only have record of two cases. One died. The other, they sent a Caller, but it doesn't say exactly what he asked for. Tender Odani, may she rest peacefully, was lazy with record-keeping."

"I'll have to talk to a Caller, then." Avi's voice was hard as flint, ready for a battle.

"Manoet can't anymore, so it's Jerohn or Enari."

A long pause followed and I managed to lift an eyelid a

fraction. Avi clenched and unclenched her hand. "Jerohn's the best. As soon as you said 'Caller,' I knew we'd need him. My pride isn't worth Tenjat's life."

"How about I bring Jerohn down here?" Lilit asked. "Jerohn won't dismiss me out of hand. And if he sees Tenjat, well, Jerohn's not heartless."

Avi sighed. "Thank you, Lilit."

I cracked the other eye open as Lilit disappeared into a vein. Avi tucked her cropped, obsidian-black hair behind one ear, shifted the weight on her feet, then fidgeted with her hands.

"Thank you," I said.

Avi jumped. "Oceans, Tenjat! You startled me. How long have you been awake?"

"Just now."

She dropped to my side and pressed the back of her hand against my forehead. "No good, Tenjat. You're scalding hot."

"From what Lilit says, I'm not getting better on my own." I weakly tried to laugh. I felt like I was melting into the bed, but I was lucid again. I'm not sure that was a kindness. "What's a Caller?"

"Someone who can make additional treasure appear in Hell. It's dangerous, and Called treasures usually only work once. Tenjat, I'm sorry I didn't notice during the trial. I'm sorry—"

A hard, flat voice cut her off. "You should be."

A trim man in Handler's clothes—I presumed it was Jerohn—had appeared with Lilit near the doorway. He folded his arms. "Didn't take you long to mess things up, did it, Avi?"

"How was I supposed to know he was poisoned?"

"You just apologized for it. You weren't sincere?"

"Of course I was!" she snapped. Then she took a deep breath and stretched her fingers out. "Now's not the time to be petty, Jerohn. You're the best Caller we have, and this man needs your help. He never did you any wrong, never caused you any trouble. Won't you help him?"

Jerohn met my eye. In one ascertaining look, he soaked up my burning face, my aches, my stomach cramps. "Poor wretch."

I didn't argue to the contrary.

"Let's continue this outside. We'll only stress the patient in here," Lilit said in a clipped manner, more command than suggestion. They closed the door, muting any further arguments. I let my eyelids do their job and block out the dimmed, vein-scattered light.

"Eflet!" I sat up, thrashing. She'd been about to explain what the treason was. Why we had to flee. Why the nagas follow her. "Eflet, Eflet!"

A pair of strong hands held me down. "You were dreaming again. Calm down. You're going to be fine." His breath smelled like salt. "We'll know in a few days if it worked."

"Thank you, Jerohn. I owe you," said Avi.

"I don't need any debts from you. Take better care of your muck next time." A handful of footsteps, and the door slammed shut.

"Eflet . . . ?" She'd been about to speak.

"I'm here," Avi said. "Calm down."

"Eflet . . ."

"Who's Eflet?"

"Sister." I felt clammy all over. "She didn't want me to come." At least that's what I tried to say, but my voiced sounded garbled. I was her last piece of family. But she didn't trust me with her secrets. The treason. What Mother died for.

"Stay calm. Jerohn Called you some medicine." She dabbed my forehead with a cool cloth. At least I had Avi watching over me.

"You must have been a good sister."

She stiffened. "I'm an only child."

"Who . . . takes care of your parents?"

I'd never seen Avi mad before, but her lips pursed into a thin line. "I don't have any."

I didn't manage to ask her how they passed. I threw up. All down my front. Whatever Jerohn did made me feel worse—left my stomach churning like a river full of nagas.

Avi and Lilit cleaned me up. Avi spoke softly. "I've looked at your records, Tenjat. How you escaped Island Ita's conquest by daring the ocean. You're strong. You can beat this."

The next week was as hazy as the previous one. I vomited bile through my nose and mouth. I shook. I burned. But I remembered Avi the best. I couldn't see her half the time, but her soft voice was ever present. Cold towels and warm broth accompanied her. She told me stories of great battles. Tenders ripped to shreds by nagas before they could retreat into the roots. Handlers dying in glory, saving their comrades. She knew lots of stories from two hundred years ago, when carrying too many children and waiting too long between coral reef feedings left our Turtle emaciated. The soil rotted, the rivers turned gray, half of the farmers starved, and the Turtle drifted as if dead. Brave Handlers rushed blockades of nagas to gather algae and fish larvae with their nets in the wide, dangerous ocean.

"Tell me a story about our High Handler? His arms are legend," I said groggily. No one knew the javelin like the High Handler.

She stiffened, then exhaled. "But you haven't heard the story of the eighth trip to feed the Turtle."

M. K. HUTCHINS

"An eighth?"

"Yes. Eight trips before our Turtle was strong enough to swim to a coral reef and feed on squid and octopus. The nagas had gnawed away that many roots."

She told the story. She fed me. When I did open my eyes, her hair glimmered like polished onyx in the golden vein-light. And she smiled at me, like it wasn't a burden to sit at my bedside and fill the room with the soothing sound of her voice.

After another week, I could sit up and feed myself. The fever turned to a simmer, then broke all together. One morning, Lilit brought me Handler's clothes—the breeches that cinched at the knee, the fishskin-like shirt. "Avi's almost done with Handler Reliak."

"Reliak?"

"Avi's a half-Handler. Graduated after her three years as a novice, but not a master. She trains under Reliak when she doesn't have other duties—like you—but she'll be here soon. You're to start training today."

Lilit left the clothes next to my bed.

I stood. As I stretched, the aches in my bones dissipated. I was ready. The clothes felt cool, smooth, like new skin.

A knock, then Avi's voice. "You ready?"

I opened the door, and Avi pulled me after her into a wide,

circular room studded with a dozen doors—other sickrooms, I supposed. In the middle stood a waist-high circular cabinet. Lilit sat at one end, grinding something in a mortar that smelled like rotten turkey eggs. An ancient man in Handler's clothes leaned on the cabinets across from her.

"When you're back at the House of Kin, make sure to take this with all your meals, understand?" Lilit asked, scraping the stuff into a leather pouch. "Tell Gija to remind you."

The man thanked her, and left with the pouch.

From the thin, clawlike scars on his limbs, the man must have been a Handler in his youth—taxes cared for any Handler or Tender who reached old age. Lilit turned to us. "Before you go, I want to inspect your arm."

I rubbed my arms. I didn't remember injuring those in the test, and they felt fine. Only when Avi sighed did I realize Lilit meant her.

"It's fine," Avi said.

"Then let's see it."

Avi rolled up her sleeve and turned, trying to block my view. I stepped around her. A six-inch yellow gash cut across her shoulder.

"That's supposed to be *fine*?" I wished I could help cure her, like she'd cured me. "Are you sure you should be practicing with me today, instead of resting?"

"It's shallow. It'll heal."

M. K. HUTCHINS

"And it'll heal faster with something on it." Lilit rummaged under the cabinet then pulled out a jar of salve and slathered it on the wound. Thankfully, it only smelt like burnt cassava leaves. "There."

Avi rolled down her sleeve.

"How'd that happen?" I asked.

"Naga skirmish last night. They're getting restless." She gave me an apologetic smile. "I was lucky. They came after me hard, but Handler Reliak backed me up. Half-Handler Deri lost his arm. Better hurry up and get you trained."

Before we managed to leave, a graying Tender in immaculate clothes stepped from a vein into the infirmary. She spotted Avi and smiled. Her voice sounded like wet sand. "How are you?"

"Fine." Avi brushed past her.

I hurried to catch up, glancing back as the infirmary door closed. "Who was that?"

"Master Tender Manoet."

"Is she . . . ill?"

"She used to be able to Call, like Jerohn. Her last Calling went poorly—tore up her throat. She's been sickly since," Avi said tersely. She took a sharp right. "I could take you to the Hellroom through the veins, but you need to learn your way around. See how the walls are different colors?"

Her tone didn't allow for more questions about Manoet. I nodded as we turned from a passage as pale as the inside of a cassava root to one the color of Avi's deep brown eyes.

"We use the wood colors to orient ourselves. You'll get the hang of it." A lattice of golden veins overhead lit our path. We took a left and descended a tight spiral staircase uncomfortably reminiscent of twisting through the dizzying golden veins.

We passed two Handlers, but they wrinkled their noses and brushed past us. I glanced over my shoulder, but they turned a corner. "Looks like Jerohn's not the only one who doesn't like you."

"Don't let it bother you."

Were they just jealous that she'd been able to claim both Handler and Tender treasures in Deephell? "Why—"

Before I could ask where the animosity came from, Avi pulled me through a door into a room nearly identical to the one I took the test in. "This," Avi announced, "is called a Hellroom. Tenders pull together a number of veins to make a strong current. From here, Handlers can travel to and from Deephell without a Tender to take them."

Maybe I wouldn't want to talk about why people hated me, either. I let the question drop.

"We use Deephell for all training," Avi continued. "It *almost* feels like being underwater, and imps don't normally congregate near the roots. Unlike in Nearhell, where you're lucky if the nagas give you a moment's rest before attacking. Are you ready?"

I pointed to the pair of javelins strapped on her back, tipped with gray chert. "Shouldn't I have one of those?"

"Not until you've mastered some basics." She grinned. "Go on. I'll follow you."

I stepped forward as boldly as I could pretend to be and touched the vein.

I spun, ripped upward, up through the Tree . . . and burst into the cold, black mist of Deephell. Somewhere, I must have turned around and gone *down*. Avi appeared right behind me, the root veins of the Tree glowing softly under our feet.

"How do you feel?" Her whole being shone brilliantly, just like before.

"Good." It was true. After two weeks in bed, I floated in cool mist. I felt *free*. I grinned, and turned to see Avi match my expression.

"It's wonderful, isn't it?"

I nodded. My hands were gray, almost like the mist. Maybe after I robbed Hell, I'd glow too.

"There's so much to learn—swimming, hand signals, dives, javelin maneuvers. You have to work fast. You were a farmer, right? I'm sure you noticed that the soil's turned poorer."

Rud's attempted takeover of my field jumped to mind, as

well as the musty smell I'd noticed all over the island. "Yes."

"The Turtle needs to feed—badly. It's starving and the land suffers. It's only getting worse." Her expression hardened.

At least with Jesso, Eflet wouldn't go hungry. I nodded.

"We're nearing a coral reef. The nagas know the island is weakest, most vulnerable, before the Turtle feeds. They're already attacking more frequently," she patted her injured shoulder, "but just before we reach the reef, they'll swarm and try to kill the Tree. Master Tender Manoet thinks we have five weeks until that battle. Hopefully we'll win, and hopefully that's soon enough to keep this season's crop from rotting."

Five weeks. My lungs felt cold.

"We lost four half-Handlers to the nagas last time we fed. Since half-Handler Deri was injured in the attack the other day, we only have eight full Handlers, a dozen half, and a dozen mucks like you."

I remembered the funerals of the four half-Handlers, green-and-blue banners hanging limp in the rain during the procession.

"You're one of a small group, Tenjat. All of us will fight— even the mucks. So. Are you ready to work hard?"

"Let's get started."

A quarter-grin cracked her face. "Good. Hand signals first."

M. K. HUTCHINS

She explained that while there was a treasure that granted speech underwater in Nearhell—a jade-studded knife—they only had one Handler with that gift. Everyone else relied on signals. Clenching my fist, then quickly stretching my fingers wide meant *retreat*. Clapping my shoulder meant *I'm injured*. There were dozens of them—rally down, rally up, rally to me, and advances in all directions. She even taught me back-up chin signals, in case my hands were full, but advised me that these smaller movements were harder to see in battle.

Once during the training session, an imp charged me. I floated, helpless, while Avi coolly slashed it open. The imp dissipated into smoke. Avi assured me again that Deephell, with its occasional imp, was a much safer place to train than naga-infested Nearhell, but I still kept half an eye on the swirling mists below us after that.

Midday, we returned to the Hellroom and Avi fetched us a lunch of mashed cassava with shredded cassava leaves. Avi spent the afternoon teaching me basic swimming strokes. I practiced kicks like a turkey snapping its beak to launch myself up, and used my arms above my head the same way to shoot me down. These were supposed to navigate me quickly in battle.

By the end of the day, my muscles ached. I knew hand signals and some swimming strokes, but neither of those would fend off the nagas when they attacked.

"Good work today, Tenjat. I'm sorry to move through so much so quickly, but I don't have three years to make you battle ready." She favored me with a sad smile. "Tomorrow I'll be gone. I'm still a half-Handler and have training of my own. Practice your hand signals whenever you have a spare moment—breakfast, lunch, before bed."

"What will I do while you're gone?" I felt like I only opened my mouth to ask questions.

"Handler Het will give you mundane tasks, usually scrubbing down corridors. He's not the most pleasant of fellows—maybe that comes from being in charge of the taxes—but the day after, you'll be with me. Better show you to the mucks' barracks and mess hall."

I swam to the glow above me—to the tip of a vein. I twisted, spiraled, down, down . . . except it really had to be up, didn't it? I spilled into the Hellroom and landed on all fours. I breathed, waiting for the room to still, but I didn't throw up. By the time I rocked back on my heels, Avi stood in front of me.

"You're getting used to it." Her infectious, crooked grin returned. "Follow me."

Whatever Eflet thought about the Handlers here, she was wrong. I'd trust Avi with my life—she'd already saved it twice. Once by defending me from the imp's attack and again by nursing me back to health.

M. K. HUTCHINS

I followed Avi through a number of multi-hued corridors to a door at the end of a hall. The walls didn't muffle the commotion of jeers, snorts, laughter, and periodic thuds from inside. When she swung the door open, everything fell silent. Except for one more thump. These apparently came from mucks jumping off top bunks, and the poor fellow couldn't stop midair.

At first, I thought their silence was out of respect, but nearly all of the dozen mucks sneered at Avi or exchanged knowing glances. The mucks ranged from a scrawny twelve-year-old to a broad-shouldered young man a year or so older than me. I didn't recognize any of them. Either they came from the other side of the island, or they'd simply managed to avoid contact with Jesso and anyone associated with him.

Avi ignored them and gestured me to a lower bunk near the door. "I believe this is the one reserved for you. The mess hall is on the first right down the hall. Can you find your way back to the Hellroom we used?"

"I think so."

"Good. I'll see you the day after tomorrow, then." She smiled and made as if to pat me on the shoulder, but thought better of it and left.

The other mucks pounced.

"She hate you, or what?" asked a muck with a beakish nose.

"Avi-tavi-ravi has a little muck now, eh?" called someone I couldn't spot in the corner.

Another with a thin mouth asked, "She kissed you yet?"

"Glad it wasn't me!" laughed a fourteen-year-old with too-white teeth.

And then, one louder voice: "Shut up!"

The boys stilled, and the broad-shouldered muck stepped forward. He was tall, maybe eighteen, and the muscles under his Handler's shirt left me no doubt that he didn't let other people do his dirty work.

"You Avi's muck?"

"Yes!" I stuck my chin up in the air. I didn't know what was wrong with these mucks, but I wouldn't be ashamed of having the best half-Handler on the island as my trainer.

"You ain't going to make it to Handler. You going to drop out and be a hub. I give you a month. Or are you two *already* hubbing?"

Words—most of them colorful—flashed through my head, but my fist acted faster than my mouth. I threw a punch at his face.

M. K. HUTCHINS

CHAPTER
10

THE BOY EASILY sidestepped my blow. He laughed. "See? More suited to being a hub than a fighter. It took you what, two weeks to start training? Little Daef over there"—he pointed at the scrawny twelve-year-old—"only needed two *days* to get over being dizzy. You've done a lot more with Avi than go to Hell."

My neck tensed. "I was poisoned. I'm no hub."

"I didn't hear that, cuz I don't listen to no hubs. Did anyone else hear that?"

"Nope!" said one boy.

"Hear what?" asked another.

I glanced over all of them. "Don't you realize we'll be fighting nagas together in five weeks? This is moronic."

A few of the boys shuffled nervously, but the big one

grabbed a friend to play a game of pebbles drawn in chalk on the floor. Everyone else followed his lead and returned to their evening games, ignoring me.

I sat on my new bunk for a while, watching them as they diligently didn't watch me. Then I wandered to the mess hall. Here, the wood shone a glossy nutbrown. A few long tables and benches sat inside, plus a serving table. Except for me, it was empty. Apparently everyone else had already eaten. I loaded myself up with what was left at the serving table— sweet cassava drinks, stewed pumpkin garnished with its own roasted seeds, and savory beans. I nibbled my meal away until I couldn't prolong going back to the barracks.

The other mucks didn't look up when I entered. I lay on my bunk and tried to sleep, but my back hurt and my hands were cold.

Was there something wrong with Avi? Everyone seemed to hate her. Somewhere in my wonderings, Lilit crossed my mind. The medic Tender, at least, liked Avi, and Lilit had a sound head on her.

I rolled over again in my bed, my too-full stomach flipping as I worried about Avi, Eflet, and the coming naga battle.

The next morning, I lay in bed and watched the other boys pour out to the mess hall for breakfast. The barracks were semicircular and contained eight bunks for a total of sixteen

M. K. HUTCHINS

beds, each protruding from the living wood of the Tree. Here the wood was the color of perfectly crisp cassava cakes. Other than the beds, a basket for each muck's spare clothes, and the chalk-drawn games on the floor, the room was bare.

These mucks fit Eflet's description of Handlers as bullies, but they were just mucks. Training would turn them into something more. *Maybe she lied about knowing what our treason was, trying to get me to stay.* She'd looked desperate enough. *Except, other than hiding why we'd fled Island Ita, I never knew Eflet to lie.*

I stretched out my aching arms, legs, and back. I was pulling on my shirt when someone squeaked, "Hello."

I turned. It was Daef, the twelve-year-old the burly muck-leader singled as pathetic, but not as pathetic as me. He must have taken the tests young.

"They . . . they pick on me, too," he said, fidgeting. "Especially Kosel. He's the big one."

Daef's eyes, feet, and hands all looked too big to match the rest of him. *Maybe when he grew into them, Kosel would leave him alone.*

"I'm . . . sorry," I fumbled, not sure what to say, or what he wanted. I'd already proved I couldn't fight Kosel.

He looked up, eyes bright with curiosity. "*Has* Avi kissed you?"

"No! Why would she?" I asked, incredulous.

"You don't know, do you?" He stared, awed by my ignorance.

"That Avi's a girl? I noticed that." I didn't understand why he made a big deal of it. Getting both Handler and Tender treasures sounded rare, but Avi was dedicated and I wasn't a hub.

Daef glanced nervously at the door. "Do you want to meet me, before dinner, in the first-floor Hellroom? It'll be empty, and I can tell you then."

At least someone was willing to explain, albeit in private. "Okay."

"So . . . we can be friends, then?" he asked. His too-large, hopeful eyes reminded me of a dog Jesso once kept, begging for scraps.

"Sure. We can be friends."

Daef gave me directions to Handler Het's workroom, so at least I wasn't late. Niches in the wall held a number of flat, cotton-wrapped parcels. A broad desk dominated the center of the room, not unlike the counter in Lilit's infirmary. Except, of course, the infirmary had Lilit and this place had Het: a bald man glowering at me from behind the desk, a wet ink brush in his stubby fingers.

I lined up next to the three other mucks in the room.

"Inat, Hegal." he stabbed his pen in the direction of two other mucks. "Corridors. Tenders' level."

Those two bowed, then scampered off.

"Varo, Tenjat. Hellroom duty. Someone failed a test this morning—bottom Hellroom. Now get out of my sight!"

Het dipped his brush into a split conch shell, then slashed a few angry strokes across his paper as if we weren't present. We left through the door we'd come through.

"Great," Varo grumbled, refusing to look at me. "Just what I wanted to avoid."

He'd played games with the burley muck, Kosel, last night. "You really care what that big lout says?"

Varo didn't respond. We stopped at a supply closet. He grabbed a bucket and jammed it into a spout made from the living wood of the Tree. When he pulled the handle back, water flowed out. His bucket filled in moments.

"How does that *work*?" I asked. "Tenders made that, right?" They pulled up water for the island's springs and streams— why shouldn't they be able to make this? "Is it fed from a reservoir above this room that the Tenders keep filled, or does it somehow pull and filter water directly from Nearhell?"

The water didn't smell salty; it couldn't be straight ocean water.

Varo grunted. He either didn't care, or didn't care to tell me. The spout filled my bucket as quickly as his. I followed Varo as he stomped all the way to the Hellroom.

Acrid, half-digested cassava plastered the room. Even the

ceiling. The stench hit me in the gut. For a moment, I thought I'd be ill. Heat prickled down my scalp.

Then Varo tossed his bucket over the mess. The tang of soap competed with the reek of vomit. I swallowed, and set to work. By lunch, my knees were soaked, I smelled horrid, and I wanted to slap Varo with a wet rag for turning away every time I entered his line of sight.

At last, we finished and headed to the mess hall. Novice Tenders popped from the veins in the wall, carrying platters still steaming from preparations by those in the House of Kin. Spiced beans, stewed pumpkin, and heaps of fruit. With the other mucks around, not even Daef would look at me. So I took my huge plate and sat at the end of the table. The mucks could hate me all they wanted, but it wouldn't stop me from enjoying this feast.

I hadn't gotten far before I heard a voice behind me. "Tenjat."

I turned, startled. A Handler with a broad face and solid jaw stood behind me. He looked maybe a decade older than me.

"I'm Jerohn."

I stood. This man had saved me from the poison. "I . . . I have a lot to thank you for."

"Don't mention it. Are you finished eating?"

The gaze of the other mucks burned the back of my neck, but they stayed silent. Was there a right answer? I reluctantly turned from my half-finished meal. "Yes."

"Good!" He grinned, his friendly face disarming. "I've recruited you. When you're not working with Avi, you're going to report to me, not Het. I've already talked to him."

The mucks muttered, but I couldn't hear what they said. Jerohn headed for the door. "Follow me."

I scrambled after, the pit of my stomach twisting. Jerohn didn't like Avi. Was this some kind of ploy against her? Would she have told me to stay?

But Avi wasn't here to ask. I followed Jerohn up an impossibly long spiral of stairs the color of good silt. He opened the door at the top and ushered me inside.

Luscious yellow sunlight flooded the room from an arched window on the opposite wall. Wisps of green leaves and blue sky played across the opening.

"Go ahead." Jerohn nodded at the window.

I rushed to the window and stuck my head out. A cool wind teased my hair and the leaves. I looked up and green blanketed my world. I looked out and caught a glimpse of the glittering surface of Hell. The thatch-and-pole homes I could pick out on the Turtle's back looked small as toys.

"Amazing, isn't it?"

I pulled my head back inside the window. How long had it been since I'd tasted cool, fresh air?

"I requested this room particularly. It's easy to forget what being a Handler means if you never look outside the Tree. You're a young novice—you still have connections out there?"

I nodded.

"Remember that you've risen above that world, even when conditions are . . . difficult." He frowned and appraised my face.

"Um, yes sir."

"You've had it especially rough." He sat on the low couch that ran against the wall. The room was twice as big as my old hut. Comfortable.

"I'm better now, though." I stood straight and tried to look like the epitome of health.

He smiled sadly at me. "Come, sit."

I did so. From a shelf next to the couch, he pulled out a flat, cotton-wrapped parcel.

"Have you seen one of these before?"

I shook my head.

"This is a book, a codex. Handlers don't just fight for the Tree. We rule the island. Het works with tax records and assigning mucks cleaning duties. Ental and Torjan settle disputes between farmers. I keep histories."

"Oh." I chewed the inside of my lip. I had dealt with Torjan when I claimed my land, and I understood the necessity of taxes, but what use were histories?

"When we try something new in battle or find a new treasure,

I record it here. I'd love to know what kind of treasure makes a Seer. I can only hope Avi told you about robbing Hell?"

"Yes." Why wouldn't she have? "There are some treasures, like sight, that I have now, and others I have to rob from my cache."

Jerohn snorted. "Inelegant, but accurate. There are also treasures that are expended after one use. Each time we need one of these treasures, it must be Called."

"Like you did to heal me." I remembered that much from my fever.

"I knew you were bright. Yes, I'm a Caller. Only a few of us have the ability. I looked through these codices," he patted the one on his lap, "to find the right treasure to Call. The records weren't perfect, so I had to try four things. These codices contain hundreds of years of Handler and Tender lore. Master Tender Manoet keeps her own version of events, as does Lilit—duplication is good. Oh, and Het keeps a tax ledger, but taxes are boring."

Jerohn unfolded the codex until it lay across both our laps. Black and red lines, thick and thin, in the shapes of hands, heads, animals, and brushes filled the first several panels.

"This is the current codex. Today, I'll record what I Called in Hell for your recovery. Can you see why this is important?"

I peered at it. The lines were elegant, but that's all they were to me.

"I want to teach you how to do this," Jerohn said.

I blinked at him.

"Not interested?"

"N-no—I mean, I am." Codices, apparently, had helped save my life. "I wasn't expecting . . ."

"Not even all of the full Handlers can read. It's not the most important skill you'll learn in the Tree. It won't help you survive the coming naga battle. But it is a skill worth having—and one that isn't dependent on your combat training. If you only learned this"—he gestured at the page—"you'd always have a place in the Tree."

"I'd be honored." It sounded better than scrubbing Hellrooms.

Jerohn folded the codex up. "I won't have time to teach you everything before the naga battle, but I'm going to start you on inks. My half-Handler already knows how to make the bark-paper and bind a codex. If I die fighting, the two of you can continue my work. Most Handlers have a specialty, and this is mine."

"You said it contains centuries of knowledge?"

"Yes."

I stared at the codex Jerohn held. Surely in the history of Island Gunaji, nagas had unnaturally followed someone, like they did with Eflet. Maybe I didn't need my sister's trust to get answers. Maybe I could find them here.

M. K. HUTCHINS

CHAPTER
11

JEROHN LED ME across the room to a row of codices sitting on a shelf carved into the living wall of the Tree. "These seven, plus the current record, give the history of the island from the First Handler."

It seemed like a tiny space for all of history to sit in. Maybe they wouldn't have anything about nagas stalking a particular human. He gently removed the cotton wrappings from several of them.

"Can you see the covers?"

I nodded. They were made from snakeskin—some glittered like new leaves in the rain, others were an ashen brown. He pulled one of the latter kind from the shelf, its cover crackling.

"This one is the oldest." Jerohn unfolded the first section. The ink was nearly the same color as the paper. "Not good, eh? It's why the previous volumes have all been recopied."

He waved his hand at some of the greener codices.

"This particular codex has been copied twice before now. Each time leaves small errors in the text."

I nodded.

"That's why the High Handler agreed to let me recruit you away from Het. Usually Handlers only have their half-Handler's help, but mine's busy making paper. I needed someone to help me experiment with inks."

"Inks that will last a long time."

Jerohn smiled again. He smiled easily—his broad, square face was suited to it. "Yes—ink that lasts as long as its paper does. I hope to leave the perfect ink recipe as my legacy. I'm keeping a small codex. Every time I try a new ink recipe, I write down the recipe in that ink. If the recipe survives, it's good to use. If not . . ."

"Then it was worthless to begin with."

"Good, good. One of the ingredients I'm working with is gallnuts. That's where I'd like your help, for now."

"Gallnuts?"

"Disappointed with me already?"

I swallowed. I hated gallnuts. Gathering them from the

trees around my field, burning them to kill the bugs inside—it reeked. "No, sir."

"Once, the Archivist used ink from cuttlefish he hunted," Jerohn said. "Two hundred years ago, they started using ground charcoal and various liquids. It smudges. The oldest codex mentions that the First Handler had a robe dyed black by the dye of a thousand gallnuts. There has to be pigment in those things—and I *will* find it." For a moment, his eyes held none of their regular warmth. "Come."

Jerohn led me into a side chamber, full of small containers and several large vats. "Chal, my half-Handler, makes paper in here. I can explain all of this later." He gestured at piles of shredded bark, mallets, and other things I didn't recognize. Jerohn handed me a small basket and a mortar and pestle, then grabbed two pots. We left, and he sat me on the floor in front of the couch. "The basket contains some large gallnuts I collected from the Tree. Crack them open in the mortar. Dump the bugs into one pot, then grind the shell to powder and collect it in the other."

Simple enough. I opened the basket. These were bigger than my fist, smooth, and darker than Eflet's hair. I took one, set it in the mortar, and cracked down on it with the pestle.

The pestle bounced off. It took me another four steady whacks to get a crack. The next blow creaked, but a hairline fracture ran the length of the gallnut. I took careful aim and swung the pestle down. The nut split in half, but I'd swung too hard to stop before the pestle smashed through the larvae in the middle of the nut, spraying bits of squashed bug and bug fluid into my face. Part of it landed in my mouth.

It burned. My stomach twisted and I ran to the window. Lunch departed. When I finished, Jerohn stood with a cup of papaya juice behind me.

"Well, I would have suggested one of the empty pots first, but at least it looks like it'll rain soon. Poor artisans. We're right above them, you know."

I took the cup and smiled. Why had I been scared of Jerohn?

I was gentler with the next nut, taking my time with three dozen taps. I dumped the wriggling larvae into the pot. Jerohn said the Handlers would use it to bait fish to the Turtle when we arrived at a coral reef. Even people who lived near the center of the island might venture near the shores then. Birds, dolphins, colorful coral—even from a safe distance, there was plenty to see.

I pounded those two gallnuts into dust for a small eternity. Jerohn sat on the couch transcribing the old codex, only sitting up to stretch the kinks in his neck. While he carefully painted each symbol, he told me about the record he was copying. The current one was written by Island Gunaji's First Caller. She'd claimed a flute in Deephell, but it took her

M. K. HUTCHINS

two years to figure out what the treasure actually did. After that, she kept a record of everything she Called—including the medicine that saved me from the imp's poison.

Eventually Jerohn drifted into telling stories about pranks that he'd played on his master as a half-Handler, then, to my delight, he retold exploits of High Handler Banoh. Battling nine nagas at once and winning. Dueling a High Handler from an invading island with only a spindle whorl. Stopping a feud between the Hari and Desohn families with wisdom sharp as a javelin. Jerohn told the stories better than even Gyr.

My arms burned and I smelled like bug guts, but this beat scrubbing Hellrooms. Eventually Jerohn cleaned his brush and came to inspect my work. He ran his fingers through the gallnut powder. "Perfect."

A novice Tender stepped out of the wall, bearing a tray of cassava cakes from the House of Kin. She set it on the table and disappeared just as quickly. Delivering food seemed to be a novice Tender duty, just like scrubbing corridors and Hellrooms was a muck's responsibility.

"Ah. Would you like some dinner? They're stuffed with turkey and spices—far nicer than the stuff in your mess hall. On rare occasions, we even get venison. I daresay you de-serve it."

Dinner. I was supposed to meet with Daef before dinner.

I glanced at the window, but already the sky cooled toward twilight.

"Something wrong?" Jerohn asked.

I was already too late—surely by now Daef had gone to eat. I'd have to find a way to silently apologize. "Not at all."

I took a cake. Jerohn was right—these put the mess hall to shame. And the mess hall's fare was richer and more abundant than what farmers could regularly afford. In three years Eflet would be eating this well too. I devoured three cakes before realizing I was probably being rude. I brushed the crumbs off on my breeches, but couldn't resist grabbing another one. "I was wondering . . . in all those codices, is there any record of nagas following someone?"

"Following? Nagas always follow people."

The succulent turkey snagged in my throat. "I mean, following one person. More than normal. Acting strange."

"Not that I can recall." He pursed his lips. "Maybe. I can look."

Jerohn took a cassava cake and, thankfully, didn't ask why I wanted to know. "How's your training coming?"

"Avi's a great teacher."

Jerohn frowned. He apparently disagreed. "We're going to need every hand to fight when the nagas swarm. Train hard, Tenjat. I'd hate to save you from poison only to watch you fall to a naga's claws."

～ ～ ～

M. K. HUTCHINS

I slipped into the barracks late. The other mucks ignored me, but before I lay down, Daef managed to catch my eye. I shrugged an apology.

Daef tilted his head to the side in question, and mouthed *tomorrow?*

I nodded. Daef whipped around, and engrossed himself in folding his spare set of clothes.

Having a real bed still seemed odd; I gratefully collapsed onto my soft mattress and pulled the sheet over my head. I tried not to think about Eflet's secrets, or why everyone—including the amiable Jerohn—disliked Avi. I needed sleep.

Tomorrow, I had training.

When I entered the Hellroom, Avi stood bent over with her hands flat on the floor. "Ready to stretch?"

I tried to mimic her position, but I could barely get my fingertips to the ground.

"How was your first day in the barracks?" Her voice took a nervous edge.

"None of them seem that concerned about the upcoming battle."

"They've trained longer than you, so they think they know what to expect. Don't let their overconfidence dull your training."

Avi kept stretching. She didn't explain why they'd all sneered at her. Might as well ask outright. "Is there a reason all the other mucks distrust you?"

"I guess they don't like having a girl be a Handler. Probably jealous that I'm better than the lot of them with a javelin." She stood, pulled one leg up behind her, and changed the subject. "Did you practice your hand signals when Het didn't have you running?"

"Er."

She scowled at me. "Didn't I tell you about the battle? Reliak told me we've caught a good current. We've got less than four weeks now."

Less than four weeks. I swallowed the lump in my throat. "I meant to, but Jerohn recruited me."

Concern pinched her eyebrows together.

"It was interesting. He worked on a codex while I ground gallnuts for him."

She snorted. "Couldn't find any real work for you?"

"It's real. He's making a new kind of ink."

Avi's expression didn't change. Feeling defensive, I said, "I'm sure whatever specialty you and Handler Reliak work on isn't any more important."

"We coordinate Handler and Tender actions and develop new ways to integrate the two groups' abilities."

"Fighting tactics?" Jerohn kept those in his codices.

"Mostly optimizing vein placement. That limits strain on the Turtle, makes hauling water easier. Having good launch points for naga battles is critical too. But if the roots sprawl everywhere, another island could snag us, melt their veins into ours, and invade the Tree from the inside. Handler Reliak used to be in charge of external defense, but High Handler Banoh promoted him to this because it's more *important.*"

"Oh."

Avi shook her head. "*Books.* Bah. Let's go do some work."

She yanked me into a vein. I twisted upward—I mean, downward—and spilled into the gray mists of Deephell.

Either talking about Jerohn put her in a foul mood or her shoulder wound was bothering her. Avi only briefly reviewed the hand motions, then she drilled me on the leg and arm snaps until the monotony of it made me want to scream.

Avi motioned for me to stop. "These strokes are great for a quick burst of speed or stopping your momentum, but it's a clumsy way to travel with a javelin."

"You're going to teach me how to use a javelin today?" I eyed the pair on her back.

"No. The javelin will fall into place once you know how to swim."

Maybe I wasn't a proficient swimmer yet, but if I was going to be fighting nagas soon, I wanted all the practice I could get with a weapon in my hand. "Shouldn't we—"

"Listen to your trainer?" Avi cut in with a disarming smile. "That's an excellent way to get to the javelin faster."

So I watched her every movement and followed every word. Avi showed me how to hold my arms at my side and kick my body like a dolphin, using the snapping motions we'd already practiced to change direction. And then we drilled. Drilled and drilled.

By the time we spilled back into the Hellroom, I had aches on aches, especially through my arms, already sore from grinding gallnuts yesterday. That whole time, we'd only rested briefly, once, for some cold cassava cakes Avi nabbed from the House of Kin.

Avi gave me a small smile. "Maybe I pushed you too hard. Sore?"

"A bit." I bent over double, hands braced on my knees while I caught my breath.

"Go get some dinner and rest. We'll have more training in the morning." Avi paused, as if waiting to walk me out.

"I'm fine. Really. Just going to stretch a bit." I raised my hands above my head to prove it.

Avi nodded. "You're a good muck."

She left through a vein. I stretched a little longer — maybe that would keep soreness away tomorrow — but I didn't head to dinner. I had a meeting with Daef.

Finally, I would get some answers.

M. K. HUTCHINS

CHAPTER
12

DAEF HUDDLED IN the corner of the Hellroom we'd agreed to meet in, hugging his legs. His eyes were as wide as a startled rabbit's, but as soon as he saw it was me in the doorway, he deflated. His arms fell away from his body and his shoulders sagged. "I thought one of the other mucks was going to find me! You took long enough."

"That's how long we usually train," I said.

"Really? I bet she's training you on special maneuvers already!" His eyes flashed with excitement. "Tricks and fancy kicks . . ."

"No. We just do swimming strokes."

Daef laughed as if I'd made a joke, then stopped with his mouth partway open when he saw I wasn't kidding.

"Oh. Are you that bad at swimming?"

If I was, Avi hadn't said. I sat across from Daef. The knot of current-rich veins that could pull us to and from Deephell glowed on the wall between us.

Daef rubbed the back of his neck with one of his too-large hands. "I won't laugh again. I'm glad you're in the barracks. The muscled jerk has someone other than me to pick on."

"Thanks." Was that supposed to make me feel better? "You mean Kosel, right?"

"Yeah. He used to be my neighbor, y'know? Always had a great time with his brothers beating up on me. Then I made it here, thought I was set for life. Two weeks after they made me a muck, Kosel took the test. He wasn't going to—his brothers all had and hated it—but once he saw a runt like me get in . . ."

"He followed you."

"Yeah. I've been here longer, but it doesn't matter. He's a lot older, y'know?"

I clapped him on the shoulder. "It's worth it," I said. "You're a Handler now. You'll catch up."

"I wish Kosel wasn't here to catch up to." He looked at me and brightened. "But it's a lot better now! I mean, if we all don't die in the naga battle, the Handlers want to graduate Kosel early to a half-Handler, and I've got

M. K. HUTCHINS

loads of time left, so . . . so we can be friends."

"Friends." We gave each other a solemn nod. At least I had one ally in the barracks.

"I promised to tell you about Avi, huh?"

"Yeah." My throat tightened. Avi . . . Avi had knelt over me and fed me soup, had saved me from that imp in Deephell. I didn't know what I expected, but I didn't want there to be anything bad about Avi *to* know.

Daef crossed the room and sat next to me. He dropped his voice. "Well, men are usually Handlers, right? Women are all Tenders. Don't want us always around, tempting Tenders to take a hub, right?"

"I thought it depended on what treasures we found in Deephell."

Daef shrugged like that didn't matter. "The test for being a Tender is if you can travel through the veins from one point to another — veins without a current."

I nodded. Avi had explained that too.

"Well, Avi had passed the Tender test, pulling herself from one room to another. But before anyone could stop her, she jumped back in the veins and plunged into Deephell. There wasn't a Handler to guard her, like our tests."

My pulse quickened, thinking about the imp diving at me, teeth gleaming cold. "And?"

"The Tender administering the test, Lilit, she went for a

Handler as fast as she could. Y'know what they found when they reached Avi?"

If I knew, I wouldn't be asking. I shook my head anyway, letting Daef revel in his story-telling.

"Avi waiting for them, two imps dissolving next to her."

Now he had my undivided attention. "She was armed?"

"Nope. Fought them with her bare hands. Admittedly, both of them were small imps, the other Handlers say, and she did get poisoned."

I couldn't fathom why he said it like some piece of dirty gossip. Taking on two imps by herself? I'd done nothing more than scream and flail. Quiet pride warmed my chest. I had the best trainer in the entire Tree. Maybe I shouldn't begrudge that she insisted I master swimming before touching a javelin.

"And they let her be a Handler, because the Tree needs Handlers more than Tenders right now. I don't know what's so scandalous about her," I said, finishing the story for Daef.

"That's not how it happened. Some Handlers wanted to throw her out of the Tree altogether for her stunt. They brought it before the High Handler."

"And he let her stay?"

"Yes, but with a punishment." Daef fidgeted. He wouldn't look at me.

"Which was?"

He squirmed.

"Daef!"

He grimaced. "Once she was a half-Handler, she had to watch over the tests for a year and choose her own muck."

My heart dropped to my stomach. "And her time ran out so she got stuck with me." Me, the sickly muck she didn't trust with a javelin. Avi deserved better.

"No." Daef stared at his toes. "It hadn't been half a year when she chose you."

I peered at him, confused.

"Handler Het, who insisted there be a punishment, liked this one because he hoped she'd pick someone she liked, make him a hub, and get herself kicked out."

With a wrenching feeling like tumbling into twisting gravity from the calmness of Deephell, I wondered if Avi chose me because she found me detestable, or because she didn't.

"So." Daef cocked his head to the side, "does she like you?"

I didn't have an answer. Avi and I worked well together, but suddenly, that made me feel like I'd swallowed mud. "Thanks for letting me know."

Better to find out sooner than later. Better to hear it from a friendly source.

Daef still stared at me in the way you look at molding food, deciding if it's still good to eat. "So?"

"So what?" I asked.

"Have you guys . . . y'know"—Daef spun his oversized hands

awkwardly in the air—"spent time dulling the pain of shame?"

"Of course not!" I snapped. "We're in the Tree. We don't have anything to be ashamed of. We're *Handlers*."

"Right. Right, of course." Daef laughed. It sounded forced. "Just curious. Sorry."

"Avi trains me like any other half-Handler would," I firmly stated. Of course, I had no basis of comparison. I'd never trained with anyone else. That snagged my thoughts. *Did* she treat me differently?

I probed Daef with questions about his training for a few minutes. He was more advanced and his trainer gave him more breaks, but other than that, our days in Deephell were similar.

"The other boys are probably all back in the barracks by now." Daef fidgeted. "I don't want . . . y'know . . . them to think I talked with you."

I silently sighed. I couldn't really blame him for publically avoiding me. It's not like either one of us—or both of us together—could do anything to stop Kosel. "You go first then. I'll wait around here for a while, so Kosel won't suspect."

"Thanks." He stood. "We should do this again. Not too soon. That would be suspicious. Ten days from now?"

I nodded, sure I wouldn't be able to match his chipper tone.

Daef practically bounced out the door. I slumped against the wall, feeling less than buoyant. I'd spent my life running away from all things husband, and I thought I'd beaten it weeks ago when Avi, face shining like a goddess, told me I'd passed the test.

Avi picked me either because she thought I'd make a good hub, or because I was obviously too slow and stupid for her to ever be tempted. I hated even the *possibility* that she might fancy me as a hub. But my mouth tasted just as rancid when I hoped she loathed me. Avi saved my life. Avi was a brilliant, brave Handler. I ached for her respect as much as I feared getting kicked out of the Tree.

I watched Avi during our next day of training for signs of affection, weakness. She smiled. Did she want me as a hub? Was she floating closer to me than necessary?

I had a life to build for myself and for Eflet—even if Eflet would rather fester in poverty.

"Concentrate, Tenjat!" Avi snapped as I fouled the strokes for switching directions a second time. "Did you not hear what I said about the nagas swarming? We had another skirmish *last night*. The Turtle has to feed at the coral reef. The nagas will *all* swarm before we get there, and we're going to need everyone, even incompetent mucks like you, to fight!"

Maybe she did hate me. I should have been relieved, but I felt nauseous.

"Tenjat—" Avi began, then froze. Her feet flashed copper,

and as if that light were a solid wall, she kicked and shot past my head. She whipped one of the javelins off her back.

An imp. Clawed hands and feet, a face full of teeth. I snapped my legs together in the stroke Avi had taught me, following her.

Avi jabbed, but the imp turned, pinning the weapon between his spiked elbow and his side. Avi swore.

I reached for the other javelin still on her back, but it botched Avi's attempt to grab it herself.

"Idiot!" she screamed at me, then kicked off my chest. We both drifted a few feet from the imp.

The imp turned his claws and teeth toward me.

Avi's feet flashed copper. Once again, she streaked through the mist, the second javelin in her hand. It pierced the imp's back, dissolving it into gray smoke.

Avi's obsidian-sharp glare frightened me more than the imp had. "Idiot. Idiot." A shallow cut oozed blood across her hand. "I'm a half-Handler, you're a muck. I have *two javelins* and you have nothing. It is my job to train you. It is my job to keep you safe. How can I do that if you throw yourself at imps?"

Her fist trembled on her javelin shaft. No, I didn't need to worry that Avi wanted to make me her hub. She hated me.

"Maybe I shouldn't bother training you. You're going to get yourself killed when the nagas swarm."

M. K. HUTCHINS

CHAPTER
13

AVI DRILLED ME the rest of the afternoon. Hard. I felt too queasy afterward to manage more than plain cassava cakes in the mess hall. Then I collapsed in my bed, grateful for once that no one wanted to talk to me.

The next day, she drilled me nearly as hard, worry lines between her eyebrows. I didn't complain. She didn't want to make me a hub and I should have been happy with that. But how could I be happy that this remarkably talented half-Handler was stuck with an idiot muck? I felt like a burden to the person I respected most in the Tree. At least all the drilling and my burning muscles helped me focus on something besides her contempt.

Avi fetched us cold cassava cakes for lunch again,

disappearing into a vein and returning a minute later. I couldn't stand eating under her silent, worried stare, so I asked her about the copper flashes.

"I claimed a pair of copper shoes from Hell's Treasury—that makes me a grabfoot. I can turn the mists solid under my feet for a moment."

"Useful."

"Only sort of. The shoes are copper, not silver or gold, so they don't work in Nearhell. I have to make sure I don't get lazy here. Kicking off of something is a great asset: you get speed, you change direction fast, and nagas can't do it. In Nearhell, you're in trouble if you end up in open ocean. Stay close to the roots."

I nodded and let the conversation die off. No point in bothering her with more questions.

The next four days blurred together. Avi drilled me on all the hand signals and swim maneuvers until I saw them when I closed my eyelids and they filled my dreams.

Then I had another day off—Handler Reliak needed Avi's help with something about the upcoming battle. I headed to Jerohn's.

"Ah, Tenjat!" Jerohn set his codex down. "I heard you'd be joining me today. Excited to grind up more gallnuts?"

"I suppose."

M. K. HUTCHINS

"I know. Not the most exciting thing. *More* interesting, though . . ." Jerohn walked over to the small shelf of history records. Rain pelted the leaves outside the window. "I skimmed for records of odd naga behavior. I'm afraid I only found an excellent example of why your work with the inks is so important."

He pulled out a codex with a faded snakeskin cover and gestured me to join him on the low couch. Near the back, he unfolded the pages a foot. "Here. Three hundred years ago, a man washed ashore claiming to be from Ceibak. The record says that he could play with nagas in the shallows and they wouldn't so much as mark him. A transcription error if I ever saw one. The original probably said the nagas covered him in marks. Or that he pretended to play with nagas."

Ceibak. Maybe it meant to say that nagas followed him everywhere, like they did Eflet? My eyes settled on a drawing. Prickles ran up my breastbone. Eflet had drawn something just like it before. "What's that picture, next to the words?"

"A diagram. The crazy man *insisted* that a Seer founded Ceibak and showed them that the world is different than what we know."

Odd. Eflet mentioned Ceibak often enough, but she'd never once mentioned a Seer. Then again, I'd done my best to ignore everything she said about the mythical place. "Can you read the labels out loud?"

Jerohn frowned. "The clouds at the top are the Heavens.

Here's what he calls the Upper Realm." Jerohn's finger passed a flat line and continued downward to some waves and a picture of a Turtle. "Here's us, with Hell beneath."

"What's the Upper Realm supposed to be?"

"He has it mixed up with Deephell. The notes aren't clear, but the man said the people of this 'Upper Realm' buried treasures and that Handlers travel *up* to the underbelly to claim those treasures."

I stilled. I always felt like I traveled up when I went to Deephell. I pointed to a circle with radiating lines. "What's that?"

"The sun. He claimed it perpetually circled around the Upper Realm. Supposedly it set in the Upper Realm's west, to appear in the west here, travel across our sky, and rise into their east."

I peered at the picture. A land where the sun appeared in the east instead of the west. Strange.

"Complete rubbish." Jerohn closed the codex. "I hope that kind of error fills you with terror. Be diligent with your inks."

Grinding gallnuts gave me too much time to think about the past—about when I'd seen that picture before.

We'd been on Island Gunaji for only a few months. Arja wanted Eflet's help with making cassava flour and sent me to fetch her. I told Arja if Eflet wasn't working, she wasn't feeling well. Even as a child, Eflet was steady, calm, hardworking. She was the only thing in my life that never changed.

But Arja insisted. I found Eflet in the clearing, sitting on a split log next to Jesso. Jesso beamed at me, fatherly. I stiffened. He wasn't my father. I left my father and brother on Island Ita and my mother in the ocean.

"Arja wants your help, Eflet." I turned my back to Jesso as best I could.

Eflet gestured to scratchings in the dirt—a Tree and Turtle overshadowed by a line the sun circled, like I'd seen just now in Jerohn's book. "We were discussing Ceibak, if you'd like to join us."

"Take a seat." Jesso smiled and patted the log next to him.

I glared at Jesso and turned to Eflet. "Why are you coddling him with Ceibak lies? *I'm* your family. *I'll* take care of you."

"Jesso's been more than kind. You could at least be polite."

"He's a *hub*."

Eflet's face hardened. She started to speak, but Jesso raised a hand. He didn't have the decency to get mad at the insult. "I've been called worse. I have work to do. I'll let Arja know you'll be along soon."

Jesso left me alone with an angry Eflet. "He takes us in, feeds us, and that's how you treat him?"

"Have you *seen* how many children that man has?"

"And why is that so wrong? Look around you! Where is there a greener, happier place on the island?"

"His children *slow* the island!"

"What if they didn't?"

She may as well have demanded that crops grow without planting or for the sun to appear in the east in the morning. "Children slow us."

"Nagas slow us more." Eflet gestured at the drawing. "Would marriage be evil if children didn't hurt the island? We could change our world, Tenae. Never fight the nagas. All the fields could be green and bounteous. No one would have to be ashamed of being poor or having children."

"Ceibak nonsense!" Wishing wouldn't keep us fed or miraculously destroy the nagas.

Eflet sighed and kicked her image into dust.

That memory gnawed at me. Eflet knew the same picture. Had there been a man that the nagas ignored? Should it have said followed?

I paused my gallnut grinding to stretch out my hands. Ceibak nonsense, indeed. Maybe I felt like I was traveling up . . . but some Ceibak enthusiast could have heard that from a Handler and made this picture up.

Except that didn't explain how Eflet's diagram matched the one in Jerohn's book. Had Eflet been preaching Ceibak on Island Ita? Is that why we had to flee? I started grinding again. My stomach churned, and not from the stench of bugs. That couldn't be the secret. Mother, dying for Ceibak madness?

It was a relief when Jerohn spoke, pulling me from my thoughts. "Dinner will be here soon. Go wash up."

"Thanks."

By the time I'd cleaned up, a novice Tender had dropped off bean-and-turkey-stuffed cassava cakes and a spicy dipping sauce. Jerohn and I sat cross-legged on the floor, the tray between us.

"This is delicious." I thanked him. "Lots better than what I used to eat."

"Your mother was a bad cook?"

I couldn't remember my mother's cooking. "My sister did the best with what we had, but . . ." I fumbled, embarrassed. Fancy spices and turkey had been beyond our meager means.

Jerohn waved a hand. "Forget it. I know what you're trying to say. We all come from some hub's wretched farm, Tenjat."

"Do you ever see them? Your family?" I asked.

He shrugged. The rain had slowed to a patter. "Some in the Tree do. Some even put a member up in the House of Kin." Jerohn laughed. I bit my lip. That's exactly what I aimed for, after all. "But me? No. They're a bunch of hubs, and hubs' wives, and hubs' children. We're different."

"Some try. To be better," I stuttered, thinking of Gyr. "But they still . . . well, not everyone can pass the Handlers' test. Not everyone can be an artisan."

Jerohn shook his head at me. "You're too close to it, my friend. Leaving is hard for some. Some mucks don't finish because of it."

"Not me." The only thing worse than being a hub was being a self-made hub, someone who had a choice to be something more and rejected it. Exactly what Eflet wanted me to do.

"Good. After you graduate your three years of training, you'll be a new person. You won't be a farmer anymore. You'll be a half-Handler."

I fidgeted with the cassava cake in my hand. "You didn't miss anyone?"

"I'll admit, I went back to see my family. Once, and only once. When I graduated to half-Handler and could go, when I still thought they were worth knowing." He shook his head. "You see things differently after three years. I wasn't one of them anymore."

"You haven't kept up with them?" Even if Eflet hated me when I could see her again, I'd still be her brother. I'd still want to know she was fed, warm, and well.

"We all have a past, but we don't have to talk about it here. We're all part of the Tree now."

"It's rude to ask?"

"A little. Don't worry about it! Here, have another cassava cake," he tossed me one, and I caught it. "Just don't go pestering everyone about where they're from, all right? You already know the answer. All our stories are pretty much the same."

I finished the cold cake I already had, then started on the fresh one. "I asked Avi once—at least now I know why she looked so upset."

Jerohn laughed. "She's worse than most, Tenjat. I don't know what her life was like on the outside, but she once punched a half-Handler for being too nosy."

I frowned at the cassava cake in my hand. "She said she was orphaned. It must have been hard."

"There are a fair number of people here who were, I think. Orphans always come out for the tests. Those with two living parents sometimes feel like they can't leave them, especially if they don't have siblings."

"Were you an orphan?" I immediately bit my tongue. "I didn't mean to—"

He chuckled at me. "No, no, I wasn't. It's fine. You're not going to get thrown out for asking. You just might annoy people."

I ate the rest of my cake, wondering what his family had been like. Lots of siblings? None? Arja's brother had abandoned her. He could be Jerohn, for all I knew—he'd certainly be somewhere in the Tree, if a naga hadn't killed him.

I wanted to ask, but I didn't want to know. The thought of Jerohn abandoning his sister and parents to poverty left a sour taste in my mouth.

"Something wrong?" Jerohn asked.

I wanted to laugh—what *wasn't* wrong? The Turtle didn't have enough Handlers for the upcoming naga battle. My sister didn't trust me because I wanted to make a good life for both of us. And the devoted Avi chose to train me because she considered me an oafish idiot. I hated feeling like a waste of her talents.

"I know you're in a difficult position . . . but I'm training you too. You'll always have something to offer the Tree." He gave me a sad smile and I finally understood the motivation behind it. He hadn't requested to train me because he saw promise. He pitied me—the poor fool who ended up as Avi's muck.

Pride burned in my throat. "I'll be a good Handler, too. I have a good trainer."

Jerohn missed the bitter edge to my tone. His smile deepened, probably mocking my naivety.

I wanted to deck him. I didn't have to meet the other trainers to know Avi was good. I'd seen her dive through

Deephell to skewer imps. I'd endured her drills. I'd felt her determination. She hadn't given up on me, the sorriest muck to enter the Tree, even when I lay delusional in Lilit's infirmary.

Avi was amazing. I worked hard. Between the two of us, I was not going to be a failure.

Over the next three days, I pushed myself ruthlessly in training. We did everything—snapping kicks, dolphins swims, and drills that involved following Avi's hand signals. Maybe seeing that strange Ceibak drawing had me on edge. Maybe it was that conversation with Jerohn. Or maybe it was knowing that each of Avi's smiles were false.

"It's a careful balance," she said, "watching the nagas and looking for signals. During a coordinated fight, a Tender can also send signals through the roots—rapid flashing means retreat."

She swam closer to me, every stroke as precise as if she'd been born in Deephell. Being near her, aching for her respect and knowing I didn't have it—it felt like the imp poison eating my body all over again.

"I'm not retreating. Drill me again."

She smiled. "Tomorrow we'll start work on the javelin."

I didn't smile back. I worked until my arms and legs burned, then worked some more. Avi's every perfect maneuver reminded me how clumsy I must seem to her. All that hard work did nothing to quiet my frustration.

At the end of the day, we spilled back into the Hellroom. I'd already marched halfway out the door before Avi called for me to stop.

"Shut the door, Tenjat."

I did so and glared at the floor. I wanted to sit in the mess hall and eat under the open, honest contempt of mucks whose opinions didn't matter.

"Is something wrong?"

"No."

At least she managed to frown. "You've been on edge. Did Jerohn . . . say something?"

I heard the unspoken question. *Did he tell you about my past, why I picked you?*

"Shouldn't I be on edge? Working hard? Aren't we close to the reef?" I snapped. I'd suffered an entire day of feigned smiles and worried glances—she didn't need to state out loud why she'd become my trainer.

"We're about a week out, but—"

"Good." I left. I couldn't stay and we weren't friends— even if I did want to ask if she felt like we spiraled *up* to Deephell, like Jerohn's codex showed.

I was almost to the mess hall when I realized I told Daef I'd meet him today.

I squeezed my eyes shut. I didn't want to go. I wanted to hit something. Pick a fight with Kosel. I slowly turned around, going out of my way to avoid my Hellroom so I wouldn't run into Avi.

I shouldn't have snapped at her. Avi was only doing her duty for the Tree and Turtle, same as me. I wondered if I'd upset her. But I couldn't imagine Avi—the girl who'd taken out two imps bare-handed—caring about what some lowly muck said.

Halfway to my meeting place, I heard shouting at the front door.

"Calm down," said the half-Tender guarding the door.

"You have to come! There's a mob! They're already burning our home!"

My heart stopped. I knew that voice: Lyna.

CHAPTER
14

"I CAN'T DO anything to help unless you tell me more details," the half-Tender said, sounding annoyed.

"They're burning our home! They're—"

I jogged around the corner and Lyna fell dead silent, her pleading eyes latching on to my face. Soot streaked her cheeks and her dress—a pretty, embroidered dress with a red sash, a bride's sash.

"Jesso's farm," I said.

Lyna nodded, mutely.

I shoved passed the stout half-Tender. "Novice!" her voice cracked after me. "Novice! You are not allowed to leave the Tree!"

With a grim nod to Lyna, I ran.

"Novice!" she screeched. I didn't care. Eflet was at Jesso's. So was Gyr.

The late afternoon sun had turned yesterday's hard rain all to steam. The muggy warmth reached to my bones, long chilled by the darkness of Deephell. I ran fast, faster. I was in the artisans' village for only a moment, then through the flat expanse of grass that surrounded them, past one of the three pools where the Tenders drew up water. Sickly farmland next, the dying soil turning gray like mold-eaten cassava — worse than when I'd left for my test. Then I ran through the forest, flecks of mud clinging to my legs. Twilight fell around me as the sun rose into the east. I prayed I wouldn't step on any snakes.

Halfway through a dank stretch of forest, my chest tightened. I tried to resist, but my strides slowed. I jogged, jumping over trees when they lay across the path. I was lucky I didn't split my foot on a rock.

I smelled Jesso's farm before I saw it. Wet wood and wet cassava gave way to wet, thick smoke. My stomach churned. I fell out of the forest onto a graveyard of cassava: juvenile stems stripped bare, charred, and bent — like skeletal fingers groping up from the musty ground.

I jogged past, unable to tear my eyes away. Cassava was life.

Then I found the house. It was ash, white-black rubble

on its earthen platform, the storage vases broken, the cassava flour turning the mud pale. My heart throbbed in my ears. Where was everyone?

Footsteps trampled the rain-softened land, far too many for Jesso's family. I breathed slowly. I had to think, think—

I heard a scream suddenly choked off, and the thinking ended. I ran to the clearing where, a month ago, I'd eaten honeyed wafers with Lyna.

Handlers, Tenders, and Jesso's family filled the clearing. Gyr lay in the center on a clean cloth. Lilit held his puffy thumb between her hands.

"You're lucky it's only one thumb bone. Think about how much more fun it would be to set an arm."

Gyr panted, holding his side. His voice sounded strained. "Do you have *any* idea how much it hurts to scream with half a dozen broken ribs?"

"You've only got two, so you don't know, either," Lilit said calmly.

I stumbled to his side. "Gyr, what happened?"

He turned and a pain-filled grin spilled across his face. "I thought you weren't allowed out until your training ends."

"He's not." Lilit cinched a brace around Gyr's thumb. She stared down her long nose at me. "Avi's going to skin you alive. Quite foolish, running out."

Of course the Tenders and Handlers would beat me here.

M. K. HUTCHINS

They'd used the veins that ran through all the trees on the island. "I . . . I wasn't thinking."

"Of course you weren't." Lilit shook her head. "Avi's with the other Handlers, rounding up those responsible. She'll be back soon."

"Who's Avi?" Gyr asked.

"She's . . ." I fumbled.

"She?"

I was hot, tired, hungry, and feeling stupid for arriving late and useless. More tersely than I meant, I asked, "Is Eflet safe?"

Gyr, oddly, didn't call me on sidestepping his question. He shifted uncomfortably, then winced and grabbed his ribs. "When will that start to feel better?"

"Later," Lilit mumbled, still working on the splint for his thumb.

I punctuated each word. "Gyr. Where. Is. Eflet?"

Secrets or no, she was my sister. Right now, those secrets seemed like nothing to knowing if she lived.

He turned his eyes down, away from mine. "She wasn't here. She's perfectly safe. Unharmed."

"She's not living with you anymore?" My voice cracked. I'd made a deal with Jesso. I'd thought he'd keep it. Keep her safe, fed. I'd only been gone a month.

"No. No, she lives here." He squirmed like something

sharp needled his back. "She's safe. Isn't that enough?"

It wasn't, but I'd find her after asking questions. "What happened here?"

"Lyna's wedding. Lots of guests, eh?" Gyr chuckled, and instantly regretted it. He put his uninjured hand to his ribs.

I glanced around the clearing. Handlers stood watch while Gyr's sisters and Tenders alike bandaged his brothers. "I've never been to a half-burned wedding before."

"They'd started the Bride's Evening, got Lyna dressed up."

The night before a bride's wedding, she stayed up all night with her unmarried sisters and friends, celebrating their last hours before the groom took her away to his home. On the island, the distance was usually short, but it provided an excellent excuse to stay up and eat honeyed wafers and candied fruit.

"Then a mob showed up. Caught all the men, tied them up, started burning things. I showed up as they were rounding up the girls."

"Showed up?"

He winced, suddenly awkward. "The field Jesso wanted to give to you? I was working over there."

"All right."

"Anyway, yeah. Lyna escaped and ran to the Tree, but I guess you know that last part."

From behind me, Oja, Jesso's nine-year-old, piped up,

"Lyna got away because Gyr came and fought the bad guys!"

I turned in time to see her dramatically smash her fist into her palm. "Is that so?"

"Yeah! He punched them and Lyna got away." Her enthusiasm faded quickly, though. Her voice softened. "That's why they beat Gyr up. Gyr, then Father."

"Jesso's hurt?"

Gyr closed his eyes and nodded.

"Where is he?"

Oja pointed across the clearing. I hadn't noticed the still body with all the other people around. A dozen running steps brought me to his side. He lay limp as a dead fish, eyes closed. Bruises blotted his face, arms, legs—everything I could see.

The sweat turned cold on my back and my gut felt like I'd just spilled out of Deephell. I'd never liked Jesso, but I didn't want to see him beaten or burned. Not on the eve of a wedding, not ever.

Jesso's eyes cracked open. "Tenjat." His voice sounded like bark scraped against bark. "How'd you get here?"

"How'd you get like this?" I asked. I couldn't imagine kind, fatherly Jesso doing anything to provoke such an attack. I resented him for always acting fatherly toward *me*, but he didn't deserve this.

Jesso took my question more literally than I'd intended.

"Oh, the mob put me in a circle. Took turns kicking me while someone fetched cassava syrup to boil. Took their time about it, for which I'm grateful. The Handlers got here before they tossed it on me. Well, much of it." He gave a self-deprecating chuckle, then clutched his ribs, turning on his side.

I could see the other side of his face now. Raw blisters marched down his cheek and across his neck. I winced in sympathy. "Is . . . anyone else this bad?"

He collapsed flat on his back. His voice rasped softer now. "No. Gyr fought them before they could tie him up—he was trying to protect me. I don't think anyone else has injuries worse than a few scrapes."

I glanced around the clearing again. Lots of bandages, but everyone except Jesso and Gyr milled about on two feet. Most of the Tenders had already left.

"Why would anyone do this to you?"

Jesso blinked slowly. He had to be exhausted, in shock, something. "Garums' cuttings won't take root. Soil's too bad."

"That doesn't have anything to do with you!"

Jesso shrugged weakly. "I'm an infamous hub. They didn't see any reason *not* to blame me. Said they wouldn't let any more of my children marry and weigh down the island with more souls."

He was right—he was an infamous hub. But I'd never

imagined others would attack him like this for what he was. My gut twisted again, looking at the blisters.

"It wasn't Panti," Jesso said.

I blinked. "What?"

"Panti. I know you were worried about Lyna marrying him. But it was Bavi."

I exhaled slowly. Bavi was a calm, intelligent man who'd chosen to tend his ailing mother rather than take the test. Lyna could be happy with him, I thought. "Good."

"You've always been a good friend to my children." Jesso smiled again, a crooked smile with burns on one side of his face. "I appreciate that. Not everyone thinks like you."

I blinked. Was he calling me a hub? There was no reason to scorn his children. Everyone had a father; they had the misfortune of having an infamous one. "Do you know where Eflet is?"

"She wasn't here," Jesso said.

I scowled. I'd heard that already. "Where *was* she?"

Jesso winced, his expression remarkably similar to Gyr's from earlier. He didn't want to tell me.

Just then I spotted Avi crossing the clearing. Her eyes tightened on me and her stride lengthened. No, she wasn't pleased I'd run out of the Tree. I swore silently. Avi wasn't going to give me time to check on Eflet.

"Jesso, promise me. Promise me Eflet is safe."

"Safe and happy," he said. "I promise. I'd never lie to you, Tenjat."

Looking at his bruised and burned face, at the sincerity in his eyes, I knew it was true. I couldn't respect Jesso's choices, but I could trust him.

Mere words still didn't feel like nearly enough, but I didn't have time for anything more. I stood to face my trainer.

CHAPTER
15

"WOULD YOU LIKE me to chastise you here, or back in the Tree?" Avi jammed a fist on her hip.

I swallowed hard and straightened my spine. "I need to check on my sister first."

"I'd sooner leave you looking like Jesso's twin than indulge your rule breaking." Anger tensed every inch of her.

I couldn't win this argument. At least I hadn't lost anything by asking—she already thought me a hopeless muck. "Tree."

She grabbed my hand, marched me to a tree, and pressed her palm against it. A slim thread of gold seeped out between the ridges in the bark, then Avi pulled me through it with her—gliding through tight, twisting spaces down to the roots, then back up an even tinier vein. We spilled into a neat, unfamiliar room. A lattice of veins, thin as spiderwebs, shimmered on the ceiling, illuminating the smoke-gray walls, a sunken bed, a loom, a chair, and a small chest. An arched window overlooked the star-studded ocean.

"Didn't you think?" Avi burst. "Shoving aside a Tender and running from the Tree? You could be expelled!"

I swallowed hard. I had no defense. If I'd been thinking, I'd have begged the Tender to take me to Jesso's farm immediately.

She slumped into the chair. "Tenjat, you're such a muck."

I supposed I was. I sat on the floor, fiddling with the cotton weft dangling off the loom.

She sighed. "Don't you know that what we do here is important?"

"Yes."

"Then why'd you do something so . . . so . . ."

I bit my lip. Eflet was why. Gyr was why. Lyna, thank the gods she wasn't married to Rud's cousin, was why. After seeing Jesso lying there so badly injured, even he was why. But that was wrong and that was weak, and Avi wouldn't understand.

"I'm sorry," I said.

"You have to focus! Four times this year, we've had to pass by coral reefs because a bigger island was already there. This time, we don't have a choice. Our Turtle's not strong enough to make it anywhere else. There will be a

M. K. HUTCHINS

naga battle in a week and a half. You'll be part of it."

She didn't have to yell at me; I knew the Turtle needed to feed. I'd smelled the dying soil and seen the aftermath of scared, angry men with only Jesso to attack.

"Can we do what they did two hundred years ago?" I asked. "Take nets, fight past the nagas, gather food for the Turtle?"

"They had forty Handlers—*full* Handlers, Tenjat. We have eight. We'd all die."

That shut me up.

"Garums' fields aren't the only ones not taking to their new planting—the cuttings are *rotting*," Avi said.

"How many fields?"

"Maybe one in ten. The overfarmed. The Garums should have cleared forest for new fields years ago." Avi paced. "They're scared, and fear makes people stupid. We don't even know how to punish them. They don't have the cassava to pay back what they destroyed. Jesso was a wealthy man."

Was a wealthy man. The words hit me. I'd depended on him to keep Eflet fed. "Jesso and his family. Do they have enough to survive on?"

"I'm not sure. Handlers Ental and Torjan are in charge of farmer disputes—they'll make sure no one starves while they sort this mess out. They'll send cassava flour from the Tree's stores if they have to."

I exhaled. "Good." Then I shook my head. *Good* was not the right word to describe what had happened at Jesso's.

"If the Turtle doesn't feed soon, the Garums' attack will only be the beginning," Avi said. "I know you worry about your sister, Tenjat, but this is *exactly* why you need to forget she exists and focus on training. We do what we have to so the island can survive."

Including working with someone she found detestable, to make sure she didn't turn me into a hub and get us both kicked out.

"Doesn't that mean the Tree can't afford to expel me?"

"You're impossible." Avi shook her head. "Handler Torjan will give his report to High Handler Banoh tonight. As your trainer, I'll be allowed to speak. Torjan doesn't have anything against me and I'll put in a favorable report."

"I thought you were mad," I said.

"I am. But you're right. We can't afford to lose anyone." Avi gazed out the window, her cropped hair falling across her cheek. "It's time for me to report."

And probably time for me to return to my bunk. I stood. "Wait, there's no door. How am I supposed to get to the barracks?"

She raised an eyebrow. "You *want* to go there? So you can be pestered by the other mucks until a verdict's reached?"

"Guess not." Actually, I doubted it would matter. What would they do—ignore me more vehemently?

M. K. HUTCHINS

Avi shook her head. She touched a vein in the wall and vanished.

I sat in the chair and examined the loom. Avi must have made it from the living wood of the Tree. Whispers of gold veins patterned the high polish of its elegant frame—it all seemed too perfect for mortal tools. The half-finished cloth displayed no picture, no curving lines—just tight, neat blocks of blue and green. Meticulous perfection.

It was good weaving, but less than fascinating to look at. I dragged the chair to the window, watching the dark, endless ocean and waiting. We had to be higher than Jerohn's room. From here, I could constantly feel the sway of our starving Turtle's swimming. It reminded me of floating on the waves of the vast ocean with Mother and Eflet.

My mind drifted to the diagram in Jerohn's book and Eflet's words about Ceibak. Maybe it wasn't just a fantasy for hubs. It was a fantasy I'd like too—an island safe from nagas, where everyone always reaped a bounteous harvest and no one was poor. I chewed my lip. Without a need for Handlers, I supposed I'd have to teach Avi how to farm. Maybe outside the Tree, I could show her that I wasn't wholly incompetent. Earn her respect. We could be friends and the entire island could be well fed.

But we didn't live on Ceibak. Gyr's broken ribs proved that.

"You're back sooner than I expected." I stood.

"I told you there wasn't much of a choice."

I nodded.

"Torjan talked to everyone at the scene. They're all your family?"

Embarrassment instead of rage heated my cheeks at the suggestion that Jesso and I could share blood. It should have been anger, but after seeing Jesso half-dead, I couldn't manage it. "They're taking care of my sister, until she can go to the House of Kin. She's the only family I have left."

"As soon as Torjan mentioned that, I knew you'd stay. The High Handler has a soft spot for families."

"Does he have a family?" I asked.

"A brother. Waln. He lives in the House of Kin."

The evening coolness rustled past the leaves into the room. "Strange. I'd never thought about High Handler Banoh having family."

Avi snorted. "So he appeared out of the air, full grown without any parents? He's human, like the rest of us."

"*Not* like the rest of us. He's legend."

"He's a good fighter, but that's all." Avi's voice was heavier than stones. The spiderweb-thin veins in her room cast watery light, making her look twice her age.

M. K. HUTCHINS

"High Handler Banoh let you stay, be a Handler. Why do you detest him?"

"Because everyone else thinks so much of him."

I didn't understand her. "Did you *want* to be a Tender instead?"

"No. The Tree needs Handlers the most right now. If, at some time, they need Tenders more, I'll switch. I claimed a golden spindle whorl from my cache in Deephell. It means I'm the only person in this Tree who can navigate veins this small." She gestured at the walls and their hair-thin veins, then sighed. "Which reminds me. Time to get you back to the barracks."

Avi took my hand and pulled me through the veins to the barrack door.

"Training tomorrow. Get some rest." Avi gave me a half smile, and I tried to return it. I'd made an idiot of myself. Avi had done a great job picking me for her muck. Had my incompetence been that glaring during my test? Screaming and flailing had seemed like a good idea at the time.

I trudged inside.

"Heard you got in big trouble," jeered Sosib, the fifteen-year-old muck with the beakish nose. He actually looked at me.

Kosel rammed his elbow into Sosib's side.

"Ow!"

After that, the mucks averted their gazes from me. Some whispered loud insults meant for my ears, though directed to their neighbors—things about failed mucks going crazy and running out of the Tree to find a farm and a wife. Things about lover's spats. Stupid stuff. Avi was more dedicated to the Tree than any of these mucks.

"You all know we're a week and a half from the coral reef?" I asked no one in particular. "Bickering with each other is idiotic."

No one made any sign of hearing.

As I slumped onto my bunk, Daef caught my eye. His creased frown asked if I really had stumbled into trouble. I dusted my shirt off to signal I was fine. A half grin and a cocked eyebrow replaced his worry. I stretched, then waved one hand in a circle: *tomorrow*. Daef seemed to understand, because he happily squirmed down into his bed and fell asleep.

I couldn't drift off so easily. Jesso and Gyr had both promised Eflet was safe, but why hadn't she been at Lyna's Bride's Evening? I couldn't get rid of the gnawing thought that something wasn't right. But I couldn't do anything about it now.

The next day I trained. No talking, no smiling, no breaks. Avi hadn't picked me for my conversational skills, so I might as well shut up, work hard, and save her from my voice. We started with javelins. She was right: with the swimming strokes in place, holding the javelin was simple. It wasn't as exciting as I'd imagined—just a new set of drills.

When we'd finished, she smiled, mirror-bright as she floated in the middle of Deephell. "Nice work."

"Thanks." No smile in return. She didn't want it. Especially after yesterday. I left and found Daef where we'd met before.

"I can't believe you're still here!" he cheered when I entered. "Did you really run out of the Tree?"

"Yeah," I said with a glum shrug. "Pretty stupid, huh?"

"I wish I had. I know I'm not supposed to, but I want to see my family, y'know? Make sure they're okay. I guess if I checked on them every week, I wouldn't be focused on training. I know I'm going to have to fight soon . . . but that seems so unreal."

The knot in my stomach tightened. I should have found Eflet first, then asked questions.

"You okay?" Daef asked.

"I didn't get to see everyone." I leaned against the Hellroom wall. "And I should have."

"Oh."

We kept talking about life outside the Tree. He told some stories about his older brother and sister, and I told him about the time Jesso lashed together several branches into a hoop and hung it from a high tree. All of his kids, plus Eflet and me, competed to see who could throw a rock through it from the farthest back. Telling a happy story about Jesso seemed right, after yesterday's mob.

"I know no one likes to talk about where we're from," Daef said, "but well, shouldn't we? That's why we're here, right? To protect the Turtle? I mean, we support the farmers."

I wished Eflet were here. She'd say farmers supported Handlers. I actually missed arguing with her. "No one likes to be reminded that they came from a hub's home."

"We *all* came from a hub's home, and now we're the defenders of hubs. We ought to care about them, eh?"

I blinked. Everyone else in the Tree seemed to distance themselves as much as possible from hubs and everything else outside.

Daef hugged his knees and stared at the floor. "Maybe I think too much. I don't have anything else to do, with the other boys always picking on me."

"Daef, you're one interesting muck. And not in a bad way." He was right. Gyr deserved my respect, regardless if he married. And Jesso deserved protection, even if he was the island's biggest hub.

"Thanks."

"When do you want to meet again? Two days from now?" I asked.

He smiled again. "Yeah. I'd like that."

"I'll tell you more stories about Eflet."

"And I'll tell you about the time my older brother beat up Kosel!"

"Really?" That was a story I'd enjoy hearing.

Daef giggled. "It was great!" And then, more somber, "I wish my brother were here now."

"Yeah." I thought of Eflet, Mother, Ven, and Father. Before I left for the tests, I missed most of them. Now I missed all of them. "I understand that."

Training with Avi continued the same for the next week. Drills. More drills. When she told me I'd have the next day off to work under Jerohn, I almost asked if I could help her and Handler Reliak. I didn't want Jerohn's pity.

But Avi didn't need me to trip her up. After breakfast, I walked into Jerohn's.

"Hey," he said with a small, sideways grin. "Doing okay? I heard about your . . . adventure a few days ago."

I flinched. "Yeah . . ."

"Don't feel bad. They let you stay, and you won't do something stupid like that again, will you?"

"It was for my sister," I said, chin level with the floor. "Not stupid."

He cleaned his brush in one of the compartments of the

halved shell that held his ink. "Tenjat, you haven't been here long enough. You want to help your sister? Forget all about her. Focus on the Tree, on the naga battle. I know Avi doesn't make you work hard, but—"

"Avi drills me until my teeth are numb."

Jerohn laughed, a full belly-rolling laugh. "Is that what she says? Didn't you just *start* javelin?"

"Avi's dedicated to the Tree. She's teaching me and she's teaching me well."

Jerohn set down his brush. "You're a good man, not likely to be distracted by a pair of pretty eyes. Surely you've heard her history by now? If she cared about the Tree, she would have accepted her assignment as a Tender."

"Avi would gouge out her eyes with a turkey claw if it would save this island."

"Avi's nothing but a would-be hub-maker."

"She's the greatest Handler on this Turtle!" My face was hot, my voice too loud. "She'll be the High Handler one day if the council of Handlers has half a brain between them."

I saw how hard Avi worked. She served as a Handler because that's what the Tree needed. If the Tree needed a Tender, she'd be a Tender. She deserved recognition, even if it was only from the clumsy muck she detested.

Jerohn's joviality turned cold. "*Avi,*" he practically spat her name, "causes nothing but trouble. Special arrangements,

M. K. HUTCHINS

special room, no barracks for her—do you think all that's worth it for a barely competent slip of a girl? And now she's making a husband out of a promising muck."

"I'm no hub!" My throat felt tight. Somewhere in the back of my head, I knew I shouldn't shout, but I'd endured day after day of Avi's fake smiles, knowing she hated me. Jerohn taunting that she liked me *too* much seemed unbearably cruel.

He laughed—bitterly. "Do you know she had to pick her trainee? Het wanted to see her turn a muck into a hub instead of a Handler. Funny, eh? Looks like she's got to you."

"Avi's not that stupid." Avi was brilliant.

"She's *really* got to you," Jerohn said.

"I'd say she's gotten to *you*. Get all riled up when she's mentioned. She's better than you, isn't she? Wish she'd make you her hub so she could teach you how to swim rather than flail in Hell? It must hurt to be bested by a 'barely competent slip of a girl.'"

His lips drew thin. "I felt sorry for you. I took you in to learn the trade of inks and writing so that no matter how much Avi ruined your training, you'd still know something useful, could still make a life here for yourself. I'd speak more carefully if I were you."

"I don't need your pity, *hub*." I spun around and strode out.

CHAPTER
16

JEROHN DIDN'T SAY anything or call out after me. I stomped down to the barracks. For once, they were silent, empty. Everyone was training or scrubbing halls for Het.

I sat on my bunk. Then I lay on my bunk. Turned over twice.

I should have waited to bicker with Jerohn until after dinner. It was going to be a long day and he always had meat in his meals.

How long until my rendezvous with Daef? Hours, hours, hours. I'd just have to sit here, alone.

Then I realized I had liberty to rummage through Kosel's basket. I could hide his clothes. Tear them up so he got in trouble? No, but some boys brought little treasures from home. Maybe I could steal something and barter for a truce. Maybe he'd beat me up instead. I creaked the door open and looked down the hallways. All clear.

I'd never come to the barracks at midday before, so no one else would either, right? I envisioned Kosel ramming his fist down my throat for sneaking into his things. No, that's why I should act now. How much better would it be to eat dinner chatting with Daef than alone at the end of the table?

The basket was small and flat, woven from palm fronds. I unlooped the cord that held the lid down and flipped it open. Two shirts, two pairs of breeches, a comb. A stash of stolen cassava cakes—interesting. A few colored rocks. *Maybe* he'd be embarrassed about colored rocks? Enough to shut up?

A bit of red cloth peeked out from underneath the breeches. I tilted my head to the side. A *proposal* sash? I reached for it, just as the door slammed open.

"Tenjat!"

I jumped around. Avi. It was only Avi. I closed the lid and hastily looped the cord back into its place. "Yes?"

"So it's true? You walked out on Jerohn?"

I stood. "I did."

"Tenjat!" She waved her hands wildly as she spoke, as if she were slapping invisible versions of me. "You *just* got permission to stay, after the mess you made running out of the Tree! Now this. I was checking Deephell for safe routes to the treasure caches and in bursts Jerohn, high and mighty, to inform me my muck's disgraced himself again, how he's going to the High Handler. Did I do something to upset you?" Every muscle from her temples to her shoulders was tight. "We talked about this. About focusing! You insulted him before you left?"

"I called him a hub."

Avi ground the heel of her hand into the space between her eyes.

"He said he took me on because you're incapable of training anyone. I disagreed."

"*That's* what this is all about?" Avi asked, wide-eyed.

I didn't know how to interpret the surprise on her face. I pressed my lips together and nodded.

She laughed, a ringing sound that made the whole room resonate. "You delightful muck!"

"I'm not in trouble then?"

"For showing loyalty to your trainer? No, no." She exhaled. "Jerohn knows that. He must have been trying to worry me before I heard the real news. Did you really call him a hub?"

I scratched the back of my head. "I . . . guess I did."

She threw her arms around my back and hugged me. Warm, soft, real. Oceans, I hated to admit it, but I liked that. Avi, next to me. She smelled sweet as copal resin. I raised my hands to hug her, to hold her closer, but my hands hovered

M. K. HUTCHINS

just over her back. I wasn't supposed to like this. To want this.

Avi stepped back, beaming, before I could decide what to do. "You're wonderful, Tenjat. I wish I could have seen his face."

Cool air separated us. I coughed nervously and tried to pretend nothing had happened. "You could walk up and repeat the insult—I'm sure the result would be equally amusing."

Avi beamed. "Maybe I'll try that. Since Het's not expecting you anyway . . . well, you don't want to sit around here, do you?"

I didn't know how to tell her I wanted to finish rummaging through Kosel's basket, so I nodded.

"Handler Reliak and I were checking routes through Deephell. Want to watch?"

My eyes widened. "Really?"

"Anything for you today, Tenjat." We started down the corridor. In the most amiable tone, she continued, "Now, describe Jerohn's face. Every last muscle."

I had her laughing all the way to the Hellroom.

I heard Reliak's gruff voice before I saw him—it seemed to radiate from the expanse of Deephell. "Took you long enough. Brought the muck along to feed to the imps, eh?"

"He called Jerohn a hub!"

"Oh, did he now?" I finally located Handler Reliak, a bit above us and to the left.

"Jerohn was insulting me," Avi said, swimming up. I followed.

"Real surprise there."

The most visible part of Handler Reliak was his scraggly white eyebrows. The rest of him appeared dim as soot, just like I did in Deephell. Something about his face seemed familiar, though.

"Anyway," Avi said, glowing brightly as usual, "this is Tenjat. Tenjat, my trainer, Handler Reliak. I told Tenjat he could spend the day watching us, as he managed so cleverly to extricate himself from squishing bugs for Jerohn."

"Ah, but now your spy is revealed." Reliak's barrel chest gave his voice resonance. "However will you keep tabs on the nefarious Jerohn now?"

"Pin him to a wall with my javelin? Then I'd always know where he was."

"But then you'd have to look at him all day."

"Point."

People like Jerohn and Het might hate her, but I smiled to see that at least Avi had a trainer who appreciated her.

Handler Reliak peered at me. "Are you that little refugee boy from Island Ita?"

That's where I knew him from—he'd been part of the trio

M. K. HUTCHINS

that heard my fabricated story of fleeing a conquest when Eflet and I washed up on Gunaji. "Yes, sir. You have an amazing memory."

"The Treasury was kind." He tapped the side of his face. "In any case, I'm glad we were right not to throw you back in the ocean!"

"How are the two Tenders from my hearing?" I hadn't yet met many Tenders besides Lilit and, at least as far as I knew, I'd never run into those two. Handlers and Tenders seemed to largely occupy different parts of the Tree.

"Asal died getting Handlers out of a naga battle four years ago. Meraja retired to the House of Kin not long thereafter," Reliak said, solemn.

I awkwardly stumbled over giving him my condolences.

"It's all past," Reliak said. "Come on."

I followed him and Avi into Deephell. It was less exciting than I'd imagined. Mostly, it felt like we were swimming in place, though the glow of the roots did dim. Then Reliak swore.

"Imps or other islands' Handlers?" Avi asked.

"An imp swarm. Let's turn around."

I followed wordlessly until we all spilled into the Hellroom.

"I thought we might be able to take the mucks to rob Hell today," Reliak muttered.

Avi leaned toward me. "Sometimes the imps gather in

clouds and merge to make larger creatures. It's safer to wait until they move."

"I . . . didn't see any imps."

Reliak tapped the side of his head again. "I've got jewel-encrusted gold coins in Deephell. I see *much* better than most folks."

I chewed that over. If he had such good vision, maybe he knew why it felt like we spun upward though the veins, but landed down in Deephell. But I didn't want to ask about Ceibak or Jerohn's codex directly. "Have you ever tried to rob the Heavens?"

"Heaven?" Reliak stared at me, confused.

"We go down the roots to rob Hell. Couldn't we go up the branches to rob the Heavens? Or at least ask the gods for advice?"

Reliak frowned, his eyebrows pinching into a shaggy line across his face. "I don't think the gods like that. I tried once. Got flipped around and ended up here."

"Oh." I felt dizzy. Deephell *could* be somewhere above the Tree.

I spent the afternoon sitting behind Avi and Reliak in a small room, not unlike a Hellroom. Avi and a tall, athletic Tender named Lasyna sat on the floor, hands pressed against the deep-red wood, apparently moving root veins. They

M. K. HUTCHINS

described the vein's positions to Reliak and Avelo, a stout, gray-haired Handler in charge of external defense. All four of them debated the best strategic launch points and how to minimize damage to the Tree during battle.

Most of it washed over me. I couldn't follow the jargon. My thoughts drifted to the diagram in Jerohn's book and the one Eflet had drawn years ago. I was annoyed at myself for letting it bother me. What did it matter if Deephell was up? Up or down, it wouldn't help us defeat the nagas or feed the Turtle.

Still, I wished Eflet was here to explain what the diagram meant. Even if her explanation were wrapped in Ceibak wistfulness.

At least Avi looked happy, especially when her face wrinkled in concentration. She was good at this work. Her unique perspective as Handler and Tender allowed her to make suggestions even stern Handler Avelo nodded at.

She shouldn't be wasting her talents training me.

When they finished, I asked Avi to stay a moment longer. Everyone else filed out, leaving us alone in the deep-red room.

"Something wrong?" Avi asked.

"You're good. At all of this."

She frowned, confused. "Thanks. You needed to talk to me alone to say that?"

"You don't have to train me. There's got to be a half-Handler to pass me to."

"You think someone else would do a better job?" she asked, not angry—curious, I think.

I didn't break eye contact. "I know you're frustrated. I know you hate this."

"Hate what? That the Turtle is starving? That we don't have more time?"

I sighed, still staring straight into her concerned cassava-brown eyes. "Me. It's fine. I understand."

"Tenjat," she said slowly, patiently, as if to make sure I was really listening. "I train you because I'm a Handler. What are you talking about?"

I tried to sound casual, unhurt. "I've heard your history, from the other mucks. How Het made you choose. You're obviously dedicated to the Tree."

She pursed her lips. "You think I chose the candidate I found most distasteful."

"Didn't you?" For the first time in weeks, I wondered if her lovely, crooked smiles were fake. Weren't hiding contempt.

The vein-light played off her hair, gold against obsidian black. "I'd planned to pick the candidate who seemed the most dedicated to the Tree. True, I did ask the tax collectors about you, and it seemed you had every reason to come and few to leave."

"But?" I remembered running out of the Tree to Jesso's. She couldn't have been impressed.

"You glow in Hell, Tenjat."

It was my turn to be confused. My hands were gray in Deephell. "No, *you* glow."

She frowned. "I see myself as being almost the same color as the mists—the same as everyone else appears. You didn't notice the other two Handlers at your test, did you?"

My gut twisted. *Three* people saw that little display?

"And Reliak—he was gray to you, wasn't he?"

I nodded.

"*That's* normal. I asked the other Handlers if they saw you glowing and they made Lilit check my skull for bruises."

"Why am I different?" I asked.

"I don't know. *That's* why I picked you. I want to find out. The only things that glow like that in Deephell are the treasures we steal." Her eyes sparkled. "I think that makes you special."

My gut wobbled under her gaze. "You don't hate me."

"Of course not! You're my comrade-in-arms. I'm trying to keep you alive for when we fight nagas together. I'd rather not see you die."

Avi's comrade. I couldn't think of a nicer title. If her arms were around me again, I'd hold her tight, both hands on her back.

Except . . . except it was probably better not to hug her at all. We were both dedicated Handlers, of course. It had just been a moment of excitement over spurning Jerohn. But the other mucks and Handlers might see something that wasn't—couldn't be—there. We were comrades, not something lesser.

I pushed away the memory of her copal-scented hair and focused on what mattered. Avi didn't hate me and she didn't want to make me her hub. She wanted the exact same thing I did—for me to become a good Handler. "Thank you, Avi."

She laughed and shook her head. "Mucks can be so *strange.*"

By the time I arrived in the mess hall, it was empty. Apparently the meeting I watched ran longer than everyone's training. I grabbed the last three cold cassava cakes off a platter and cheerfully munched them down. Avi didn't hate me. What was cold dinner compared to that?

I strode to the barracks, grinning. All traces of that grin disappeared after I opened the door.

Daef lay curled on his bunk, Kosel and three other boys surrounding him. Kosel rammed his fist into Daef's stomach.

CHAPTER
17

THE OTHER MUCKS sat elsewhere, backs carefully turned.

"Didn't we tell you not to talk to that hub?" One of the other boys spat at Daef's face. Somehow, they'd found out about our conversations. I didn't know how and I didn't care.

I squared my shoulders and shouted across the room. "Kosel! You're such a hub."

The room froze. Neat trick, that. Kosel hadn't turned around, but he bristled.

"Yes, you, Kosel," I said, with as much swagger as I could manage. "Who else in here is weak enough to be a hub? Only you."

I itched to take another swing at him, but I knew how that would end. Bitterly, I hoped the red fabric in the bottom of his basket was what I thought I'd seen. Kosel turned around, arms clenched from shoulder to fingertip.

I forced myself to grin. "Ah, I see I'm not invisible anymore. Have I been stepping into your territory? Talking to a girl you like? I'm sorry, but Avi's not interested in hubs."

The rest of the mucks winced. One waved behind Kosel's back, trying to warn me to shut up if I didn't want my ribs coming out my nose.

Kosel's footsteps thudded against the wood floor as he marched toward me, fist cocked for a punch.

"It's true, of course. I bet he even has a wedding sash in his basket."

Kosel gritted his teeth and swung. I ducked it. Avi's training *was* working. "Go ahead!" I shouted to Kosel's pals. "Take a look."

If I was wrong, I'd earned myself a beating and a visit with Lilit. But I'd earned Daef a respite, too. He sat up on his bed and wiped his bloody nose on his sleeve.

Kosel's mouth was a thin line. His eyebrow twitched. "You'll shut up!"

"Yeah, Kosel's no hub!" yelled Varo, one of his lackeys.

"Then open his basket."

Varo laughed. "You really think there's something in here?" He kicked Kosel's basket with a hard thwack.

"Stop!" Kosel yelled, spinning around. I'm sure he

M. K. HUTCHINS

mistook the noise for the basket lid hitting the floor.

"That's interesting." I tried to sound casual, but my body tensed like I'd been drilling, "If there's nothing to be worried about, why so concerned?"

Even his friends peered at him with confused eyes.

Kosel laughed nervously. "I didn't want you ruining my basket, Varo. You've got a mean kick."

"Look inside," I said.

Kosel glowered. "I'm going to rip your ears off, Tenjat."

"So you admit to being a hub?" Varo's eyes hardened. He ripped the basket open. "Let's see."

The room froze to watch. Kosel gritted his teeth, but if he charged Varo, who'd believe his innocence?

Varo tossed out a set of clothes, then the colored rocks and comb. Kosel had apparently already devoured his stashed cassava cakes. The next thing Varo pulled out was a long red sash. He threw it at Kosel. Then a second sash. Then a third.

"*Three*, Kosel?" Varo snapped. "Three! Why not throw them away before you came? It took that many failed proposals for you to try the test? There were three girls more tempting than the life of a warrior?"

"There was only one girl." Kosel's fists tightened at his sides. It was the wrong thing to say.

Varo sneered. "You're disgusting. You run away to the Tree to hide from her, or what?"

No wonder Kosel hated hubs so much. He was one.

Sosib, the beak-nosed muck, laughed. "How much did you spend on all that red thread?"

I was so tired of that sound—of mucks laughing at mucks. "Sosib, can we hold off tormenting each other until *after* the nagas have their chance to chew us up?"

If any of us survived the battle. A couple mucks nodded, but most fidgeted uncomfortably.

"Maybe nagas think hubs taste better," Sosib chortled, turning back to Kosel. "You offered her three sashes, and she *still* sent you off?"

"She came from a bad family. I was stupid." He shot a glare at Daef. "I learned better, quickly."

"Not quickly enough." Varo spat on the sashes. From the way Kosel's gaze lingered on the red cloth, he hadn't learned at all. He still missed her.

"It was Reja, wasn't it?" Daef's soft question sliced through the air like a well-thrown javelin.

Kosel's face pinched at her name. He glared at Daef and stalked off to his bunk.

"Who's Reja?" Varo asked.

Daef squirmed with the self-awareness of ten pairs of eyes watching him. "My sister. We used to walk by the river, collecting pebbles if the water was low. Kosel would follow us, pick up pretty rocks of his own—sometimes he'd throw them at me, sometimes he'd offer them to Reja. I thought he was making fun of us. I thought he was there to tease me."

Daef awkwardly rubbed the back of his neck. We all heard what he didn't say: Kosel was trying to get Daef to leave, so he could court Daef's sister. "She's . . . she's very pretty," Daef offered, as if that would make Kosel's stumble less grievous.

Sosib grinned and opened his mouth. I cut in before he could speak. "Does anyone want to practice hand signals together? It couldn't hurt."

The other mucks looked at me like I was crazy. More training, when they didn't have to? Only Daef bounced over to my side. The other mucks resumed their games, conversations, and bunk-jumping. Except Kosel. Kosel lay on his bed, still as a corpse. His reign was over.

I ate breakfast with a fellow muck for the first time.

"Looks kind of . . . lonely, doesn't he?" Daef asked.

I glanced over to where Kosel sat alone. "Broke his heart good, didn't she?"

Daef smiled fondly. "Reja loved doing that. Lead someone along just a bit—flutter her eyelashes at them. She's real pretty, Tenjat." He paused, spoon halfway to his mouth. "I wonder if she didn't mess with him because he taunted me. She did that once before. A guy who made fun of me for being so skinny. Started flirting with him, got him to follow her everywhere with his big, sad eyes, then *smack*!" He *thwapped* his spoon flat against his porridge. "Told him she hated him. She doesn't want no hub—keeps trying to get an artisan to apprentice her."

I wish I could say I looked at Kosel sitting alone and pity swelled in my heart. But I didn't. Truth was, I thought about Avi. She could have been like Daef's sister, leading weak, would-be hubs along and then smashing them down, laughing with her pretty eyes. She was too good to be anyone's wife.

She was my comrade instead.

"I should have seen it earlier." Daef popped a whole cassava cake in his mouth.

I shrugged. "Sometimes we're all blind."

Sanyl, a tall fourteen-year-old muck, plopped next to us on the bench. "*Oceans*, it was great to see Kosel's face yesterday." He grinned and picked up his spoon. "Just great."

"Sure was," I muttered, and kept at my breakfast.

Sanyl continued. "If you'd told me you were going to do that, I wouldn't have believed it! I woulda said, not that sorry muck. Then you got him!"

"You do realize we're here to fight nagas?" I asked him.

"Yeah, but you were still impressive—you completely slew Kosel! Did you let him knock you down on purpose, so your attack was that much more devastating? Daef didn't have the gall to do it himself, so he asked you when you showed up?"

Daef squirmed. "I . . . I didn't know."

I wanted to snap at Sanyl to lay off Daef, but then I'd sound like Daef's mother—probably the last thing he needed.

Sanyl shook his head. "Kosel. What a hub. I always hated him."

"I couldn't care less if you were his best friend. We'll be nearing the coral reef in . . ." I paused and glanced at Daef. I'd lost track of time, training with Avi.

"Three days," Daef offered.

My gut turned cold as I realized he was right. "See?" I said to Sanyl. "We'll be fighting naga *soon*. Worry about that, not Kosel."

Sanyl blinked at me. "You are intense. That's why we have *training*."

Overconfident muck. If fighting nagas was safe, the Tree would have fewer graves outside and more living Handlers.

Avi taught me a new maneuver. She positioned me, legs bent to the chest, feet facing flat out. Then she grabbed my hands, bunched her legs, and pressed her feet against mine. "On the count of three, kick your legs straight and let go of my hands. One. Two. Three!"

I kicked against her feet, launching outward. The cold

Deephell mist brushed my face like iced spiderwebs. Avi shot the other direction, but immediately used her copper grabfoot to fly parallel to me.

"This is useful in battle. If nagas bear down on both of us, we can shoot away, then flank them. We'll drill this now. In battle, there won't be time to line up toes, so it's important to—" Avi paused. The roots below us were flashing rapidly. Avi had taught me some of the root signals Tenders could employ, but I didn't know this one.

"Oceans," Avi muttered. "Training's done for today. I'm needed."

"What's happening?"

"We must be closer to the coral reef than everyone thought."

CHAPTER
18

AVI PULLED ME with her through tight, thin veins, skillfully twisting away from the currents that tried to tease us back to larger pathways.

We dropped into a room I'd never seen. It was broad and circular, dimly lit by the few veins stretching across its black wood. Several heavy bars barricaded the only door. Two half-Handler guards stood there, javelins at the ready.

"Is there an attack?" Avi demanded of the nearest person, a middle-aged Tender taller than either of us.

"We've run into another Turtle leaving the coral reef."

My chest froze. We couldn't retreat. The Turtle had to feed.

"*But,*" the Tender continued, "it's the same size as ours.

Master Tender Manoet is negotiating for a Market. Island Baska is abundant with food, and a little extra cassava in our pantries might settle some of the unrest outside."

I exhaled. A Market. There'd be trading, games, general festivities. I didn't have to worry about battling the nagas yet.

"We're close to the reef, then?" I asked.

The woman nodded. "Three days. Five if we stop for two days of Market."

I'd take every extra hour of practice I could get.

Then Handler Avelo tapped her shoulder and she turned from us. A dozen total Handlers, half-Handlers, and Tenders lounged in the room. Avi was the only one to bring a novice, but she didn't send me away. Some of them played games drawn in chalk on the floor, others munched from the low table full of round cassava cakes and toasted pumpkin seeds. Lilit sat by one of the game boards and waved us over. "Brought the young 'un?"

I frowned at that. Lilit laughed. "I'm not remarking on your age, but your status. We talk about novice Tenders like children. I suppose you prefer muck?"

"Yes." Muck sounded natural. "Are we supposed to be loafing?"

Lilit nodded at the door with the guards. "Through there is the Isolate Vein. The rest of the root veins we groom to grow straight down, making it difficult for another Tree to

M. K. HUTCHINS

snag us from a distance and board us through the veins. The Isolate Vein is the exception — we send it out when we want to communicate with another Turtle."

"But, as the name suggests," Avi continued for her, "the Isolate Vein doesn't connect with the rest of the Tree. If they tried to board us, they could only come out through that room."

"Which is why we're here, just in case. Manoet and her two assistants are in there, negotiating the terms for a Market. It's grueling work, talking through a vein."

That explained why the veins in this room were thin and stopped before the door. "Isn't Master Tender Manoet . . . sickly to begin with?"

"Yes, but she's good at negotiation. And she *is* the Master Tender — she didn't let anyone change her mind."

"Anyone up for a game of Bump?" Avi asked abruptly.

I frowned at the board of concentric hexagons, cut with intersecting lines like the ones in the barracks. "Bump's played on a square board."

"I've seen that variation. You must be from near the tail of the Turtle," Lilit said, arranging the playing stones. I could barely tell the light from the dark with only the thin veins overhead. "Let Avi play first and watch a round."

The morning turned into my most relaxed in the Tree. I felt like I ought to be practicing something serious, but I couldn't quite manage to suggest it with Avi smiling at me. Real smiles. I snacked. I watched games, I played games. I could almost forget how soon the nagas would swarm, how close we were to the coral reef.

I was finally beating Avi on our third game of Bump when the door opened.

"That didn't take long. I didn't even have to take a turn at guard." Avi stood, then glanced at our half-finished game. "I win."

"What? I'm two pieces ahead and—"

She scattered the playing stones with her foot. "Oops. Did I do that?" She grinned at me. "I guess we'll have to play a rematch sometime."

I should have been mad, but I couldn't scowl at that face of perfect innocence.

Master Tender Manoet stumbled through the door, wisps of graying hair slipping from her braid. A pair of other Tenders held her up.

"We've come to an agreement." Manoet's voice sounded worse than when I'd heard her before, like gravel. She nodded at the stocky, middle-aged woman next to Lilit. "Tender Avret, prepare a ferrying vein. We're having a Market with Island Baska."

Tender Avret gave a sweeping bow, touched a vein, and vanished. A Market. I could go see Eflet. Make sure she was safe. And I could get answers about Ceibak, our treason, everything. I could tell her about what being a Handler was really like, how much the island needed us, and how I was right to come here.

"You need to rest," said one of the Tenders holding Manoet.

She shook her head. "Take me to the High Handler. He'll want to know."

"Talking through the vein took too much out of you!" the Tender on her other side protested.

"I'll sleep afterward."

The Tenders frowned. I agreed with them. Manoet's face drooped and her posture looked haggard enough for a woman twice her age. She needed a few days in Lilit's infirmary, at least. Lilit must have been thinking the same thing; she likewise frowned, then disappeared through a vein, probably to go prepare medicines.

Avi ferried a few Handlers to wherever they needed to be, then returned to me. "We don't have to stay here, now that they've pulled back the Isolate and are working on a ferrying vein. Do you want to see?"

"See what?"

She grinned and took my hand. "I'll show you."

Without warning, she touched one of the veins and pulled us through it—tiny, twisting, thin as a thread. We appeared in her smoke-gray room. She pulled me to the arched window.

Across the sparkling blue waters of Hell rested Baska's Turtle. Their Tree was a thin line, reaching to the Heavens. Green spread under that, ringed by paler blue, with dark shadows where the Turtle's limbs stretched under the water. The Turtle's head had just risen for air—it shone like an island of amber, divided by pearl-pale lines.

"Beautiful," I said.

Avi grinned. "Same size as ours. A Market instead of a battle. The gods smile on us, Tenjat."

We couldn't risk a Market with larger Turtles—it might be a ploy to board us. But we could trust that a Turtle our size wouldn't risk a conquest they might easily lose.

Last time I looked out this window, night hindered the view. "I can see so *far*. How far above Jerohn's room are we?"

"Jerohn?" Avi laughed. "That pathetic thing? He lives way, way down there." She leaned halfway out the window and pointed to the right. I sighted along her finger and the world spun. I couldn't find the ground. Just ocean and leaves . . . and then my eyes adjusted and I marked the edge of our Turtle, and a dot that must have been a hut.

Avi grabbed my shoulder and pulled me back. "Careful, there. I didn't know you had a thing about heights."

"I don't." My feet felt like porridge under me. This wasn't height, it was godhood. The way the floor swayed up here with the Turtle's swimming didn't help.

Avi escorted me to the bed. "Lie down before you hurt yourself, silly muck."

"You're enjoying this, aren't you?" I asked. I certainly was, despite being dizzy.

"Quite."

"Sadist."

"Of course. Why did you think I wanted you for my muck?" I lay on my back now, and she sat next to me, brushing the hair out of my eyes. "I wanted to watch you throw up and pass out, of course. I slipped something in your food to make sure you would."

When she giggled, her nose crinkled.

"Well, if I had to have a torturer . . ." I smiled. She smiled. Warmth blossomed in my stomach. This was nice.

I sat up. This was *too* nice. What was I doing here, sitting on her bed, alone in this room? I wanted something cool to drink, but of course didn't see any such thing. Time to change the topic. "I've been worried about my sister since the attack on Jesso's." I'd never heard Reshla, Jesso's flirty daughter, prattle about mobs, so it seemed safe to assume that was an unromantic topic. "I'm glad that, with the Market, I'll finally have a chance to check on her."

Avi inched back. I breathed easier. "Check on her? Tenjat, you're a muck, confined to the Tree for training. A Market doesn't change that."

"I . . ." I swallowed hard. At least I'd managed to turn my stomach into a cold knot. "Avi, we're battling the nagas soon. I need to see Eflet before then."

"Perhaps not seeing her will motivate you to stay alive."

I bit my lower lip. I had questions for Eflet too. About that diagram. About why she thought an island existed where no one starved and good men like Gyr didn't have to be ashamed. About why we fled Island Ita and why Mother died. "I'll concentrate *better* if I'm not worried about her."

"Why would you want to leave the Tree? It's ugly out there. Hubs, marriages, children bound like slaves to aging parents. Hubs slow us. They may as well be nagas."

Hubs were people, not monsters. "Without hubs, no one would be here. Everyone has parents."

"And because you were raised by a hub, it's all right to sympathize with them?"

I jerked back. "You'd ask a man to hate his own mother?"

Avi glared. I took that to mean she despised hers.

"Not everyone can be a Handler, Avi."

She turned to the window, jaw tight. Avi's anger baked into me, making my skin itch.

"My father, he was a Handler once. On a different island," I began.

Avi nodded. "The one Island Ita conquered, right?"

I paused. I wanted to correct her, to tell her the truth of

M. K. HUTCHINS

why we'd left, but I didn't know the truth myself.

"Tenjat? You were saying?" she peered at me, confused by my odd silence.

"Umm, right." We could have that conversation another day. "A naga bit his hand, crushed it during a battle. He was still young—I guess not a full Handler yet—so the Tree refused to care for him. They kicked him out. Without a wife, without children, he would have died. I still revere him as I would any Handler here. I can't hate him."

"At least his heart was in the right place."

"Weren't your parents'?" So many parents had to be like Gyr or Lyna. They'd both end up married to someone, but they bravely postponed the inevitable. "Some never have the opportunity to become Handlers or artisans." Farming was honest work—my fields had been my pride before I came here.

"Do you think a man like Jesso ever took the test? Do you think *he* does the best he can for this island?" Avi demanded.

"I . . . guess not." But not all hubs were like Jesso, and even he didn't deserve that mob. "What part of the island did you grow up on?"

Avi glared, lips tight. "We don't need to talk about me."

"I wasn't trying to pry." I sighed. "You're the one who diverted the conversation away from my sister. I just want to check on her."

"I saw her."

"When?"

Avi's shoulders stiffened. "On the night the Garums attacked Jesso's. She's healthy enough. Now you can concentrate."

"Healthy?" An odd choice of words. Why hadn't she mentioned this before? Gyr and Jesso had avoided talking about her too. "What's wrong with her?"

For a moment, I thought Avi hadn't heard. She spoke softly, still not looking at me. "Your sister knew . . . knew that in three years, you could put her up in the House of Kin?"

"Of course!" Eflet was my only kin; who else would I send?

"She believes in Ceibak, doesn't she?"

"She likes the stories, yes. Eflet may have some strange ideas, but . . ." I bit my lip. *But I almost believe her because I feel like I travel* up *when we go to Deephell. Because somehow, Jerohn's ancient book illustrates her story. Because the more I learned, the more it felt like something was missing.* I was insane for almost saying it.

"I knew someone, once, who liked the notion of Ceibak, of lots of children." The dappled sunlight played across her cropped hair. "It's all a vile lie, to justify a hub's shame. No wonder your sister gets along with Jesso."

I shrugged. "She doesn't think what he does is wrong."

"That man has a sickening number of offspring." Avi shook her head. "I know you love your sister, but she's wrong. This

M. K. HUTCHINS

island can't afford people like Jesso. We're slower than we should be. Easy prey. I don't like that people attacked Jesso . . ."

My stomach sank. "But you think they were right to do so."

Avi nodded.

Jesso didn't deserve broken ribs. Neither did Gyr. "Eflet's not like him."

"Really?"

"She just likes Ceibak stories. The idea. She's different."

Avi turned around. "Or is it just that she's your sister?"

"Eflet doesn't have two armfuls of children!"

"Yet," Avi muttered. More clearly, she said, "Tenjat, I know it hurts. But sometimes the people closest to you aren't worth knowing."

"Eflet is—"

Avi waved her hand, cutting me off. "Talking about Eflet is just upsetting you. You need to concentrate."

"Let me go see my sister, then." I took Avi's hand. Warm. Calloused from holding a javelin.

"No. I need you focused. Lose that, and I don't know what chance you'll have to survive the nagas."

"Avi—"

She pulled away from me. "You've left the Tree once. You will not do so again. Ask a hundred times to see Eflet, and I'll answer the same. *No.*"

CHAPTER
19

"MARKET!" DAEF SHOUTED in greeting at the mess hall the next morning. He bounded to where I sat and plopped down next to me, a bowl of bean soup in hand. "Do you think people on Island Baska play Bump? Do you think there'll be a tournament?"

I pushed my soup around with a spoon. "Doesn't matter. We're stuck here."

Daef didn't slow talking. "I *love* Bump. Last time we had a Market, the islands held a children's tournament. Entry fee was a bag of cassava flour. Mother told me no, so I stole it."

"Really?"

He grinned. "I think she wanted to flay me to death. Then I won the whole tournament—ten bags of cassava and a pair of pretty pots to put it in. Do you think I still look young enough to play with the children?"

"Not with those greedy eyes."

"Maybe we can play a few games this morning." All the Handlers and Tenders were busy with the Market, leaving us mucks to our own devices. A real day off. Most of the mucks seemed excited, but I couldn't hope to enjoy today, not after I'd imagined spending it with Eflet. I wished I could have trained in Deephell. Concentrating on the island's defense would be easier than sitting around worrying about my sister.

When we finished eating, I told Daef I'd be in the barracks soon for a few games. After he left, I started through the hallways. Up, to Jerohn's room of codices.

I pressed my ear to the door. No noise. I swung it open.

As I'd thought, Jerohn was gone, helping with the Market. I ran my fingers over the cotton wrappings of his codices, until I found the right one. I knelt next to his low couch and carefully unfolded pages to the diagram. I traced my fingers over the picture: the Heavens, the Upper Realm, the treasures buried there, our Turtles, then Hell. Too bad Jerohn never taught me to read. Maybe it was mostly Ccibak nonsense, but I still wanted to understand it. Everything and everyone else insisted we traveled *down* to Deephell, not up.

Eflet would understand what this picture meant. I would too, if I hadn't spent years not listening. Even before we fled

Island Ita, I had ignored her. Once, I was picking cotton with Ven and kept my eyes on the plants too long. Ven loved running—down fields, over hills—and he'd jogged off, out of sight.

Panic choked me. We were tenant farmers on a large estate. Ven knew not to leave the estate lands, but that still left me dashing through dozens of fields, shouting his name.

Eventually my voice died out. My lungs burned. I'd circled back nearly to our fields when I spotted him under a tree—curled against Eflet's side. She'd always had a sisterly intuition about him. I was annoyed, not surprised, that she'd found him first.

I took a moment to catch my breath. They didn't seem to notice me.

" . . . and then Kan, Hero of the People, challenged the rich man to a swimming contest to see who would rule Ceibak," Eflet said in her storytelling voice.

Ven wrinkled his stubby nose. "What's swimming?"

"Using your arms and legs to keep yourself afloat in water."

"Can't go in the water!" Ven screeched. And with good reason. His friend, Minik, had gone with her folks near the shore to visit an aunt. Minik fell in the estuary. Nagas ensured she never came back out.

Eflet smoothed his hair. Grief edged her soft words. "On Ceibak, nagas never attack. That's why it's such a nice place."

"And no one is hungry?" Ven whimpered.

"Never."

Ven hugged her tight. "Minik would like Ceibak."

When Eflet turned to me, I wasn't sure whether to chide her for giving Ven silly hopes, or thank her for finding him. I strode over.

Ven spotted me. He scowled and shook a serious finger. "You're a'posed to watch me!"

Supposed was hard for him to say. I spluttered.

"Shame on you, Tenae." Eflet raised a chiding eyebrow, but under it she was smiling. "Did you want to hear the story too?"

"I don't listen to Ceibak drivel."

Eflet's shoulders sank. "You never listen."

Even then, she was trying to teach me about Ceibak.

Ven's eyes welled up. "It's not real?"

"Of course it is," Eflet murmured, stroking his hair again.

Ven turned to me. I wasn't about to lie, but I wasn't going to make him cry, either. "Race you back home?"

"No!" Ven grinned. "To Old Man Tul's!"

Ven shot off at once, little legs light and fast on the earth. I nodded to Eflet and ran after.

I traced the picture in Jerohn's book with my finger. I couldn't count the dozens—hundreds?—of times Eflet had tried to teach me about Ceibak. She'd always been trying to teach me. But I'd never thought there'd be any truth in a fable, even if it was just this one small fact.

Maybe if I had more time to look at this picture, I could figure it out. I rummaged through the room until I found a precious piece of bark paper, an inkwell, and a brush. Carefully, I spread the codex on the floor, sat across from it, and began to copy.

But I was no artist. My lines were sloppy. I tried to copy the words, not knowing if the signs I'd made were even legible. Then I accidently dribbled ink across the wooden floor. I swore and tried to wipe it up with my hand, leaving a dark smear.

My throat tightened. What was I thinking, sneaking into Jerohn's room for a bit of Ceibak nonsense? I looked about, as if expecting a Tender to drop him through the veins at any moment. Which, of course, *could* happen. I shouldn't have come.

I stoppered the inkwell. Avi was right—worrying about Eflet made me lose focus.

Quickly, I put away the inkwell, the brush, and the codex. Again I tried to clean the floor, but the wood had soaked up the ink. At least I hadn't gotten any on my clothes.

Only my half-finished drawing was left. I folded it and nearly ran out of the room with it. How ridiculous to risk getting caught over a poor, partial copy of nonsense.

M. K. HUTCHINS

I tore it up and tossed it out the window. The pieces fluttered and spun in the breeze. Oddly, I felt heavier, not lighter, watching it disappear—like I'd just thrown away something important.

Part of me itched to open the codex again, to steal another look, but I'd already risked too much time in here chasing the shadow of a Ceibak myth. I hurried out.

By the time I retreated to the barracks, I didn't feel much like talking. Thankfully, Daef kept up enough chatter during our Bump game for three people, so I didn't have to add much more than grunts to the conversation.

Daef beat me.

Then again.

And again.

"This was all me and Reja would ever do, after our chores were done." Daef gathered his pieces for a new game. "She'd play boys from all over the island, learn their tricks, and whomp them."

I rubbed the side of my face. The way he bumped all my pieces off the board made it look effortless. "Yeah, I can see that."

"You don't seem to be enjoying yourself." Daef frowned and placed his first piece. "Should I pretend to lose a few? Reja always said people would play with me more often if I did that now and again."

"It's not you." Though losing so many times in a row wasn't exactly cheering me. At least this round there weren't other mucks around to watch Daef's crushing endgame. Inat, Hegal, and Sanyl had joined the rest of the mucks running races in the hallway, leaving the barracks empty except for Daef and me.

Daef imitated a gruff voice—his trainer, half-Handler Fajal. "'Markets are the soul of distraction! The mucks are not permitted outside.' Bah. If it's that distracting, why are the Handlers out in it?"

"Someone has to direct it."

Daef's next move bumped off one of my playing stones and neatly blocked me from doing the same to him. So much for taking his own advice and pretending to lose. "Y'know, we could do all sorts of things today and we're just playing Bump," he said. "Who would know if we snuck out?"

"Daef. I'm not getting myself expelled from the Tree." Not when there was a battle coming. Not when I could help fight and make the island a little safer, a little more like . . . well, Ceibak, in a way. At least the part about no one starving might happen, if we won against the nagas and the Turtle fed.

"You could see Eflet." Daef knew where to hit me.

I exhaled through my nose, wishing that was enough to banish the thought. I made a horrible move—horrible even for me—and Daef bumped another one of my stones off.

"I'd have to be gone hours to walk to Jesso's and back."

"Jesso's? She's probably enjoying the Market! We could slip out, find her, slip back inside."

Markets flourished at the base of the Tree—the flat lawn around the artisans' village was the only good spot for one. It meant two Markets—one on our island, and one on theirs—but it wasn't too hard to have merchants and Bump competitors travel through the ferrying vein and leave the populaces put. Eflet could be just outside the Tree.

"Hey!" I shouted as Daef took his turn, shifting a piece. "You said that stuff to distract me."

I pursed my lips and surveyed my options—I couldn't navigate any of my few remaining pieces to block Daef.

"Fine. Take your turn back." Daef grinned.

I was doomed. In this handful of games, Daef had only let me cheat when he'd win anyway. It took him three turns instead of one, but he whomped me again.

"I wasn't kidding, though." Daef said as he sorted out his pieces. "How hard could it be to slip out the front door?"

"It would be easier if we were Tenders." We could use the veins, then.

"You know any Tenders who would help us?"

Avi wouldn't. Neither would Lilit. "No."

"So we slip out the front." He waggled his eyebrows. "It'll be fun . . ."

My gut twisted. This had to be a bad idea. I shouldn't talk it through, shouldn't encourage him. "We couldn't actually walk through the Market. The Handlers would see us."

"My family lives close to the Tree. We'll stop there and pick up a disguise. Eh? Eh?" Daef jogged over to the barrack door, his impatience plain.

It was dumb, but my head ached with questions. Why hadn't Eflet been at Lyna's Bride's Evening? Why had Gyr, Jesso, and Avi avoided talking about her? If I didn't go now, I'd have to survive the naga attack and wait more than two years before I could make sure Eflet was safe, learn why Mother died, and ask about the Ceibak drawing. I knew I'd said the wrong thing as soon as the words passed my mouth. "I'm in."

Daef's grin split his face in two. "All right. I have a plan."

CHAPTER
20

"That's the plan?" I gaped.

"Well, yeah. Easy plans are harder to mess up, right?"

"*Walk out of the Tree and hope no one notices* isn't much of a plan."

Daef wrinkled his nose. "You got a better one?"

I chewed my lip. "Doesn't a half-Tender always guard the door?"

"Yup."

"And how are we going to get past her?" I asked.

"I have a plan . . ."

It probably wasn't the brightest thing I'd ever done, but I hid around the corner while Daef continued to the door.

"Umm, 'scuse me," he said. "Some other mucks ruined everything laid out for breakfast. Big food fight. Now there's nothing left to eat. I looked for another half-Tender or Tender to grab more food from the House of Kin since I can't leave the Tree, but they're all busy with the Market."

I didn't recognize the half-Tender's voice. It was nasally, but in a not-unpleasant, humming sort of way. "I'll check the House of Kin for any more cassava cakes for you, kid. I'll leave it in the mess hall." She sighed. "Mucks are so gross. I hope their trainers all scold them until their ears bleed."

After a pause, Daef called back, "She's gone through the veins. Let's hurry."

I ignored the sinking feeling in my gut and ran out the front door with Daef.

Warm, beautiful morning air swept over me. I wriggled my toes in the moist grass. The coolness of it would fade as noon triumphed over daybreak. Daef was right. This was worth it.

"Ha!" Daef slapped my back. "Told you it would work! I knew it wouldn't be hard to convince her mucks were dirty troublemakers."

I'd wanted to go with the simpler lie that the other mucks had eaten everything, but the House of Kin had outdone itself today—twice our number of mucks couldn't have eaten it all before lunch.

Laughter drifted from around the other side of the Tree, along with the aroma of roasting turkey and cassava chips. The Market was over there. A few people sat nearby, eating snacks or talking, but no one I recognized.

"Where's your house?" I asked. "We still need disguises."

He dragged me toward a starboard path, rambling excitedly. "She won't suspect a thing! No one will be looking for us."

Bean soup and cassava cakes did, in fact, plaster the mess hall. Daef and I used every remnant of breakfast to paint a catastrophe in there.

"All the other mucks will get blamed for our mess," I said. "They'll be furious if they find out we did it."

"Jealous, you mean!"

Perhaps it was a combination of his slight build and big feet, but Daef had a nearly-silent stride. We strolled down the path, ignored by those going the opposite direction to the Market.

Fields flanked us. Even this close to the Tree, the soil looked gray and smelled like rot. The crops were dull, stunted. Everything would shrivel if the Turtle didn't feed soon.

We reached a broad expanse covered in neat rows of sickly cassava stems. A platform full of whitewashed houses with thickly thatched roofs sat in the middle of the fields.

"This was my home." Daef spread his arms wide.

"That's quite a lot you left behind." I stared. I wondered if all of Jesso's children could even farm it.

"Yeah, not too bad, eh? Maybe I wouldn't have left, if Kosel wasn't always bugging me. I should thank him one of these days."

Daef led us down the broad path to the houses. A fire crackled in the outdoor courtyard hearth, where an old woman stirred a pot of pumpkin stew. "Daef," she said, voice creaky. "You've graduated already?"

Her wrinkled brown skin clung to her like well-loved leather. Daef fell into her open-armed invitation for a hug. "Not quite, Grandma. I came . . . for a visit."

"Oh ho, now," she chuckled—a burbling noise from the back of her throat, "Sneaking out, are we? Doesn't surprise me one bit."

"Yeah, something like that, Grandma. Where's everyone else?"

"At the Market, of course. Well, I think Tova's still here, but she's taking a nap with the babes."

"Who's Tova?" I asked.

"My brother's wife." He dropped his voice to a whisper, "And a real shrew. Has the face to match."

"I'm not quite that deaf, you know," his grandma frowned. "She's a lovely girl."

M. K. HUTCHINS

Daef rubbed his cheek. "I guess your sight went before your hearing, then, Grandma."

She laughed and swatted him lightly with her stirring spoon. "Oh, you're a rascal, Daef."

He told her we needed plain cotton tunics and broad hats to hide ourselves. She shuffled inside one of the buildings.

I frowned. "Hats and tunics?"

"The Handlers won't notice us if we look like famers."

"It doesn't sound like much of a disguise," I said.

"Do you have better?"

I didn't. Part of me wanted to retreat to the Tree, but I was already outside. I'd quickly find Eflet at the Market, *then* sneak back inside the Tree.

Grandmother happily supplied us with clothes and we took turns changing in their elegant house — plastered walls, neat shelves of cassava flour, glazed bowls from the potter's. When the Turtle was strong, their land had to be extraordinarily productive. There were benefits to living far away from Nearhell and close to the Tree where the Tenders replenished our streams. Not even Jesso's shamefully huge family could grow enough cassava to afford this kind of opulence. I stepped outside in my disguise. The loose tunic and trousers, uncinched at the knees, felt like relics of my distant past, instead of something I'd been comfortable in a little over a month ago. A fishskin-tight shirt and cinched breeches were now normal, not this. "I feel like an idiot."

"Kinda fun, isn't it?" Daef grinned. He'd probably grin at the nagas, too.

I shook my head. We hiked back to the Tree and around to the other side—to the Market.

It looked like half the island was here. Stands dotted the lawn, merchants called wares, and contestants sparred with staves in roped-off arenas. The scent of everything from honeyed pumpkin seeds to smoked turkey assaulted me. Too bad we couldn't pay for anything.

We passed a stand displaying a number of lavish goods, where a merchant called to the crowds around other stalls. "I have cassava, I have feathers, I have jade! We are kind to our slaves, and we pay well! Have too many children? A debt to pay? A pretty daughter? We'll pay more than a suitor would in bride-price! Come one, come all!"

Desperation lined the merchant's face. The crowd around the other stalls kept their backs solidly turned to him.

My throat tightened. Most of the small islands didn't bother with slaves. That's one thing I liked about Island Gunaji. Island Ita had plenty of slaves—taken from families that couldn't pay their taxes.

He pointed at me. "You! I'll give you an excellent price for your little brother there!"

Daef laughed. I didn't. I stomped to the front of his

stall. Maybe I shouldn't have, but the thought of someone dragging Daef off made me want to punch him. "No one here will sell you their family. Go away, old man. You're ruining the Market."

"Please, please don't yell." He wrung a hat in both hands. "We're . . . we're out of slaves. We haven't had anyone sell to us in a generation. We're gentle. We'll pay well. Please. Anyone. Children, especially. Women. Especially the pretty young ones."

"You're sick." I spat on his face, and turned.

He called after me. "We're not bad people! We're trying to *help* you. We'll pay anything you like. Jade, feathers, fine green-tinted obsidian. Twenty, no—thirty!—bags of cassava flour for your little brother."

"Thirty?" I peered at him. Something wasn't right. At least on Island Ita, thirty bags of flour was an outrageous price for a skinny thing like Daef. Daef didn't protest as I walked back to the stall. I didn't see any slaves here, organizing his goods or helping call out to passersby. It was just this man in a stall full of fineries.

"Thirty is a wondrous price, yes? I can pay in cassava cuttings instead, if you'd rather. Once your Turtle feeds, it should grow nicely."

"I'm not selling." I gestured at his stall. "Where are your slaves?"

"I . . . I don't own any myself."

A slaver who didn't own slaves? Ridiculous.

"Or you treat them so badly you wouldn't dare show them in public." My stomach twisted as I thought of my father and little Ven. Either or both could be slaves now. "You beat them toothless, don't you?"

"No! Please. Please. Thirty-five bags for your brother. He seems a delightful person. He'll have a good life with us."

"I'm not selling him."

"Yourself, then? I'll pay the same for you."

Oddly, I saw nothing but sincere concern in his eyes. "You have a quota to meet?"

"No, no. Please. You, him, both . . . you'd have a good life with us." He sniffled, then started to cry. "Please."

A slaver, feigning sadness to make a purchase. I'd known a slaver on Island Ita. He didn't have a soul left to feel. Yet the man before me looked so sincere.

I hadn't come to argue with pathetic slavers—I needed to find Eflet. I turned to go.

But Daef was gone. I spun about, frantically searching for him in the crowds.

I slammed my fists on the slaver's stand. "Where is he?"

"W-what?"

"I've figured out your game. You distract me. You talk. And while I'm not watching, you had someone kidnap him!"

The lines in his face deepened. "No. No. I wouldn't do that."

"Where—" The demand froze in my throat. A Handler walked toward us—Het, by the bulk of him. A number of the people around the other stands watched the slaver and me, muttering to each other. I'd made too much of a racket.

I slipped past the stand selling honeyed pumpkin seeds and merged into the crowds. Maybe the slaver hadn't lied. Maybe Daef had wandered off. I passed a juggler tossing chert knives in the air, a stand with twenty-three varieties of dried turkey and rabbit, and a team of tumbling ribbon dancers as colorful as macaws. No sign of Daef. The artisans from the other Tree sold fabrics and pots, while locals set up stands of fried bread and fresh juice.

I gave the roped-off ferry vein a wide berth. From a distance, it looked like nothing more than a lawn with a spot of gold at the center. Someone had mentioned it at breakfast— to get the merchants and goods from one island to another, the Tenders set up a vein that traveled only from this one spot on our Turtle to a similar location on theirs. Handlers guarded it. I didn't get close enough to see which Tenders were ferrying folks back and forth.

Maybe I should have been watching the ferry vein. Any slavers would transport their cargo through it, wouldn't they? I frowned. *Someone* would recognize Daef if they tried to move him, but I'd heard no commotion over there. The old slaver must have told the truth. Daef had wandered off.

But wandered where? I saw a dozen places where I'd be happy to while away a morning. Maybe he'd gone to listen to the drums and flutes.

After I passed a food stand selling cassava with roasted chilies, I spotted it: a Bump tournament. Dozens of pairs played on clay boards in a roped-off area near the edge of the Market. I sprinted.

A portly woman with a switch in her hands stopped me before I reached the ropes. Her voice came in a droning wheeze. "Sorry. We're already in the second round. Non-competitors are *not* allowed inside."

"I don't want to play, I—"

"Want to help someone cheat? No. The spectators," she waved her branch to a crowd on the other side, "stand over there. Nicely. No running."

"I'm looking for someone. A skinny boy, age twelve."

She pointed at one of the players. "Him?"

Daef. He sat on the grass next to one of the Bump boards, playing a girl I recognized from my part of the island. Daef kept his hat low, over his face. Either that worked a lot better as a disguise than I thought, or no one in the crowd realized he shouldn't be out of the Tree.

I took a step forward, but the woman held the switch out

in front of my chest. "*No* crossing the ropes. We've made our agreement, and you can't pull him out of it."

"Agreement?" I peered at her.

A smug smile creased her face. "I'm the tournament director. He showed up late with no entry fee, but promised that if he lost, I could sell him to the slavers to recoup the cost. I had eight of the players witness, so you're not getting him back."

CHAPTER
21

I TRIED TO blend in with a part of the crowd where everone looked reassuringly unfamiliar. My throat closed as I watched Daef play. He'd made an agreement with witnesses. Not even the Handlers would save him from that.

From here, I had to strain to see his board. Daef played with his typical flair, bumping two of his opponent's stones off at once while simultaneously ruining the man's next move. His opponent—a burly, middle-aged man—swore and knocked over the table. The portly tournament director dashed over and declared his forfeit.

Maybe Daef could do this. Maybe he could win. I leaned to the woman standing next to me. "How many rounds are there?"

"Seven."

I swallowed hard. Five more games?

Daef spotted me and jogged over, grinning ear-to-ear. He leaned on the rope barrier and waved. "Did you see that last move?"

I navigated my way up through the crowd so I didn't have to shout. "I lost you. I can't believe . . ." I trailed off. I sounded like a nagging older sibling. "Daef, did you really offer to sell yourself if you lost?"

"Yeah. I didn't have an entrance fee and they'd already finished the first round."

"Daef!"

He shrugged, still grinning. "Guess I'll have to win."

Maybe he didn't understand. Maybe he'd never seen slaves. I glanced uphill at the ferry vein. It sat closer than I liked. I pulled my hat lower. "We don't want to draw attention to ourselves. You should have stayed with me."

"I thought you were behind me and by the time I saw you weren't, well, I wanted to make the tournament before it started. Even then I was late. If I stayed with you, I probably would have had to offer to sell both of us to cut into the forth round." Daef laughed like I'd suggested something ridiculous.

Then the tournament director announced the new matches. "Rendat and Mil. Daef and Hania."

"That's me!" Daef waved cheerfully and jogged to his board.

I glanced up at the ferry vein, then watched as Daef and his opponent laid their stones. Third round. Four rounds after this.

I should have been looking for Eflet. This was my chance to figure out why Gyr, Jesso, and Avi wouldn't talk about her—and demand to know why Mother died. But I couldn't leave Daef alone. When he lost, I'd have to do something. Maybe smashing up the boards would create enough of a distraction for him to escape?

I tried to think of something more elegant, and more likely to succeed, than rampaging through the tournament. The slavers couldn't have Daef.

Every decent plan involved finding Avi and begging her to use her Tender abilities to sneak him inside the Tree.

Daef breezed through the third and fourth rounds. Then he spent the entire quarterfinals with a serious crease between his eyebrows and his lips bent down. I'd never seen him frown while playing Bump.

The crowd around me grew for the semifinals. I recognized his opponent; Yura was a white-haired, stick-thin grandmother who lived not far from Jesso. Both she and Daef made their moves slowly, whittling away at each other's stones, until each had only four left.

M. K. HUTCHINS

The people beside me muttered nervously. "It's close. So close. Maybe—oh, I think that was a bad move on the little guy's part."

I gritted my teeth and tried to block out the sound. I should have found Eflet rounds ago. Now my feet felt like Hell itself had lashed them to the ground.

Move by move, Daef navigated his pieces around the board. He took one of hers; she took one of his.

Then he bumped one of Yura's, leaving her with only two—not enough to form a row. He'd won.

I exhaled. I hadn't realized I'd held my breath. Yura graciously bowed, then Daef did, and they chatted as the other match finished.

"At least she took it well," the man next to me muttered.

The boy next to us, about my age, replied, "I'd be cursing up a storm if I were her. What a runt! He must have cheated."

"Did you watch that game?" the man asked. "You could only call that cheating if good moves are cheating."

Maybe Daef could do this. Maybe. Maybe.

The tournament director waved her switch in the air. People in the crowd pressed tight around me. "Here it is! The final match! The lovely lady versus the little man!"

Those around me cheered, most with great hollers, some—like the boy next to me—with weary, polite clapping.

Daef bowed a few times, grinning, and took his seat. I'd

been so focused on Daef that I hadn't noticed his opponent.

The young woman had an uncanny beauty. Even the curve of her neck was elegant, poised right next to an even more alluring neck. I glanced at the crowd of young men around me—were they here to watch the game, or watch *her?* To their abundant clapping, she gracefully reached out and deposited her first piece with equally dainty fingers.

I didn't care how lovely she was. She had to lose.

Daef chuckled and slapped down his first piece. No one could hear what they were saying, but they talked an awful lot. He'd lose a piece and she'd laugh, bright eyes twinkling. Daef would laugh too. Oceans—this wasn't a game! Well, it might be a game, but it ended in slavery if Daef didn't win.

I swallowed the dryness in my throat. Yelling at Daef not to let a pair of pretty eyes muddle his strategies would only distract him. And I doubted he'd hear me. Crazy muck.

He lost a piece, she lost a piece, he lost another one. My nails dug into my palms. I strained on tiptoe for a better view of the board. They whispered merrily as she took another piece. He only had three pieces left—too separated to make a row before she struck. He blocked her once, but it was a desperate last move. She destroyed him.

The director practically glowed. "And the lady is the winner!"

Everyone else clapped. It had been an excellent game. Even Daef heartily applauded her.

I felt sick.

The director's face glittered with greed as she eyed Daef. Then she strode forward along with the porter carrying the prize of a fine vase of cassava and a jade pendant.

The winner stuck out her elegant hand. "I'm sorry. I forfeit."

The director blinked. "Excuse me?"

"This young man played a marvelous game. I am sure only my fortune in going first allowed me to win. I forfeit."

Daef leaned toward the porter, apparently giving him directions of where to take the winnings. I gaped—as stunned as the director—as the young lady linked arms with Daef and strode away. I chased after, but I couldn't make much headway through her crowd of admirers. Luckily, Daef saw my plight, excused himself with a bow, and came to meet me.

"You little hub—flirting your way to freedom!"

Daef giggled. Giggled until his eyes teared from not breathing.

"Daef!"

He managed to calm down, but a grin still cracked his face. "I saw her there before I offered to sell myself. I knew one of us would win."

"And you thought you could endear her to forfeit for your sake in one match?"

"Tenjat, that's Reja. *My sister.* Grandma would flay her

alive if she let me get sold." Then he sighed. "It's not fair, y'know. She's had Grandma to practice with and I've had you."

"Gee, thanks."

He steered us toward a massive tree on the edge of the Market. "Grandma's better than both of us, y'know. Just doesn't like the crowds. Anyway, my sister said she'd come meet us here after shaking off the would-be hubs."

"I need to find Eflet."

"Reja said she'd bring food . . ."

That won me over—I'd search better with something to eat. The sun hung halfway across the sky. We sat beneath the tree and waited.

Reja arrived shortly with a dozen steaming cassava cakes in a basket. "You must be Tenjat. Daef's told me so much about you. All in the last few minutes, of course."

"Good things, I hope."

"Oh course!" She managed to plop next to us and look graceful at the same time.

I couldn't deny that Reja was beautiful. A month ago, I would have scowled and run away to find lunch elsewhere. But, oddly, I didn't find her threatening or embarrassing. Her too-perfect smile reminded me of Avi's crooked one. I wished Avi could enjoy a meal with us too. Well, an Avi who wasn't furious I'd snuck out of the Tree. Again.

M. K. HUTCHINS

Reja tossed a cassava cake to each of us. "Quite naughty of you to sneak out of the Tree, Daef, but I'm glad you did. *Even* if you made me suffer the shame of forfeiting, it's good to see you."

I munched on the cassava cake. Sweetened with honey— very nice.

"Do you like my disguise?" Daef asked her, tugging the brim of his hat.

She clapped her hands. "I told all those men following me that you were courting me. Oh, how they fumed!"

Daef was a scrawny kid—I could imagine their pain. "That's cruel."

"And *terribly* fun." Reja's grin looked like Daef's, except Daef's mouth wasn't half as pretty. "I hear you're not entirely kind yourself. Daef told me what you did to my poor beau, Kosel."

I rubbed the back of my neck. "Self-defense."

"Of course." She patted my shoulder.

We ate all the honeyed cassava cakes, then she helped us scour the Market for Eflet. We slunk behind stalls and shifted through crowds, hiding whenever we saw a Handler or Tender.

No luck.

By twilight, my feet were raw. Reja hugged Daef good-bye, then Daef and I trudged back to the Tree. Daef planned to make a lot of noise so the half-Tender would step outside to investigate, then slip back in while she wasn't watching. If it was the same half-Tender from this morning, it wouldn't matter if Daef's scheme worked or not—I doubted she'd embarrass herself by telling everyone she'd let two mucks through in the first place.

"I'm glad we escaped today and got to see my sister," he said.

"At least one of us did." I tried not to be bitter it wasn't me.

Daef sighed, scuffing his too-large feet against the ground. "I guess my plan wasn't perfect after all."

And in that moment, it became less perfect still. Avi stalked down the path straight for us, lips pursed tight and arms crossed. My stomach tried to eat my heart.

"Daef and Tenjat—*what* are you doing outside?"

M. K. HUTCHINS

CHAPTER
22

"ER . . . DO YOU think we could run?" Daef asked.

"She said our names. Don't think that would help."

I kept walking toward Avi. Slowly. Like someone had tied rocks to my feet.

"I finish my duties. I go to check on you. And I can't find you," Avi ranted. "I look in Deephell. In our Hellroom. The barracks. The mess. *Everywhere*. One of the mucks said he hadn't seen you or Daef since morning. So I came for an evening walk. Because surely you weren't stupid enough to leave the Tree. Surely I wouldn't find you outside."

I winced.

"We didn't mean to get seen," Daef said.

"Obviously!"

Daef seemed undisturbed by her rage. "Well. How about you go inside, we'll sneak back in, and then it will be like you didn't find us?"

Avi glared at me. "I thought you learned after last time. They could expel you. We're a couple *days* from the naga battle! If you and Daef aren't there to fight, we'll be that much weaker."

"So . . . so maybe they won't expel us." My voice sounded small and pathetic, even to my ears.

"They should have expelled you already, Tenjat. Maybe they'll let Daef stay, but you . . ." Avi massaged the back of her neck. "You were both in my room all day. Understand?"

"What?" I stared at her.

"Tell anyone who asks that I have a nice Bump board, and I took you both there and let you play. You were never outside. You never broke the rules."

Daef tilted his head to the side. "Y'know, I don't think that will work. Didn't you say you asked a muck where we were?"

"Then tell him I forgot. It was a long day, after all."

"Hmm." Daef scratched his arm. "I don't think that's a very good lie."

"Then *make* it sound good. C'mon."

Avi grabbed both of us by the wrists, yanked us to a nearby tree, then leaned against it. A pinprick of gold surfaced on

M. K. HUTCHINS

the bark and we disappeared inside. We squeezed through the vein, twisting down, then up, until I was thoroughly ill. Avi dumped us all into a quiet side hallway. After giving Daef terse directions to the barracks, she yanked me back into the veins and shot us up to her smoke-gray room with the vein-decorated loom, bed, and chair.

"I don't understand you," Avi said. "You escaped capture and slavery from Island Ita—miraculous that nagas didn't eat you. You passed the Handler test. You broke the rules once and got to stay. So much good fortune—and this is how you act?"

I stared at my mud-speckled feet.

"Answer me, Tenjat. Why? How could you betray the Tree like this *again?* Daef's just a kid. You know better."

I bit the inside of my lip, chewing my words. "Eflet—"

"Eflet! I told you to focus *on the Tree, on your training!*" Avi emphasized each word by smacking the back of her hand into her palm.

"I can't focus. Not without seeing for myself that she's fine." And getting some answers. "I promised to take care of her."

Avi collapsed on her bed. "You're a fool."

The words stung. I turned away, only to be drawn back by Avi's sigh. "I thought I could enjoy a conversation with you, then end this miserable day. I spent half of it on guard duty at the ferry vein, listening to Jerohn whine. He's turned paranoid about his inks, sure that someone snuck into his room to steal some."

I coughed awkwardly at that, but thankfully Avi just kept talking. "Then I scoured the beaches for some herb Lilit needed—Master Tender Manoet's taken very ill, ever since her negotiations through the Isolate Vein. *Then* I had to sit on council for the Garum family."

I stilled.

"They didn't have anything to pay Jesso back with, until now." She closed her eyes. "The other island keeps slaves. Garums still couldn't repay, and so . . . well, it's done now. Jesso has as many cuttings and as much flour as he did before, plus extra to cover his lost home. I'm sure with everyone worried about food, he'll get good trades on his surplus flour."

I felt sick. "Jesso wouldn't want the Garums sold."

"Doesn't matter what he wants. The Handlers see that justice is served. It has been."

At least on Island Ita, slavers claimed their wares were worse than hubs, the dredges of humanity that couldn't support themselves in the present, let alone old age. Purchasers treated their slaves accordingly. No humiliation, no pain, seemed too small or large for them to inflict—everything from urinating in slaves' food to carefully-planned mutilations to floggings that usually resulted in a slow death as the wounds festered. Starving on Island Gunaji's failing soil would look like a luxury to the Garum family.

The sun faded in the eastward window, its evening-orange light twisting through thousands of leaves. The floor swelled with the starving Turtle's swimming.

"What do I do with you, Tenjat? You won't follow my orders. That could get us all killed in a fight."

"I'll listen to you during battle."

Avi snorted. "You think you can learn discipline in three days?"

"In three days, I'll be fighting for Eflet's safety. You won't have to worry about me."

"You should stop thinking about her." She spoke softly, but raw bitterness oozed from her words.

"Earlier, you said some people aren't worth knowing." Maybe this wasn't safe ground, but I'd already started. "Who were you talking about?"

"My parents. Like you, they put something else above the good of the Tree."

"Avi, I want to be a great Handler, I—"

"Then act like it."

I bit the inside of my lip. Being a Handler and taking care of my sister weren't exclusive.

Avi sat up on the bed, her gaze soft. "Do you think I want you to become one of *them?*"

"Them?"

"A hub. Living outside the tree." She shook her head. "I *like* training you. I *like* being in Deephell with you. I *like* . . ."

Avi stood and, without warning, hugged me fiercely. I should have shouted; I should have pushed her off. Instead, I wrapped my arms around her back and savored the warmth of her cheek against mine. She still smelled like copal. For all her lean athleticism, Avi felt soft against me.

"You scared me today," Avi whispered. "Don't abandon me again."

"I won't."

She kept holding me. I didn't push her away. I wanted to slip my mouth around to hers and thread my fingers through her hair.

Oceans, I *was* a hub.

But I didn't step back. I wanted this memory, this moment of Avi's arms around me. Selfish of me. Hub-like of me. But we'd fight the nagas in two days. After that, if I survived, I had to request a new trainer. I couldn't stay with Avi. I wanted to be a Handler, to provide a good life for myself and my sister. Avi's presence persuaded me there might be another life I'd like better.

This might be my last quiet moment with Avi. It *should* be my last quiet moment with Avi, if I was going to focus like she always admonished me to.

So I memorized the warmth of her, the smell of her, and

M. K. HUTCHINS

told myself even if I was secretly a hub, that didn't mean I had to act like one. It didn't mean I'd end up outside the Tree.

I was a muck, a Handler-to-be, and in three days, I'd fight nagas and prove my worth.

When Avi finally stepped back, she told me to stay focused, then sent me to the barracks.

The mucks smelled faintly of bean soup, but no one accused me or Daef of fouling the mess hall. Either they were scared after how I'd handled Kosel, or Daef had taken Avi's false alibi and turned it into a believable epic. If anyone could do the latter, it was Daef.

I spent the second day of the Market doing what I was supposed to. I stayed inside. I played some Bump. I drilled hand signals with Daef when I tired of losing at Bump. Then he and I started repeating things our trainers had said.

"You can't let yourself get out in open ocean. Stay near the roots, where there's something to kick off of," I said. I wished Nearhell had some safe, quiet spot where I could actually practice kicking off roots before the battle.

Daef nodded. "And where you can have your back to something. Nagas are good at ambushes."

As we talked, the other mucks slowed their activities. Listened. Kosel sat up on his bunk and added softly, "Don't throw your last javelin. Not unless there's already a Tender waiting to pull you out."

The entire barracks fell silent. Sosib sneered. Other mucks fidgeted and stared at the walls, the floor, anywhere but at Kosel.

We couldn't afford to treat him like the enemy. I opened my mouth, but Varo spoke first. "And don't leave for battle without at least two javelins to start with. Sometimes throwing a javelin is the only way to save yourself—or another Handler."

Varo looked at Kosel without scorn for the first time since he'd turned the three red sashes out of Kosel's basket, then sat by me and Daef. After that, another two mucks joined us. Then another, and another, until everyone, including Kosel, sat on the floor, listening and talking together.

Two days from now, the nagas would swarm. Apparently, the other mucks finally realized we'd be fighting together, not against each other. I would have laughed with relief at the happy scene, except the topic of conversation constantly reminded me that not all of us would return from the ocean.

In the morning, several people stood at the barrack door after breakfast. Avi, Reliak, Jerohn, and four half-Handlers: Ori, Bokan, Indon, and Varehn. The former two leaned against the wall, bored, the latter stood alert with grim faces.

Reliak stepped forward, his white eyebrows pinched in a serious V. "Today, we take you all to rob Hell. Usually, robbing Hell would wait until you graduate to a half-Handler, but as you are all aware, we have a battle coming, and you sad mucks will be fighting early." His gruff voice echoed across the barracks. "I have a treasure of clear sight. I have been searching for imp-free paths to the Treasury. There aren't any."

My chest tightened. Jerohn stepped next to Reliak and continued. "Imps do not swarm like nagas. In large numbers, they mold themselves into new, larger creatures."

"This is the largest escort of Handlers we can spare presently," Reliak said. "If it comes to a fight, at least you'll get some practice for the nagas if you stay sharp and don't get yourself killed."

I glanced at Avi. She gave me a classically stern, focus-on-your-training look. Good. I needed to focus, and a smile from her wouldn't help.

"We have javelins waiting for everyone in the Hellroom. Now, file out!" Reliak barked.

Deephell had never felt crowded before, but a dozen mucks and seven total half- and full Handlers changed that. Their gray forms seemed to overlap each other—a tangle of limbs and eyes and chert javelin tips. Except Avi. She still shone bright as polished palm wood in these twisting mists.

No one else looked at her oddly. No one else remarked on her brightness. Avi was right—only I saw her like this in Deephell. Reliak gave the order, and we all swarmed down, away from the roots.

I resisted the urge to swim near Avi, but it didn't matter. She dropped back to me, close enough that I could have reached out and touched her swirling, glowing hair. I swallowed hard and kept swimming. I couldn't let her know what a hub I was.

"Nervous?"

About her or the imps? The former seemed more dangerous. "No."

"I know you heard Reliak and I talking about running into Handlers from other Trees," Avi said, mistaking my apprehension. I vaguely remembered that conversation. "Don't worry about it. It rarely happens, even if we're robbing Hell at the same time."

I frowned. Getting poisoned by imps was unlikely too. "How rare?"

"There's just one Deephell and one Treasury that all islands' roots reach toward, but the Treasury's kind of like the night sky. We could be on opposite sides of Gunaji, and we could both reach for adjacent stars. But we wouldn't see each other."

M. K. HUTCHINS

"The Treasury caches look like stars?" That sounded unnervingly like Eflet's diagram.

"From a distance, but that wasn't the point." Avi paused. "Up close they look like tiny skeletons or piles of dust. It's kind of eerie . . . but don't be disturbed."

If she'd meant to calm me, that hadn't done it.

We swam in silence with the rest of the group, a shifting mass of mucks and Handlers. Occasionally, I glimpsed a stray imp, watching us from a distance. We'd brought so many people with us, maybe we'd reach Hell's Treasury unassaulted.

I was wrong, of course.

"Swim right!" Reliak shouted.

I obeyed, even though I saw nothing but swirling gray mist, gray mucks and handlers, and a glowing Avi.

Reliak glanced upward. "Oceans. It's faster than us. Javelins out!"

From the mists a massive snakelike beast emerged. Fangs longer than javelins gleamed in a lipless mouth. Its scales glittered as it streamed toward us, each scale vaguely imp-shaped. I shifted my grip on my javelin, hands already clammy from Deephell's coldness.

"Rally to me!" Reliak called. "Don't show it your back!"

But the beast moved faster than we swam. It dived under our haphazard clump of mucks and Handlers, swinging one of its six clawed hands at Avi.

CHAPTER
23

AVI BLOCKED THE claws, but it knocked her away from the rest of us. The beast streamed after her.

Of course. Separate us. Destroy us one by one. That was the safe way to attack.

I kicked off the nearest available surface—Jerohn's chest—and launched toward her, javelin in hand.

Avi's feet flashed copper. She shot straight at the massive teeth of the creature. The monster must have seen the confidence in her face, because it paused and glanced behind—at me.

Avi's feet flashed again, again, again, and before the creature could turn around, she rammed her javelin through its skull.

The beast dissolved into some fifteen imps. Those that composed the head, those that Avi had skewered, dissolved into gray mist. I gaped at her skill. Why did I think she needed help?

Avi charged deeper into the creature. *"Attack*, Tenjat!"

I swam after her. An imp swung at my face, but I blocked with a sideways sweep of my javelin and ran him through. The motion felt natural after so many drills.

In a moment, the rest of the Handlers were there, thrashing through the imps. Then Reliak's voice shouted, "Rally to me! Rally to me!"

Without question, I pulled back. Once again, we made a tight formation. While we'd fought, a number of the imps had regrouped into a new creature—something with eight tentacles, each of those ending in a spike. I shifted my grip on my javelin, ready to throw.

"Hold!" Reliak shouted.

I waited. The monster considered us, then it turned and swam away with amazing speed. My chest was tight with pride, even as I caught my breath. I'd fought. We'd won.

"Casualty report!" Reliak commanded.

"None."

"None."

"None." It looked like a number of the mucks had been too slow to join us.

"Cheek, superficial," said half-Handler Indon. A shallow gash cut across his narrow face.

"Ankle, superficial, but I could use something to wrap it with," Varo said. Jerohn kicked to him and pulled some bandages from his belt.

Then I heard Avi. "Shoulder. Moderate."

I whipped around. Avi, wincing, rolled up her sleeve. A deep gash cut perpendicular across the naga wound she'd gotten some three weeks ago. She pressed her hand over the cut, but beads of blood welled between her fingers and floated into the mist, still glowing.

"When . . ."

"The teeth. Had to get close to hit it, didn't I?" she grimaced, trying to smile at the same time.

Jerohn swam to us. He shot me a disgusted glare—probably for kicking him in the chest. He wrapped Avi's shoulder. "This is temporary. You should see Lilit when we return."

"Understood."

My triumphant pride cooled. Now was not a good time to be injured—not with the battle coming. Reliak regrouped us, and we continued swimming down. I stayed by Avi's side, in case she needed me.

"You're fussing," Avi chided.

"You're *injured*. Can I help you?"

She gave me a grim smile. "Not the first time I've been cut, Tenjat."

All of us kept a tight formation, watching for other monsters, but nothing came. The mists grew warmer, darkened, and thickened. I could still swim and see a little, but it felt like tar. Every stroke seemed to suck me backward. Glowing eddies filled the space above us, as numerous as the stars. Some were tiny; some looked larger than my head.

"Welcome to the Treasury," Reliak said. "Mucks, find the eddy that *pulls* on you—that's your cache. Swim toward it. When the mists won't let you go farther, *reach*. That's how you claim your treasure, and once claimed, you'll always be able to use it. Don't touch anything else."

It didn't take long to find my cache among the other fist-sized, shining whorls; it glowed as brightly as Avi, large as my fist, and tugged at the center of my chest. I swam closer.

As I neared, I could make out the center of several caches. Some held only dustlike lumps, others doll-sized skeletons. My cache held two such dolls, one glowing, one not. Somehow, I knew, deep in my bones, that the dull gray one was a part of me—like staring at my own death and returning home at the same time. Uncanny didn't begin to describe it.

Two gold coins glowed over the eye sockets—the coins that let me see in Deephell. The rest of the treasures rested nearby, not quite touching the doll. A plain knife that would let me breathe in Nearhell. A shroud folded by the feet that would stave off poison.

Oddly, I had Tender treasures, too. Finely painted pots that would allow me to draw up water for the island's springs. A tiny loom that would allow me to shift the veins and feel what lay at their ends. And the most beautiful spindle whorl I'd ever seen: pure gold, incised with flowers. More treasures than I'd dared hope for.

The spindle whorl lay in the brittle hand of the glowing skeleton-doll next to my dull one. Copper shoes glowed on her tiny feet of bone. I'd be a copper grabfoot, like Avi. She'd never said what power claiming a doll would grant, but I supposed I'd find out soon enough. Maybe—maybe—it would make me a Seer.

I *reached*, like Reliak said to.

A tingle ran through me, a warmth. I supposed that was it. I'd robbed Hell.

Avi shrieked.

I swam to her, pulled my javelin out, and searched for the imp. There was none.

"Tenjat!" She stared at me, horror on her face. "*Your* cache! What didn't you understand?"

Reliak stared at me. A number of mucks glanced at each other, confused.

M. K. HUTCHINS

"What's . . . wrong?" The actual robbing had been unexciting. No fireworks, no flashes.

Avi pointed to the little figure holding the spindle whorl. "That's *my* cache, *my* treasure. Didn't you hear Reliak? Only claim *your* cache. It should be the only one you *can* claim."

"I did." I pointed at the skeleton-doll next to hers, feeling sick. "That's mine."

"You share a cache," Reliak muttered. "I don't think that's ever happened before, but Jerohn would know. Don't move."

Reliak kicked near Jerohn, who floated near a whorl, eyes closed, mouth moving.

"What's Jerohn doing?" I asked Avi.

"Calling. Master Tender Manoet's still bedridden from the Market negotiations. Lilit asked him to get a kind of medicine."

"Oh." I bit my lip. Jerohn opened his eyes and closed his mouth, but he now held something silvery in his hands. Apparently, the Calling worked. Reliak conversed with him in low tones.

"Avi . . . can you still use the treasures?" I asked.

Her feet flashed copper and she drifted a few inches forward. "Looks like."

At least I hadn't crippled a talented half-Handler right before the naga battle. I tried to kick against the mists, but nothing happened. Then I focused on those copper shoes, *reached* for that power, and kicked. Too hard. My feet flashed copper, I shot away, and Reliak spotted me.

"Stop!"

Both he and Jerohn swam to me. Jerohn glared, the silvery medicine clenched in one hand. "Don't do anything! What's wrong with you?"

"I seem to be fine."

"Shared treasure? I've read all the histories, and I'm sure that's *never* happened," Jerohn snapped. "You're going straight to the High Handler, understand?"

Avi sneered, good hand on her hip. "You really think the High Handler will care?"

"What if this does something we've never seen before? Makes your treasures help the nagas, or turns the imps more powerful?"

"You're being ridiculous," Avi said, turning to Reliak for support.

But Reliak frowned. "Avi, it's unknown. There's a battle coming. Caution seems prudent." He eyed her bandaged shoulder. "Lilit's infirmary, *then* the High Handler."

If Jerohn had said it, I'm sure Avi would have protested. But she didn't fight Reliak. We floated in silence while the other Handlers ensured the mucks all claimed their caches of treasures. All had knives, but I didn't hear everything else.

Kosel received the same clear vision as Reliak; Daef claimed something that gave him hard-to-cut skin. Varo got gold shoes in his cache, which meant his grabfoot would work even in Nearhell.

The mucks whispered excitedly to each other during the return trip, but I swam silently by Avi. I knew she disliked the High Handler. I wanted to say something reassuring, but couldn't find the words.

What might the High Handler do? And what did it mean, sharing a cache?

We ran across two stray imps, but they fled our pack. When we reached the root veins, Avi obediently took me and Jerohn to the infirmary.

"You're here," Lilit sighed in relief. "Come this way, Jerohn. Manoet's thrashing again."

Jerohn looked back at us. "You two stay here. Lilit will see to your shoulder, then I'm taking you to the High Handler."

Lilit didn't waste time asking questions; she ushered Jerohn into one of the sickrooms. Weak groans emanated from within.

"Manoet's bad?" I asked.

"She's been sickly for some time," Avi answered. "She insisted she was well enough to do the negotiations, but . . ." Avi trailed off, staring at her hands. "At least I know why you glow in Deephell. We each had a skeleton-doll to claim in the same cache of treasures."

"What does that mean?"

"I don't know." Avi—my brave trainer that laughed at imps—sounded terrified.

It was the wrong thing to do, it was hub-like, but I took both her hands in mine, squeezed them, and didn't let go. We waited like that, while Jerohn gave the medicine he'd Called to Manoet.

CHAPTER
24

WE DROPPED HANDS when Jerohn stepped back into the main circular room of the infirmary. He left to see the High Handler. I watched silently as Lilit stitched Avi's shoulder. Either Lilit was naturally uncurious or she didn't want to upset Avi. She didn't ask a single question as to what had happened.

Jerohn returned as Lilit finished smearing salve on the wound and began wrapping it. "The High Handler has considered the advice of all his full Handlers. He has made a decision. You are both to report to him immediately—by foot, not vein."

"After I finish," Lilit said. "Don't rush a healer."

Jerohn grumbled, but didn't push. He stood in the corner, arms crossed over his chest. Avi didn't look at him. When

Lilit finished, Avi thanked her kindly, then strode out the door. Jerohn escorted us, killing any conversation.

We stopped at a mahogany-colored door, plain as any other in the Tree except that Yasel, a wiry half-Tender with a permanent scowl, stood outside. I hadn't seen her since the afternoon I spent with Avi guarding the Isolate Vein and playing Bump.

"Thank you for bringing them, Jerohn," Yasel said. "You may go."

"I was told to bring them to High Handler Banoh."

"This is close enough."

He frowned. Apparently he wanted to be present when the High Handler gave his verdict. That couldn't be a good sign. Jerohn left, and Yasel opened the door.

Avi's neck and shoulders tightened, but she stepped inside. I followed.

Fifteen chairs were carved into the golden-red living wood of the perfectly circular wall—the exact right number for all the current full Handlers and Tenders. The knot of veins in the ceiling illuminated every sculpted armrest. Glorious, all of it, and I would have gaped in awe, if Avi hadn't stiffened next to me.

"The High Handler's audience chamber," Yasel said, then closed the door behind us.

Only one man sat in this room, in the chair directly across

from us. It had to be High Handler Banoh. He stood, smiling. His fishskin-tight Handler's shirt displayed lean, toned muscles, despite the gray of his hair. Scars crisscrossed his arms. This man was legend. "Come. Sit on the floor with me. These chairs are too stiff and formal."

Avi didn't move. "Where are the other Handlers?"

Only Avi would talk to the High Handler that way. I wanted to elbow her, to remind her whatever her qualms, this man ruled Tree and Turtle.

High Handler Banoh sighed. "They don't need to be here for me to tell you what we've decided."

Avi bristled. She crossed the room, but remained standing. I did likewise.

"Such a stubborn child," High Handler Banoh mumbled. "Won't you sit?"

"Tell me your decision," Avi ordered, not moving.

"This is a hard time for our Turtle. You must understand that."

"You're suspending us, aren't you?"

High Handler Banoh cleared his throat, not quite meeting her eye. "To determine if you are safe to battle would require many tests in Deephell, carefully weighing—"

"You just don't want me to fight," Avi snapped. "Stop coddling me. I should have been promoted to full Handler months ago and you know it."

"Until we understand what happened in the Treasury, you are a liability."

How long would that take? I glanced at Avi, but she was too busy glaring at the High Handler notice. "Jerohn already said there's nothing in his books. We may *never* understand. You might as well kick me out of the Tree and find me a hub."

The High Handler shook his head. "Avi, Avi, when things are so grave, is there a need to be stubborn?"

"Doubly so. Let me fight."

The red-gold walls seemed too cheery, too bright for this conversation.

High Handler Banoh's shoulders slumped. Slouching like that, graying hair unmistakable in the bright vein-light, he looked old. Tired. An ordinary man, instead of one of legend. "The Tenders have spotted a Turtle twice our size, headed for us. Maybe if Manoet hadn't been ill, we would have spotted it sooner."

I turned to Avi. "Twice . . . ?"

"It's on course to conquer us," High Handler Banoh finished. "If we continue on this course, they'll reach us in about a day and a half. Just after the naga swarm."

I felt hollow. We might be able to win against the nagas with heavy losses, but we'd be doomed against an invasion as well.

"That's impossible!" Avi burst. "We just met a Turtle

262   M. K. HUTCHINS

from that direction. They would have sensed it, would have warned us!"

"If they hadn't stopped us for a two-day Market, we could have fed on the reef and left before this Turtle could catch us. It does move slower, being so much larger. The island we held Market with . . . they were likely bribed or threatened into detaining us. We cannot turn around."

"I know the Turtle must feed," Avi said, "but we can't —"

High Handler Banoh waved a hand, interrupting. "The Turtle is ready to fall into unresponsive sleep and drift. It lacks the strength to turn, let alone flee. Our fate is locked."

My gut turned upside down. The slaver at Market, begging for our children and pretty young women — he'd been sincere. Offering so much jade, feathers, and cassava for slaves was ludicrous. Offering that much to save a few souls from the slaughter and slavery that awaited Island Gunaji . . . yes, *that* made sense.

I envied the Garum family, safely tucked away on a new island. The invaders might enslave a few of us, but they wouldn't want to weigh down their Turtle with too many extra bodies. After stripping the island of anything precious, conquerors usually slaughtered the remaining populace. They'd then either tow the island for extra land or let the Turtle drift. Destroying the native nation was easier than keeping a smaller, more agile Turtle subjugated.

"I want to fight," I said, voice hoarse. Maybe it was suicide, but it was the only thing I could do for Eflet. If death or slavery befell her, I wouldn't sulk in the Tree while it happened.

Avi's shoulders straightened. "I will battle along with my muck."

"I spoke to the full council of Handlers. Both of you are under full suspension. It is not safe —"

"Not safe! Do you have the luxury to pick and choose your warriors when an invading Turtle is upon us, old man?" Avi shouted.

I touched her wrist. I agreed with every word, but this man was the High Handler. He deserved some respect.

Avi jerked her hand away from mine and glared at him. "I have every right to defend this island."

"Are you forcing me to arrest you?" the High Handler asked.

"Try it, and I'll see you deposed."

He smiled. "Oh, really?"

"I'll let them all know exactly what you are, hub."

I gaped at Avi. That insult didn't belong with the High Handler's name. Was she trying to get us both expelled?

But High Handler Banoh merely chuckled. My gut turned cold.

"And who would believe you? Perhaps a few — Het seems

M. K. HUTCHINS

to hate everyone—but it wouldn't be enough to throw me from my position. Idle threats, Avi."

Her fist clenched. "I'll destroy you."

"No. You won't. You won't try, because you know if I'm overthrown right now, the island will fall into chaos. You'd ruin whatever chance we stand against the nagas and the invaders. I know you too well. You love this Turtle and this Tree, and I'm what's best for them."

"So let me fight! You're letting those who have always distrusted me to 'persuade' you to keep me from the danger."

I glanced between them, a sick foreboding growing in my chest. I couldn't be understanding this conversation correctly. The High Handler wasn't a hub.

Banoh spoke softly. "It's not danger, it's death. Avi, we cannot win. We will make a heroic last stand. You're a talented Handler and a clever Tender. You could carve out a room in the Tree they would never find. You could take a vein, go to their shore, and start a new life as a farmer."

"You want me to take a hub."

"I want you to *live*." His voice ached with concern. He turned to me, as if I might plead his case. I bit my lip. Avi wouldn't want safety if the price was abandoning her duties. Neither did I. Eflet, Gyr, Lyna, even Jesso—the entire island depended on Handlers for safety.

"You're a coward," Avi said, "and you always were."

"Island Gunaji's dying. If you save yourself, at least someone will remember her."

"You've always been obsessed with continuity," Avi sneered.

High Handler Banoh smiled softly. "I'd order you to go, if I thought you'd listen. Would it be so bad, to be a farmer's wife?"

Eflet had said something similar, but hearing those words out of this legendary man's mouth . . . the sickly feeling in my chest tightened like I'd just dropped out of Deephell.

"I don't even know how to farm!" "He does." The High Handler nodded at me. My face burned. Surely there wasn't a treasure for reading thoughts. Surely he didn't know how much of a hub I was, how nice a life with Avi sounded.

Avi turned to leave. The High Handler sighed deeply, a sigh decades older than himself. "Avi, I'm sorry. I won't mention it again. Please stay."

"For what?"

"If I can't convince you to flee, we should spend some time together. Lilit says Manoet is recovering speedily with the treasure Jerohn Called. She'll be here soon. Me, you, Manoet, and your young muck, if you'd like."

"Stop trying to play at family. You're the High Handler!" Avi glared, eyes glistening and rimmed red. "What would your Handlers think, if they saw you now?"

M. K. HUTCHINS

"I don't care what they'd think. I'd like to spend some time with you."

"Odd. I always try to *avoid* that."

"Avi—"

"You sicken me. Good-bye, Father."

CHAPTER
25

MY HEAD WHIRRED as Avi pulled me out the door, then through a vein that dropped us into her gray-walled room. She paced.

I gaped at her. "Father?"

"I'm not going to sit by. We're going to *do* something, Tenjat."

"Father?" I sunk into the chair. I'd heard the whole conversation, High Handler Banoh's own admission, and I still couldn't make sense of that word.

"Why do you keep saying that?"

"Father?"

Avi rolled her eyes. "Why am I the only person in this Tree who can see how pathetic that man is?"

"His arms are legend . . . he's saved us . . . he fights . . ." I stammered. I wanted to defend his name, but the cold truth soured my gut. The High Handler had a daughter.

"Banoh slowed down the Turtle like any other hub. *Worse* than any other hub. He didn't need a child."

What little I knew of Avi's past slowly trickled through my brain. "I thought you were an orphan."

She dug her fingers into the windowsill. "So did I, once. Until I was ten, they told me Manoet was my aunt—that way Banoh's brother could raise me in the House of Kin. Manoet took me through the veins to visit her and Banoh every week."

"Why haven't you said anything?"

"Because all the stories are true!" Avi slammed her fists down on the sill. "He *is* a great Handler. He took me to Deephell when I was five, started training me, thrilled I could see as he did. And I loved it there."

"He trained you?"

"He saw the talent, he saw I loved it. He wanted to make me happy."

My mind whirled slowly. "And so when you took your Tender test . . ."

"I jumped to Hell and killed an imp for show, yes, because I wanted everyone to know I could handle myself in Deephell." She spoke the last word with affection. Deephell was beautiful, in its own way.

"Manoet's your mother?"

Avi nodded glumly.

"I suppose that makes sense. The two of them, alone so often, discussing matters of the Tree and Turtle . . . I could see . . . accidents . . ."

Avi gave me a bitter grin. "It was no accident. They held their own little marriage ceremony. He even made her a sash. She has it hidden somewhere."

I swallowed against the dryness in my throat. *"Why?"*

"Father subverted her over time. He's a born hub."

The last word sliced through me. I was more hub-like than any muck should be. As soon as I admitted to myself that I liked Avi's company too much, I should have asked for a new trainer. But the thought of training here without Avi left me feeling hollow. "I'd appreciate the whole story."

Avi sighed. She looked out the window, not at me. "His father's dying wish was for his two boys to take the Handler tests. If one passed, the other could live in the House of Kin. Banoh took the test and passed."

"I take it his brother failed?"

Avi nodded. "Banoh left the Tree anyway. He didn't want to be a Handler—taking the test was a token gesture for his father. But his betrothed wouldn't have a self-made hub. She was better than that." Avi smiled wryly. "She rejected him and threatened to tell all the neighbors that

M. K. HUTCHINS

he'd rather be a hub than not. He'd be outcast."

Being a hub was one thing. Being a self-made hub? Having a choice? That was infinitely worse.

"With his betrothed gone, Banoh returned to the Tree and devoted himself to training, day and night. Until Manoet became his assistant, until the dream of family crept back into his mind, and he wore away at her day after day with his charm until . . . until I happened."

Her story sounded impossible, even though I knew Avi wasn't lying. "He's such a talented Handler."

"I know."

"I never would have thought—"

"No one ever does!" Avi's fists tightened into rocks. "Ever!"

"He's . . . legend, Avi."

"He's a hub."

I digested that for a long, slow moment. "He's right, though. If you told everyone, the worst thing that could happen right now is for them to take you seriously and throw him out. The Tree needs him."

"I *know*. That's why I didn't do it a long time ago."

I frowned. "Then why are you telling me?"

"Because I trust you. Because we're both suspended. Because you're not like him."

"Thanks." I stared down at my hands and hoped she couldn't sense the guilt burning my face. She didn't know how hub-like I really was. "What do we do now? Try to figure out our treasures in Deephell?"

"*Full suspension*, Tenjat. I wasn't supposed to use the veins to bring us here. No tending, no fighting—I'm not even allowed to watch the Tree door."

"It needs watching right now?" I couldn't imagine who would bother the Tree with a naga battle closing in.

"A Tender always guards it. You never know. During the Market, some deranged woman tried to break in, claiming to be a Seer. The High Handler isn't the only crazy person in this world." She punched the sill again.

I stood and laid my hands on her shoulders. "You should find something soft to hit—not me—or calm down before you hurt yourself."

"I'd be happy to punch the High Handler."

"Probably not the best idea."

Avi tore herself away from the window. "I won't take this one sitting out. They won't let us fight, but maybe we could do something more . . . risky."

"What do you mean?"

"Father was right: I *could* carve a room for myself here that no one could find. I *could* transport myself to the other island once they ensnare our roots with theirs. With your treasures, after some Tender training, you could do the same." She paced across the room, thinking aloud.

"But I could do more than survive," Avi continued. "With a bit of luck, I could travel into the invader's Tree, find their High Handler, and place a javelin through his throat. Maybe it wouldn't stop the invaders from coming, but it would slow them. It's something, at least."

I wanted to believe it could work, even though it sounded worse than one of Daef's plans. "By the time the roots are entwined, they'll be boarding. That's too late," I told her.

"You're right. I should swim to them."

Swim through the nagas infesting our island and theirs. "Even if you succeed, I don't think you'll make it back."

Not if the other Turtle had guards. Not if she had to swim through the nagas a second time. Once seemed impossible.

"I know." Avi didn't flinch.

"I want to come with you. You'll have a better chance with someone watching your back."

She hesitated for a moment, then hugged me. "Thank you, Tenjat."

If Avi and I died, at least I could tell Mother that I'd done all I could to protect Eflet. I hugged Avi tightly and ignored the part of my mind that screamed I was as hubbish as the High Handler. Avi and I wouldn't live long enough for her to know that Banoh's suggestion—running away, starting a new life together—had sounded tempting.

"The sun's getting far to the east," I said. "If we want

to go before night falls, we need to go soon."

Avi nodded and stepped back. "I can take us as far out as our root will go. We should each bring at least three javelins." She paused. "I told you how the naga target Tenders first? They treat me similarly. Use it to your advantage if you can, to skewer one from behind."

Not reassuring. I'd make better bait—Avi had all the combat experiences. "Grab one of the bandage pouches, too, like Jerohn had in Deephell."

"I will." Avi disappeared through a vein.

Impish butterflies twisted in my gut. I wanted to be gone, going, before I had a chance to think about what we were trying. We'd have to get past the nagas on both sides, and that was before finding the enemy's High Handler. Before assassinating him.

Thoughts rattled my mind: Eflet wouldn't forgive me, this was stupid, I should plan more. But I didn't want to look back.

Avi returned with a half-dozen javelins. We silently strapped them on. She handed me a belt, showed me where bandages and salves were stored in it, then tied on her own. I didn't ask where she'd stolen them.

"You ready?" Avi asked.

"As I'll ever be."

She took my hand, squeezed it, and reached for the golden vein.

M. K. HUTCHINS

CHAPTER
26

WHERE DEEPHELL WAS all smoke and shadow, Nearhell was all ink. Light from the sun filtered down in shafts full of drifting particles. Darkness lurked between. Roots, some with a faint twist of gold, descended into darkness.

Avi gave the hand signal to rally to her and swam forward. The water was thicker than Deephell mists—like swimming through mud in comparison. Avi didn't glow here. She was a silhouette next to me, nothing more. The curve of her shin and the scoop of her arm looked like it could belong to the twisting, snakelike body of a naga.

Motion snagged my eyes. In the tangle of roots below us—some thicker than tree trunks, some thin as thread—I glimpsed snaking flesh.

I signaled Avi. She glanced down. Three nagas? Five? I swam harder. The root-light flashed silver off naga irises, gleamed dully off their claws and long, twisting bodies. They swam after us.

I sucked the water in and out of my lungs like air, as the treasure I'd claimed allowed me to do, but it felt like breathing stone. My innards chilled.

Avi stopped swimming. She threw a javelin past me. I yanked a javelin off my back and turned in time to see her weapon sink into the chest of the foremost naga. Its silvery skin blackened. Then it turned to sludge and dissipated in the water. The other nagas—five that I could count—cut up through the water at us.

Avi gave the hand signal for us to kick off each other, with her going downward toward the naga outpacing its peers. The few scraggly roots above us might let me kick back and join her, but they didn't look sturdy.

I wanted to argue, but there wasn't time. We stuck our feet together and kicked. I shot upward; Avi shot at the naga. I turned and kicked off the roots, but they were floppy. I moved as slow as I'd feared.

Her dive was beautiful. The naga she aimed at swiveled to the side. Avi spread her limbs, stopping before she crashed into the knot of four nagas below.

I swam hard. The five flanked her, tails whipping. Just as

Avi predicted, they barely glanced at me. I wished I had more roots, more people to kick off of. Swimming felt impossibly slow.

Avi brought her javelin around and clipped a naga in the head. It hissed and struck. She blocked, but it knocked her toward the other nagas. Avi feinted to the right with her javelin, then bent her body in half—legs and arms going over her head to speed her downward, dodging an attack. The she straightened and thrust upward. Another naga turned black, dying.

A fourth naga grabbed the shaft of her weapon and snapped it.

That's when I arrived. I stabbed at the naga, but only got a shoulder. This one had no eyes, only a half-human mouth filled with teeth like jagged obsidian. It clawed at me, nearly taking out my neck.

Avi kicked off my shoulders, putting us on opposite sides of the nagas. Now we flanked them. I kicked forward, skewering one.

Three nagas left.

We could win. Avi exchanged rapid blows with one of them, leaving two by me.

Then I smelled Avi's blood, metallic in the water. The three nagas writhed. They could smell it too. They all fixated on her. I jammed my javelin into the neck of the naga closest to me. I kicked off its body, just before it sagged and melted away into liquid black.

With that momentum, I skewered the next naga under its clawed forearms. It, too, dissipated into ink. I looked up, but by then, Avi had dispatched the one attacking her. Empty water surrounded us—empty except for a chunk from the side of Avi's shirt, shredded and mixed with blood.

This handful of nagas had been too crazed by the blood to defend themselves, but more would soon follow the scent. The two of us couldn't fight all the nagas under the island. I put an arm around Avi and swam to the nearest root. I would continue onward, alone.

Avi signaled that we should both rally forward. I shook my head. She couldn't swim like this. She needed Lilit. I pressed my hand to a root and *pulled*. I felt a vein bend toward us. Avi had gotten us this far; she'd have to let me finish.

Avi's eyes widened. She pointed down. In the far tangle of roots, a golden vein illuminated eyes and coils of nagas. Fifty? A hundred?

They writhed. They swam toward us.

Then Jerohn's voice cut through the water. "Where are you, silly girl? The Tenders felt you distorting the root veins."

Apparently Jerohn was the Handler with the jade-studded knife that let him speak. He'd brought half-Handler Varehn and Tender Lasyna with him. They were nearer than the nagas—though that wouldn't stay true for long.

As the golden vein surfaced on the root, Avi weakly signaled for me to rally forward.

Jerohn spotted us. He signaled for the group to advance, but the Tender signaled for him to look down. Nagas.

In the moment he wasn't looking, I stuck my hand to the vein and pulled myself and Avi through.

Jerohn's group joined us in the veins. The Tender tried to pull me with her, but I yanked away. I'd like to say I was talented and strong, but I'm positive my golden spindle whorl simply granted me more power than whatever whorl she'd claimed.

Avi didn't nudge the veins. Her pulse felt faint, feathery.

Maybe I should have taken her into Lilit's infirmary and then dived back into the roots, but what chance did I stand alone against the nagas? We needed a hot meal and a place to bandage her. I knew one person who could provide both.

I pulled us as close to Jesso's farm—as close to Eflet—as I could manage. I couldn't see farmsteads from the veins, so I guessed the distance. We appeared in a stretch of forest, the sun orange and red in the eastern sky. Oddly, we weren't wet. The vein must have filtered the water out.

Avi panted, one arm against her side. "I . . . don't . . . feel . . ."

She sagged forward. I caught her, blood seeping into my clothes. I finally saw her injuries in real light. The nagas had carved what looked like a set of oversized, bleeding gills into her side. "You need stitches."

Avi's hand tightened around my wrist. "Lilit will make sure we don't leave."

"I'm not taking you to Lilit."

I opened the pouch at my side. When I smeared on the salve, Avi screamed. I wrapped her clumsily in bandages. Somehow, the outside ended up splattered in mud. I hoped the inside didn't look like that.

Avi smiled weakly up at me. "Ready to swim?"

"With you reeking of blood? Avi . . ." The plan had failed. "My sister's smart. We'll rest there. When will the nagas attack?"

"Tomorrow. Probably midday."

"Then let's rest tonight." I'd dive under the Turtle then. The Handlers wouldn't waste people midbattle to return me to the Tree. Eflet would care for Avi. "I know you don't exactly love my sister, but she can stitch this for you."

Avi's face tightened. "Tenjat . . ."

Footsteps crashed toward us. Jerohn?

"Tenjat?" Gyr called.

I'd never heard such a welcome sound. "Over here!"

In a moment, Gyr stood panting in front of us. I beamed at him. "How'd you know we were here?"

I wasn't even sure where this stretch of forest was.

"Er." He wiped his face. "The hut's not too far. Let's get her inside."

I must have looked pretty bad, covered in mud and Avi's blood, because Gyr insisted on carrying her. We reached the small field in half an hour—the one Jesso had offered to me, along with his daughter. Withered cassava-stubble covered the gray, fetid soil. I knew fields were bad all over the island, but I still stared, heartbroken. Jesso's land was always lush. His horde of children weighed down the island, but they did work hard.

"The cuttings should recover, once the Turtle feeds. We're lucky, really," Gyr said. "The handful of places that are still growing well have all been robbed. The Handlers are too busy with the upcoming naga battle to stop it all."

I shuddered. Gyr stepped onto the earthen platform of a fresh-made hut on the corner of the field.

"We should take her to Eflet," I said.

Gyr cleared his throat and looked anywhere but at me. "Well, ah, Eflet's here. She sent me to get you."

"Is this where she was on Lyna's Bride's Evening?" I asked. If she'd just been helping with another piece of land, why not tell me?

Avi groaned, clutching her side.

"Better get her inside," Gyr mumbled, avoiding my eye. I pulled aside the door of lashed sticks for him.

The first thing I saw was Eflet's long, black hair. She sat next to the fire, patting out cassava cakes and slapping them onto the hissing griddle. Part of me wanted to shout at her for the things she hid from me. But I also wanted to hug her and prove she was as real and healthy as she looked.

Eflet turned and smiled. "Tenae. I hoped you'd come."

Then her face tightened. She covered her mouth with a hand, then reached for a cup of something sweet smelling.

I stepped forward. "Are you ill?"

"Morning sick." Eflet took a few careful sips. "Gyr, lay Avi by the fire. Let's have a look at her."

Morning sick? I stared at her, but she didn't contradict the only conclusion. A thousand possibilities ran through my head. Had Jesso sold her to some prospective hub? Had she been attacked? I couldn't place her *and* a child in the House of Kin. All hopes of a good life for both of us disappeared.

"How . . . how did this happen?" My palms sweated. Heat boiled to my face. "Jesso said he'd watch you!"

Eflet calmly undid Avi's muddied bandages, waving for Gyr to fetch her clean ones. She spoke in her soothing-mother voice. "Calm down, Tenjat. It looks like you got Avi here in time, but shouting doesn't help."

Eflet's fingers were light, but Avi still groaned softly as Eflet tended her wounds. I dropped my voice.

"Tell me who did this to you." All of our dreams — Eflet

M. K. HUTCHINS

living in the House of Kin, happy, provided for—gone. It felt so good to already have a javelin on my back.

"He's standing behind you."

I whipped around, but only saw Gyr, self-consciously rubbing his neck. I felt like my own tongue was choking me. For the first time, I noticed the red sash hanging on the wall.

My dreams had never been her dreams after all. Eflet was married.

CHAPTER

27

THE STITCHES, AVI, Eflet's deft fingers—it all faded into the background. I felt as feverish as when I'd suffered poison.

"How long did you wait after I left? A day? Two? You wanted to be an artisan, Gyr. And my sister—she had a future! She was headed to the House of Kin. Did you begrudge me passing my test so much?"

"It . . . wasn't like that." Gyr inched back from me, his eyes on the floor.

"Tenjat," Eflet said, voice cool as always, "if you're going to be cross, go outside."

"We can take this outside." My fists tightened.

"*Without* Gyr. You need to stop."

"You should have told him that the first time he kissed you."

Eflet paused her work to glare at me. "You are impossible. Gyr didn't seduce me. We *got married.*"

I couldn't hold her gaze. I brushed past Gyr, outside, into the cool, dim air. The sun had almost faded into high eastern sky. I sunk onto the hut platform and rested my head against my knees. I'd imagined a rather different homecoming.

My head throbbed, my body ached. Eflet, married. And worse, Gyr had done the deed. Lyna was married too. All fallen, all gone, all that spark of youth and potential— vaporized like a single dewdrop in the full heat of the sun. I hadn't been able to stop it. Even for Eflet, the last of my family, the one I thought I could save.

Cloth rustled as Gyr sat next to me, but I didn't look up, didn't move.

"Hey," he said.

I didn't answer right away. Gyr didn't interrupt my silence.

"Why?" I asked at last, my ribs grinding my heart into flour.

He spoke low, apologetically. "The day you left, she started helping me with my pottery. She was patient, kind. She's a good listener, you know. She improved my pottery a lot, but two days later, the potter chose a different apprentice. I had no hope."

"So you took hers?"

"Jesso suggested we marry . . ."

My fists tightened.

" . . . but I wouldn't listen to him. She's your sister."

"You listened eventually."

"Not to him. To her," Gyr said. "She suggested it. Convinced me that if I had to marry, it was going to be her. We've always been good friends. It . . . it made sense."

"How long after I left?"

"The wedding?"

I nodded.

"Five days."

My gut wrenched. While I lay sick and delusional in the infirmary, she ate spiced pumpkin and honeyed cakes. *"Five?"*

"I thought I wouldn't see you for three years. What did it matter if we waited five days or five months? When Eflet puts her mind to something . . . she's persuasive. Maybe if I was a stronger, better man. Maybe if I were great like the High Handler . . . but I'm just a man, Tenjat. I thought I could enjoy my life as a hub if I could share it with her. Jesso gave us this whole field for our own." He paused. "I'd like to still be your friend."

The High Handler wasn't so great, either. I didn't reply as Gyr patted me on the shoulder. He shuffled toward the door, paused, then ducked inside. I felt as weighty as a slab of limestone, and just as unable to weather the ravages of time.

M. K. HUTCHINS

I'd hardly left, and she abandoned me. Convinced my best friend to become a hub before he had to. Was having a *baby*.

I was going to be an uncle. I'd thought, for the longest time, that if that ever happened, it would be little Ven's fault, and I'd never know about it. Ven—who might be dead or enslaved. I knew his life would be hard at best, but I thought I could lift Eflet and myself up to something better. Father put me in charge of her. Mother died for her.

And I'd failed them all.

Twilight had settled when I heard Eflet's soft footfalls on the platform. "She's bandaged. I've spoon-fed her an infusion that ought to help her rest."

I stared at the cassava stumps.

"There's dinner inside."

Stumps in gray, dying soil.

"Dinner's better warm, Tenjat."

"Why didn't you tell me?"

Eflet sat next to me. "About getting married?"

"And why we had to leave Island Ita. Everything. You still haven't answered most of my questions. You've never trusted me with the answers."

"I told you not to take the test. I said you might not recognize me when you got back."

Avi was right to tell me so little about my sister, to refuse to let me see her. I couldn't focus. "I thought you meant *older*, not . . ."

"Married? Is that so awful? Father and Mother were."

I looked up. "Mother's not coming back! Father wouldn't have wanted—"

She laid a hand on my shoulder. "This *is* what Father wanted for me, once he understood how the world works."

"Eflet, I'm not a farmer anymore," I pulled away from her. "I've seen things that would boggle even your mind. I've seen nagas underwater, I've seen the veins of the Tree, and the depths of Hell itself. I understand the world better than you think."

"Oh? I've seen more than that. I've seen the treasures you share with Avi. I've seen the Heavens. And, unlike you, I have a plan to prevent this island's destruction."

My heart stopped. I stared at Eflet, a dead spot hollowing out my chest. She *couldn't* know about Avi and me. "Eflet?"

"It's time we go inside and talk, Tenjat."

She stood gracefully and swept inside, her long dark braid trailing after.

At least Gyr hadn't married some fickle, empty-headed girl. Part of me wanted to stay outside, to spite her, her secrets, and her ever-calm demeanor. But I didn't have time to brood. The nagas attacked tomorrow—the other island, soon thereafter.

M. K. HUTCHINS

If Eflet had answers, anything that could help our condemned island, I had to hear her out.

I knelt next to Avi. Tight, clean cloth bound her entire torso. She breathed steadily, eyes closed.

"She's recovering well." The fire cast deep shadows across Eflet's face.

"Good." Dirt floor. Tattered mats. Little else but cassava and beans to eat. How could Eflet choose this over a warm, well-fed life in the House of Kin? "Where's Gyr?"

"He went for a walk. He wanted to give you some extra time to . . . adjust."

Did he think a few hours, or even days, would let me forget my sister's ruined future? I sat and stared at the flames, the twigs turning to ash. "Tell me why you know things you shouldn't."

"I'm a Seer. It's why we had to flee Island Ita. They learned what I was. They wanted to use me for war. Any Handler would."

"You've never robbed Deephell."

"Neither had you, when you passed your test. The treasures physically touching your skeleton—like your gold eye coins—you don't have to claim. I've always been a Seer."

I wanted to call her a liar, but Eflet didn't lie. Bile rose in my throat. I kept my voice low so we wouldn't disturb Avi.

"You could have warned us. If we didn't stop for a Market, the Turtle could have fed before the invaders reached us."

Eflet continued in the same patient tone. "Being a Seer doesn't grant me all knowledge, Tenjat. When I realized what was happening, I tried to give myself up to the Tree. They tossed me away from the door and called me mad."

"You should have told me before I left. I could have let the High Handler know."

"Ah. So as soon as a problem arose, you'd betray my secrets and turn me into their weapon. Do you still wonder why I kept my secret?"

Frustration burned my face. "You tried to give yourself up for this crisis! You can hardly name me a traitor for thinking the same. You should have trusted me."

"Locked in the Tree, how would you ask my permission to spill *my* secrets? That's the difference, Tenjat. They aren't your secrets to share." Eflet poked the fire with a stick. Sparks and flakes of ash twisted through the sooty air. "Mother died so I could be free and use my gift for something greater than the petty goals of one island. If there was any chance you'd hand me over to the Tree . . ."

I glanced at Avi's still form and remembered the nagas, twisting, swarming, attacking. "You're right. I would have told the High Handler about you, and I wouldn't have asked. But the lives of everyone on Island Gunaji—your own included—are at risk. I'd rather have you alive and hating me than dead."

"I'd rather be alive too. And I don't hate you, Tenae." She gave me a rare, small smile. "I hope you don't resent my secrecy for long. It's moot now, anyway. If I'm going to be a tool, better to be used by Island Gunaji and secure our escape than be captured by Island Ita."

I peered at her. "The island coming after us isn't large enough to be Ita."

"No. It's Hibu, one of Ita's scout islands." Eflet shook her head. "Let me start earlier. I can only See places and people close to gold, and only when I'm actively looking. It could be the gold from a precious necklace, earring, or coin, but mostly I use the gold in an island's veins. Island Ita's High Handler, Rydel, can track us using my kin's blood."

I flinched. "Do they have Father, Ven, or both?"

"Father for sure. They keep him well fed and, unlike the other slaves, don't beat him. He's an asset." Eflet's voice quavered. "I thought Hibu was just another island. They'd fed. They should have moved on. But they continued at us, as if they knew Island Gunaji was here. Then I spotted Rydel."

Father, alive. I stared at the dirt-packed floor, breathing slowly. Captured, but *alive*. "Ven's still free?"

"I . . . don't know." Eflet hugged her knees to her chest and stared at the fire. "For years, Ven's been hiding at Old

Man Tul's. I usually go weeks between Seeing him—he's not often close to gold. But I haven't spotted him in months, not since Tul's funeral."

Old Man Tul, gone. It seemed surreal. I hoped Ven had a chance to thank him before he passed. "Ven's hiding well, then. I knew he'd grow up into a smart kid."

Eflet's shoulders sagged. "Tenae, Rydel's both the High Handler of Island Ita and a powerful Caller. He can even change the permanent goods in someone else's . . . you call them 'caches,' correct?"

I nodded, not sure where this was going.

"He hid somewhere without gold on Island Hibu, some-where I couldn't See him, until it was too late for our Turtle to swim away. He brought and hid at least a hundred Handlers with him. Rydel's eager to discover what treasure makes a Seer, and he's finally trapped me."

I hadn't touched my cassava cakes, but now I didn't think my stomach could hold them. "Do you mean *Father's* on that island?"

Eflet shook her head. "No. I've still been catching glimpses of him on Island Ita when they move him from one place to another. It made Rydel's deception all the more convincing."

I felt ill. "You think Rydel is hiding Ven on Island Hibu."

Eflet stared at the fire, her silence confirming my statement.

"You should have told me they were *alive*." Surely they treated Ven as well as they treated Father? All these years I'd agonized over whether they'd survived or not. Eflet had *known*. Everytime I wondered out loud about them, she'd said nothing.

"And how could I have convinced you, without mentioning my ability?"

I couldn't answer that. I changed the subject. "You said you knew a way to save the island?" Her new information snapped together in my head. "You don't mean surrendering yourself?"

"No. They'd still conquer Gunaji and add it to their fleet. Island Ita's strong. Give them a Seer and they'd devastate every Turtle that floats on the surface of Hell."

I bit my lip. "Does this have to do with Avi and I sharing treasures? No one in the Tree knew if that had any effects, and they didn't help us find out."

"I'm afraid I don't know, either. It might mean nothing. No, I'm afraid my plan is painfully simple."

"What do we do, then?"

Eflet pursed her lips. "We need to travel up through the veins to what you call Deephell, but we may need Avi to do it."

"Up. It's really up, isn't it?"

"Yes."

Calm filled my chest. For once, I didn't feel the need to

argue with Eflet over Ceibak. We could both agree on this point. "I'll go. Avi and I have the same Tender treasures."

"It will be difficult. There are strange currents in the veins that far up—another reason for your Hellrooms. You may have the same treasures, but Avi has experience."

"So I take us to the Tree and we use a Hellroom."

Eflet shook her head. "The Tenders will sense that. It would take only a moment for the Handlers to arrive and ensnare us, much like what happened to you underwater. You'll have to use the thin, difficult veins."

I exhaled slowly. No time like the present. "What should I do once I get there?"

"Just see if you can make it, then come back here. If you can, we'll find Gyr and all go. I need him to Call you a certain treasure."

"*Gyr?*" Maybe I was crazy to listen to her. "Gyr failed the tests. I've seen his scars."

"He can't see in Deephell—he only has that one gift in his cache. He'd be little use as a Handler without the knife to breathe in Nearhell, but he'll be of great help in saving Island Gunaji."

I wiped my clammy hands on my shirt. "This treasure—what does it do?"

"If all goes according to plan, Island Gunaji will never fight with the nagas again."

I stared at her. An island without nagas. It sounded unreal, impossible. How could a single treasure defeat them? Eflet knew so much more than me, so much more than all the codices in the Tree. I wished she'd used that knowledge earlier. "Why didn't you try this as soon as we arrived here?"

She smiled. "Because I didn't have a Handler or a Tender that I trusted."

"So you *should* have told me everything before I went into the Tree." I tried to sound teasing instead of bitter.

Eflet sighed and shook her head. "You're impossible, Tenae."

"I'll see if I can make the trip. Watch over Avi," I said.

"Of course."

I walked through the dark fields and pressed my palm against the nearest tree, pulling out a hair-thin vein. I slipped inside.

The space pinched too tight, but I stayed to similarly thin veins. I traveled to the Tree and paralleled the Hellroom veins in my thin one. I could feel their strong current, threatening to suck me in and alert the Tenders.

It still felt like I twisted upward, up and up . . . until I ran into boiling currents that tossed me downward. Just like Eflet said. For a moment, I lost all sense of direction.

Then I shot upward.

Only to be thrown down again.

I tried a dozen more times, sometimes getting shunted to one side, then the other, until I ached. The strong, safe veins of the Hellroom tugged at me, relentless as a deep river current. Fearing I'd stumble into their pull, I retreated the way I'd come. As soon as I toppled out of the small tree near Eflet's, the world lurched to the side, like my first time back from Deephell. I vomited. Black spots filled my vision.

At least I passed out before my face hit my own filth.

Eflet must have been watching me, because I woke up in her hut with a clean face, lying next to the fire opposite Avi. I gingerly sat up.

Eflet immediately handed me something warm to drink. "Here. Don't get yourself worked up, either. You tried. You simply don't have the practice, Tenae."

I sipped, ignoring her advice. Maybe if I'd tried one more time. Gyr sat whittling in the corner, but I still couldn't bring myself to speak to him—even if their marriage was Eflet's idea.

"The nagas won't attack before midday," Eflet said, "and Hibu shouldn't be able to reach us until tomorrow evening."

"Avi will be awake before then?" Even in the cheerful firelight, Avi looked sickly.

"She should be."

"Can you . . . See that, or . . . ?" I fumbled.

"I'm no prophet. I based that comment on my past

experience with herbs and injuries. I can only See what's currently next to gold, remember? I can't See the future. Legends of Seers are exaggerated, I'm afraid."

"Oh." I paused. "If your plan involves Avi and me, how were you going to tell us?"

"I couldn't. I watched your suspension and hoped you'd remember me enough to say good-bye."

"I tried to find you at Market."

Eflet gave me a wry smile. "And, knowing you were a muck unable to leave the Tree, I never looked for you. As I said, the powers of a Seer have been exaggerated. I learned of your search afterward when you quarreled with Avi."

"You *watched?*" Ants crawled up my skin.

"Only briefly, to learn what had happened. I *did* watch your entire fight with the nagas. Gyr can tell you how I cursed at you to get out of there—a whole school of nagas coming at you!"

I glanced at Gyr in the corner, his chert knife in one hand, the block of wood he was carving in the other. "You knew? About her being a Seer?"

Eflet answered. "I told him before the wedding—I wanted him to have a choice to say no."

"As I recall, you kissed me after. Which didn't give me much of a chance to say anything," Gyr mumbled, but he looked happy.

Eflet *giggled*.

"Moving on!" I wished I hadn't asked. "What were you going to do if I didn't show up?"

"We tried to build a raft, but I doubt it would float," Gyr said. "I'm no more a carpenter than a potter."

Eflet gestured for him to join us by the fire. Strange, to see them sit and eat together. A month had changed them. Eflet hadn't laughed so easily since she was a little girl, and Gyr . . . Gyr had never sat so still, so calm.

I felt like a stranger sitting next to my own sister. She and Gyr had continued living, turning into people that weren't quite the ones I'd left behind.

The embers burned low, only dimly outlining Avi's slow breathing. We didn't belong here. The Tree was our home.

I curled up on the floor. Father lived. Ven might be as close as the invading island.

Sleep should have been impossible, but darkness, familiar smells, and warmth of the small hut all betrayed me.

CHAPTER 28

AVI GROANED. I fumbled to her side in a moment. The hut was all shadows, but outside birdsong signaled early morning.

"Avi?"

"Water."

I pulled a jug from the wall and poured her a cup. She propped herself up on her elbow and took a deep drink. "Where are we?"

The forms of Eflet and Gyr rustled on the other side of the hut.

"You passed out after Eflet stitched you."

She blinked hard and glanced about. "What time is it?"

"Morning."

Avi shot straight upright, then grabbed her side, wincing. "Tenjat, we need to go. Try again."

"Swimming will pop your stitches. The nagas will smell the blood and follow you." That cheerful comment came from Eflet, who was rolling up her mat. Gyr yawned and groggily sat up.

Avi glared at Eflet, then Gyr for extra measure. "This is none of your business. Tenjat, you coming?"

"Avi, you can't make it across Nearhell like this," I said. "We should listen to Eflet."

She scoffed as she finger-combed her hair, not bothering to look at Eflet. "With or without you, I'm going, Tenjat."

"She's a Seer, Avi."

A long, awkward pause followed. Avi's brows furrowed. She glanced between Eflet and me. "That doesn't make sense, Tenjat. If she were a Seer, she'd have gone to the Tree and—"

"I *did*." Eflet cut in. "They turned me away."

"You're delusional."

"That's what they said."

Avi gingerly rose to her feet. "I thank you for your assistance, but we have work to do."

"Eflet has a plan," I said. "Gyr's a Caller. If we take him to Deephell, he can Call a treasure to stop the nagas."

Avi laughed. "Really? If such a treasure existed, why didn't Jerohn Call it years ago? Why aren't all islands

M. K. HUTCHINS

naga-free?" She shook her head. "Tenjat, I know she's your sister, but she's a hub-maker."

I stiffened at the insult — so did Gyr. He shifted defensively toward Eflet, but my sister smiled calmly and said, "Yes. And your father's the High Handler."

Gyr gaped. Avi rounded on me. "You told her?"

I held my hands up. "I didn't breathe a word."

"If I have to save this island myself, I will." Avi stomped to the door, one arm cradling her side.

"Your mother, Manoet, can't Call anymore because she exhausted her voice gaining the treasure that cured you of imp poison just after your Handler test."

Avi stopped dead. Her arms trembled from shoulder to fist. "You shouldn't know that."

"How *do* you know that?" I asked.

"I watched the gold veins in the infirmary after it happened. Knowing what had befallen the Master Tender seemed important. It wasn't hard to piece together." She turned back to Avi. "I'm a Seer, just like I said. And we need your help to save Island Gunaji."

Avi sat, back to Eflet, and folded her arms tightly across her chest. "Speak, then. But it's impossible to exterminate the nagas, Called treasures or no."

"You're right about that. Thankfully, I don't have extermination in mind." Eflet calmly seated herself next to the hearth. She blew on yesterday's embers, bringing them back to life, and tossed on a few twigs. They smoked, then flame ran along their edges.

"I'll have Gyr Call a treasure that will let Tenjat speak with the nagas. If he can persuade them to stop biting the roots, our island would be more than fast enough to flee, even with a starving Turtle. Without nagas to fend off, the Handlers could forage on the open sea. We'd never need to risk a coral reef again."

I frowned. That wasn't the kind of treasure I'd envisioned Gyr Calling.

Avi snorted. "Bargain with nagas. That's a *brilliant* plan. At least if you're aiming for fratricide."

I winced at Avi's phrasing, but I couldn't contradict her, either. "Eflet, Avi's right. They're *monsters*."

"You just don't speak their language."

Avi stood. "I don't know why I'm listening. You're not a Seer. You're crazy."

"Tenjat can't get us to this Deephell without going through a Hellroom and alerting the Tenders," Eflet said. "Island Gunaji needs you."

Avi stilled. She'd always been so loyal to this island.

"If there's any chance that this can save Gunaji . . ." I began, my stomach twisting even as I said it. Bargain with nagas. Ludicrous. If the Called treasure did let me understand them,

I'd probably be the first Handler to hear what nagas yelled when they tore a person apart. But how could I not try?

Avi's shoulders tensed. "Fine. I'll help. But I'll talk with the nagas. Tenjat doesn't have half my training."

Endangering my own life on Eflet's word seemed rational. But I couldn't ask Avi to do the same. "I want to go."

Eflet turned to Avi. "You've noticed how nagas target Tenders—target women–first?"

She nodded. I'd seen that myself in our brief skirmish.

"Between a lingering scent of blood and that, I'm not sure they'd listen to you before they attacked. Gyr will be worn out from Calling and the nagas won't listen to me. It has to be Tenjat."

Avi turned, her short hair whipping around her ears. "Won't listen to *you*? They won't listen to *anyone*."

"They can sense that I'm a Seer. I know what they are, but I've ignored them for years. They'd devour me before I could speak."

Avi wrinkled her nose in contempt, but I'd seen the way nagas followed Eflet. "Ignored them?"

"Nagas are bits of souls who have waited too long for life. Desperation twists them into tangible, immortal monsters that vanish like smoke when impaled, but always congeal back together, given time." Eflet folded her hands in her lap. "I want to help them, but I couldn't simply tell everyone they're not just monsters. No one would believe me unless I revealed I was a Seer, and that would get me imprisoned by the Tree for their use."

I stared at her, the words moving slowly through my skull. *Bits* of souls?

"*Imps* congeal," Avi said.

"Because they're similar. Imps are the souls of the lost dead, neither in Heaven nor Hell. Those in the Upper Realm call them ghosts."

It was my turn to frown. "The imps *live* in Hell, Eflet."

"What you call Deephell is actually above us—a space between the watery surface of Hell and the Upper Realm. *Real* Hell is so far beneath the waves that any Handler who tried to step into it would be forced back up the roots by the pressure alone."

Eflet drew in the dirt, creating a picture like the one in Jerohn's codex.

"The highest realm is the Heavens, where the sun passes under the feet of the just daily—east to west. Beneath them, the Mortal World sweats and earns its bread. Under their feet, in the dark earth, they bury their dead with treasures—treasures that shine as stars in our sky. Beneath the earth is mist and waste where souls too afraid to meet their gods and their judgment roam as imps. Below this, Turtles roam the watery surface of Hell. When the sun dips under the

Upper Realm, it travels west to east across our sky.

"Far below the waves, Hell turns to denser and denser stuff. These realms narrow as they descend, like a cone. The deepest part of Hell is a single black point, from which there is no escape. The Heavens are too wide to be imagined."

Avi snorted and moved to leave. "Fancy, silly words."

If I hadn't grown up with Eflet, or heard last night about the things she'd Seen, I probably would have dismissed her just as quickly. I'd had time to let her words settle, and I'd seen the drawing in Jerohn's library.

"Avi, my sister knows things she shouldn't. If you care about the Tree, shouldn't you hear her out?" I knew she couldn't resist that argument. Avi glared, but stayed.

"If there's someplace nicer to live, why do we float on Hell?" Avi demanded.

"The gods could not judge our souls, so they placed the Turtles here and gave us a second chance at life. Without that, we'd be condemned to the limbo of the imps. And the gods, walking atop the sun, are just beings." Eflet spoke this in a reverent hush.

Avi rolled her eyes. "Why couldn't we be judged?"

"Our souls weren't fully formed."

I stared at her, long and hard. "You're saying we're from this Upper Realm?"

"Yes. Souls grow into maturity during gestation," Eflet said. "All of our souls *began* growing in the Upper Realm, but never developed into whole, completed souls."

I blinked.

"We come from miscarriages and stillborns, Tenjat. Unfinished bodies, unfinished souls. What you think of as your 'cache' is truly your grave. The things we were buried with—coins, drop spindles, knives—can give us power here."

I wanted to laugh away her statement. But the caches had looked so much like graves. That tiny skeleton felt like part of myself. I turned my hands over, stared at them. Had my life begun in such a different place? "We still have miscarriages and stillbirths here."

"True. Those soul fragments wait again for another chance to finish growing here, just like those from the Upper Realm."

"This is all lunacy!" Avi turned to me, waiting for me to concur with her.

But I couldn't. I'd seen my origins—my too-small skeleton. Everything I'd been thinking about for the last few months, since Eflet told me that she was the treason that made us leave Island Ita—it all finally made sense.

"Have you ever tried to reach Heaven?" Eflet asked Avi. "You'll find yourself in Deephell. Don't you feel like you travel *up* to reach Deephell?"

I did. Avi stubbornly shook her head. "The Treasury is *down*."

"You and Tenjat share the same treasures," Eflet said, "because you share the same grave from the Upper Realm, the Mortal World."

I shivered. Avi did too. She felt the truth of it. Feebly, she protested. "That's . . . Ceibak nonsense."

"Ceibak isn't nonsense. On Ceibak, nagas protected the roots because the island bore them as sons and daughters. They weren't frenzied into rage like everywhere else, but waited patiently to live again, helping the island in the meanwhile by foraging for the Turtle. No warriors were needed, and the island blossomed."

A place where Gyr, Lyna, and everyone else who never had a chance to be an artisan or live in the Tree wouldn't have to feel ashamed. It sounded beautifully unobtainable.

"Others have bargained with nagas," Eflet continued. "So will we."

The nagas. I'd almost forgotten about Eflet's plan. "What am I supposed to offer the nagas?" I wasn't sure I wanted to know what twisted, half-formed souls desired.

She laid a hand low on her abdomen. "Me."

Gyr squeezed her shoulder.

"You want to let them have you? *Eat* you?"

"Not eat." Eflet smoothed her skirt. "They've long hated

me. I know what they are, but I've made no effort to help them. Promise them, if they help, that I'll bear as many of them as I can before I die."

Avi recoiled and I tried not to mirror her sentiment. As many children as Jesso, maybe, if Eflet didn't die in the process.

Eflet continued, "I'm already carrying a naga soul. That may generate some goodwill in the bargaining, Tenjat."

"Carrying one of them? How could you know that?" I asked. How many secrets did Eflet have?

Eflet smiled. "It's your fault."

I frowned, deeply confused.

"Nagas usually appear as solid monsters, though they can also dissipate into their truer, soul-like state. Indeed, attacking them only forces a reversion to the latter. But naga soul fragments, twisted with despair, are *always* slower than any new fragments. The younger soul fragments beat them to bonding with any newly-forming bodies.

"But nagas that have tasted a woman's blood can smell her pregnancy and bond before newer soul fragments are aware of the opportunity. Such births are rare. Nagas attack Tenders first, hoping for a taste of blood and a chance at life . . . but unfortunately, any kind of blood in the water sends nagas into a mad frenzy."

"We've seen that," Avi muttered, unimpressed.

M. K. HUTCHINS

Eflet ignored her and continued. "Not many nagas get born with everyone avoiding the water and Tenders remaining childless. But you, Tenjat—you fed my blood to them."

All those weeks ago, when I was just trying to scare Rud away from my fields. I hadn't realized my actions would have any other effect. "Will . . . will your child be born evil?"

"Of course not. This naga's soul fragment will continue to grow and heal as its tiny body does. Given the age of his grave, Father's soul developed from a naga's. So did Tender Lilit's."

I couldn't imagine either of them as a monster.

"This is preposterous!" Avi burst.

Maybe everything Eflet had said about naga souls was just Ceibak nonsense. But it didn't matter. There were more important things at stake. I took Avi's hand. "Won't you help us? If bargaining can save the island . . ."

"You'd really be willing to try negotiating with nagas?" Avi asked, incredulous.

"I was willing to swim across Hell to assassinate Island Hibu's High Handler. This doesn't sound that much more dangerous," I lied. I tried to block out memories of silver coils and flashing eyes.

"Your sister is insane."

No more insane than Avi and I had been, thinking we could swim across Hell and invade Island Hibu by ourselves.

"It's for the good of the Tree, Avi. She's a Seer. Our plan failed. We should try hers."

Avi paused for a long moment, then abruptly stood. "Fine. You want me to escort you to the Treasury of Hell? Follow me."

She stormed out the door. Eflet sighed and followed.

Only Gyr and I remained. "Gyr?"

"Yes?"

"I'm sorry my sister pulled you into all this crazy stuff."

He shrugged. "I always wanted to avoid the boring life of a farmer. Eflet's taken *boring* out, at least."

"Okay." We walked out the door together. That's what I like about Gyr. I didn't have to say anything more than that. We were friends again.

Avi marched up to a tall tree. A sliver of dawn glowed high in the western sky, threatening full daylight.

"Come," Avi snapped. She grabbed my wrist. "Everyone hold onto me or him."

Eflet and Gyr laid their hands on my shoulder.

"Good." She pulled on the island's veins until the faintest gleam of gold showed on the bark. Avi yanked us inside.

We bobbed through the upper roots to the Tree. I anticipated the stomach-flipping rush as we dived down to Deephell—or rather, up to the mists of our graves. Instead, she navigated through a complicated system of winding veins.

I tried to tug us the other direction, but with equal treasures, Avi's skill won. We spilled out into the High Handler's chamber. He sat with Manoet in the center of the room, studying a map of the Tree's veins on a table that hadn't been here before. Whatever medicine Jerohn Called had restored Manoet—she looked hale. Their heads jerked up, eyes wide.

"I bring you a traitor, a Seer. Use her as you will in your coming battle, Father."

CHAPTER
29

"GOOD DAY, EFLET," Manoet said, her voice as hoarse as before.

Eflet bowed in reply. "Good day."

"You know her?" I demanded. How surreal, to see my sister standing calm in this room of red wood cut with gold veins.

Gyr stared, wide-eyed, at the golden veins crisscrossing the ceiling and the chairs sculpted from the living wood. His astonishment was comfortingly normal.

"We washed ashore, Tenjat," Eflet said. "Someone had to convince the High Handler to let us stay."

"*I* did that." I'd convinced Reliak and those two Tenders that we were harmless refugees, fleeing Island Ita's conquest.

Jesso adopted us until they trusted us to live on our own.

"Manoet thought our story odd, especially our survival on the raft." Eflet folded her hands in front of her. "I asked the Tenders on our committee for a private audience with her and Banoh, then explained I had some Tender abilities that let me sense veins and steer us across the open ocean. I asked for their secrecy, as I wanted the life of a farmer."

High Handler Banoh smiled, even as he traced a line on the map with his finger. He *would* like that story.

"She's helped us since," Manoet rasped. "About a year ago. She spotted an enemy Turtle we'd overlooked and saved Gunaji from conquest. You've come to volunteer then, Eflet? You have excellent vein-sense, but that won't help us now."

"I did try to warn you, as soon as I realized what was happening, but the Tender guarding the door said you were too sick to see anyone. When I asked to see Tenjat, she told me novices were forbidden visitors. When I asked to see the High Handler, she laughed. When I claimed I was a Seer, they dragged me from the Tree."

Manoet frowned. "I know your vein-sense isn't lacking, but it's brazen to name yourself a Seer."

High Handler Banoh looked up from his map, a line between his brows.

"The story I told you about why I fled was true," Eflet said, nodding at Manoet. "Except the Tender part."

Banoh frowned and folded his map. "If you were a Seer, you would have foretold our doom."

"It doesn't work like that."

Avi slowly shook her head. "I can't believe you freaks all know each other."

Gyr was still staring at the ceiling's golden veins.

"I have a plan to escape destruction," Eflet said, calmly ignoring Avi. "Time wastes. Please do not delay us."

Banoh straightened. "You know their weak spot?"

"I know ours. I need the assistance of a trained Tender. Avi, since she already knows my situation, would be ideal."

"There's been a . . . complication with Avi," High Handler Banoh muttered, folding his scarred arms over his chest.

"You're more afraid of uncertain difficulty than Island Hibu?" Eflet demanded, fearless. "Hibu's on course to reach us by this afternoon."

Banoh's gray eyebrows drew together.

Gyr tore his gaze from the veins to stare at Eflet, who rotely began explaining her plan. Gyr leaned toward me and whispered, "My wife just chided the High Handler. And I think she got away with it."

"Yeah."

"She's kinda scary like that sometimes."

I nodded. I'd grown up with her.

When Eflet finished speaking, the High Handler sat in

his sculpted chair and rubbed the back of his neck. "I could send Jerohn with you. He's a practiced Caller. You'd lose anonymity, but—"

"I have full faith in Gyr," Eflet said. "I don't want to be named in this. If we succeed, Avi and Tenjat receive all the credit."

"Ah, you do realize that Calling can be . . . strenuous?" the High Handler asked, glancing at Manoet. She massaged her throat, a reminder of the price she paid for Calling Avi's cure to imp poison.

"Completely," Eflet said.

Banoh turned to Gyr. "And you're willing?"

Gyr nervously cleared his throat, but under the High Handler's stare, his voice still came out a half octave too high. "If Eflet says I can do it, I can. Sir. High Handler."

Banoh laughed. "You know, I'm not an intimidating person, but everyone treats me like a full-fanged naga."

That's because no one knows what you are. He was a hub, just like Jesso—one who happened to be good at fighting. All the legends I'd heard since I first landed on Island Gunaji dissipated into the reality of a lean man with graying hair.

"May we continue on with the plan?" Eflet asked. "I'm not to be mentioned afterwards."

Banoh pursed his lips.

Eflet raised an eyebrow. "If you need me to See something

for you at a later date, send Manoet. If all of Island Gunaji knows I'm a Seer, one slip during a Market will inform another island. Someone will eventually try to steal me. More someones."

"She's right," Manoet said, settling in a chair next to Banoh.

Banoh laced his hand with Manoet's, without looking away from Eflet. The gesture seemed old and familiar to the two of them. Almost habitual. "I don't like your plan, Seer, but I'm out of alternatives."

Avi glared at him. "What is wrong with you?"

"Take them to Deephell, Avi. You should be able to take side veins the Tenders won't notice."

"Tell Manoet to go, then," Avi said. "She could do it."

Manoet's voice was almost too soft to hear. "If the nagas attack, I'm needed here to shore up veins and reposition roots."

Avi crossed her arms and turned away from her father, obsidian hair swishing around her ears. "You suspended me."

"That didn't stop you earlier."

"Avi, you're the perfect escort," I pleaded, stepping toward her. "Eflet doesn't risk losing her anonymity and all the Tenders stay focused on their tasks. This can happen smoothly and silently."

"And why should she have anonymity?" Avi snapped.

I laid my hand on her shoulder. "Avi?"

M. K. HUTCHINS

She softened slightly as she turned to me. Her cassava-brown eyes seemed too warm, too rich, to be real. A lump formed in my chest. I hated pushing her to help us like this. "I know you don't like it, I know you don't believe Eflet. I don't know if I do, either, but this is our only chance to save Gunaji. If it doesn't work, we're doomed anyway."

Her arms drooped slowly back to her sides, and she hung her head, resigned.

"Thank you," I whispered in her ear.

Avi sighed and walked with me to a fat vein in the wall.

"Are you ready?" I asked Avi.

She nodded glumly. I would have felt the same about this plan, if I'd only known Eflet as a crazy hub-maker. Gyr and Eflet placed their hands on my shoulder, as before.

"May the gods see you safely home," the High Handler said.

Avi exhaled slowly. I took her hand in mine, then she pressed her free palm to the vein. We spun up, up, my stomach flipping, until we burst out the top of the Tree—the journey finally making sense. I'd always felt like I was going upward because I was.

Avi shone bright as ever in the mists. "All right. Stay close together. Keep a watch out for imps."

Gyr breathed heavily through his nose, rubbing the old

wound on his back. His eyes darted about, blindly passing over our figures. "Eflet?"

She took his hand. "I'm here."

"You can see here?" I asked Eflet.

"There's gold in the veins and in many graves of the Upper Realm. That does leave some blind spots and fuzzy patches where gold isn't present, but I'll manage."

"Hmph." Avi looked over us. "I suppose the three of us will keep watch, then. I assume neither you nor Gyr can swim?"

They both shook their heads.

Avi sighed. "Tenjat, you help the hub. I'll help your sister."

I scowled at the insult, but Avi took no note. Gyr didn't deserve to be called that.

I put my arm under his and around his back. "Kick your feet back and forth to help propel us, all right?"

"Got it."

We swam upward through the mists, the padded quiet of swishing cloth the only noise.

"To the left," Eflet said suddenly.

I veered, awkwardly pulling Gyr with me. Avi did likewise.

"That should be enough. Up again."

"Down," Avi grumbled.

Eflet was right, though. The journey through the veins finally made sense. They pulled us above the Tree, and then we swam higher still.

"We need to pull right now," Eflet said. Avi mumbled something that didn't sound polite, but we all followed Eflet's instructions.

With two passengers, we traveled slowly. Gyr was clumsy and blind. Eflet's course corrections took time, but we didn't so much as see any imps. The mist floated past, silent. It was almost tranquil.

We reached the Treasury unharmed.

"Tenjat, could you bring Gyr over here?" Eflet asked.

I flipped us sideways, tried to dolphin-swim, and reverted to snap kicks.

"That's far enough. You can let him go."

I swam back a few strokes. Eflet took his hand. Calm spread over him. "I'll lead you."

"Thanks."

She cupped her hand around his, leaving his index finger sticking out. She pushed it against the tiniest of whorls. Gyr flashed with light, before returning to smoky gray.

"You're a Caller now," Eflet said with the gentle smile. "I'm afraid the next part is . . . less pleasant."

"I know. I'm ready."

"Close your eyes."

He did so, letting his body go limp.

"Can you see the flute in front of you?"

"It's . . . crude. Badly carved. Which side do I even blow on?"

"The one with the notch. Do you have it now?"

He winced, recoiling backward. "It burns, Eflet."

"It's part of the Mortal World. Things are hotter there than here. You're going to have to play it for some time — until a mortal hears you and leaves the offering we need."

He nodded, soothing his body back to a calm state.

"Here, hold your hands like this," Eflet said, pulling them out in front of him, as if he held a flute, "and I'll move your fingers. Repeat this melody in the flute in your mind." She hummed a tune I'd never heard before.

He nodded, licked his lips, then winced as he rested his mouth against the burning nothingness.

Eflet wrapped her arms around him from behind, her face nuzzled next to his. I could not hear the encouragement she whispered as she moved his fingers. Gyr's ghostly face contorted in pain. Smoke curled off his fingers.

He played and played, a melody I could not hear but could feel tugging at me. I felt a desire to make him something sweet, a food with honey, and leave it by him.

Gyr stopped playing and screamed.

"Only a little longer, dearest! The mortals hear you. They stir. You cannot stop now."

He squeezed his eyes shut and blew harder across the flute I could not see. Eflet moved his fingers and he blew, the smoke from his fingers and mouth trailing downward.

M. K. HUTCHINS

With a small *pop*, a new whorl appeared above his head. Eflet ripped his hands from the flute, then embraced him. "Well done, dearest. Well done."

He buried his face in her hair.

"Can you speak?" Eflet asked.

He answered with a muffled groan.

"Don't try yet, then. You'll heal. I'll tend to you."

He pulled away from her, kissed her on the cheek.

"Tenjat? It's your turn now."

I kicked toward her. "That's for naga speech?" I pointed at the whorl.

"It's ambrosia, a food made from honey. It will let you understand and speak any tongue, but it's only an oblation. It will perish quickly. We need to hurry."

Oblation. Avi would have called it a temporary treasure, like the medicine Jerohn Called for me. I cupped it in both hands. It swirled warmly against my fingertips, but my gut lurched in revolt.

"How did you know that song?" I asked. I wanted to hear that she'd watched dozens of other Handlers drink ambrosia, speak with the nagas, and survive. That we weren't crazy for trying this.

"It's a folk song of Ceibak, passed down along with the legends."

Now I felt like vomiting.

"Tenjat, you don't have to do this." Avi's tone made it quite clear she thought I shouldn't. Bargaining with nagas was insane, whatever Eflet said.

But Eflet's plan was the only one we had. Our only chance to save Island Gunaji. I smiled at Avi, wishing we had a casual afternoon to lounge in her room and debate the issue over a game of Bump. But already the ambrosia felt a little cooler in my hands. "Yes, I do."

I tucked the ambrosia against my side with one hand, linked elbows with Gyr, and dolphin-kicked with full speed back to the Tree, away from the Treasury. Except . . . Treasury wasn't the right name for this place. These were our graves. The underbelly of the Upper Realm.

Under Eflet's guidance, we met no imps in the mists. We reached the glow of what I'd called roots—the thinnest, forking tips of the Tree's branches. Apparently leaves didn't grow this close to the Upper Realm.

Avi reached out with one hand, eyes closed. She jostled her fingers around for a moment. "The High Handler room's empty except for him and Manoet. I'll take us back there."

We lined up behind her and dropped through the veins, lurching to a stop on the High Handler's floor. I was used to the travel by now, but I still felt queasy. Eflet and Gyr doubled up, retching.

Manoet stepped forward with steaming cups of some

herb infusion, apparently anticipating their nausea. She'd take care of them. I needed to go. Now. Before the nagas attacked.

I stepped to the vein, but Avi took my hand. Her snappish anger dissolved into worry lines. "Can you get to Nearhell by yourself? Without using any of the largest veins?"

"I guess I'll see."

"I'll come with you."

I shook my head. "Avi, if you get into the water—"

"I'll just see you through the veins," she said. "Then I'll come back here, so Eflet can tell me if . . . if you need help."

If the nagas attacked me, she meant.

I nodded. And then I swallowed the whorl of ambrosia. Warmth flooded my mouth, warmth sparkling and glittering down my throat.

Avi nervously rubbed her arms. "Did it work?"

I shrugged. I'd find out in Nearhell.

Her frown deepened. "You're really going? To bargain with them?"

I nodded, afraid that the warmth would fizz out of my mouth if I opened it.

Avi embraced me, pressing her cheek against mine so she could whisper something private: "I'll never forgive you if you don't come back alive, understand? That's an order, muck."

I nodded into her hair. She smelled like copal. I held her as long as I dared with the High Handler watching, then pulled away. I didn't see another choice. And I didn't have time to waste.

I touched a vein, slipped into its golden glow. How often had I traveled through one of these, without thinking of the beautiful light playing through them? I could feel Avi in the vein just behind me, guiding me, but I didn't think I needed it for this trip. The veins currents ran smoothly here, and the journey was short. Avi pulled back just before I reached Nearhell. I traveled that last short stretch of vein alone.

The ocean's sudden, instantaneous cold hit me like a slab of rock.

I was alone, directly under the Turtle. Roots thicker than any hut I'd lived in twisted around me, below me. Between the gigantic gaps, thin, exposed veins revealed more roots of all sizes, some twisting around other roots. The underbelly of the Turtle, when I could see it through the shadows, hung slate gray, like a sky about to storm.

The soft vein-light flickered against the waving curve of a snakelike body in the distance, against the clawed forearms of another. The light flashed across the slits of eyes. I couldn't count them. They swam for me.

My fingers twitched for the javelin I'd left behind. The waters gleamed with signs of nagas, silver and numerous as the stars. I closed my eyes and breathed slowly through my nose. The ambrosia still burned hot in my throat: the frigid water did nothing to change that.

I felt the water on my skin shift as the nagas frenzied. They'd tear me apart in seconds.

I opened my mouth, and spoke.

CHAPTER
30

"I HAVE COME to strike a deal with you," I called out, or tried to. Unfamiliar sounds wrestled my throat, as if I had an eel half-swallowed, wriggling between my tongue and my lungs, controlling my voice. I gagged.

"What. Do. You. Want?" Each word came from a different direction, hissed like streams of bubbles into my ears.

Eflet was right. They could speak. Maybe they could reason.

A tail brushed my foot, scaly and hard. A fin nicked my hand. The nagas were close enough to breathe the water I exhaled. I kept my eyes closed. I knew I'd panic if I could see them.

"Another Turtle approaches." I paused to swallow. The

words were trying to strangle me. "They have many Handlers. We are small. We will not survive. They are gaining on us. Leave us alone until we escape."

"There will be much blood."

"Many bodies in the water."

"They will bring us warmth."

The comments came as streams of bubbles hot with excitement from all around me. The last one was spoken inches from my ear. A tongue—I think it was a tongue—flicked over my cheek.

Then another voice shot out: hard, cold, and as old as Hell. "What will you offer?"

The front of my skull felt frozen. My temples throbbed.

"A dozen young people from your Turtle to eat?" the ancient one suggested. My jaw tensed. "Just your sister, then?"

The bubbles popped in my ears, each a small explosion.

"How . . . do you know who my sister is?"

"You smell like her."

"Sister, sister, sister," hissed several voices.

"Her mother was delicious."

"Sister Sees too much of us."

"We want to destroy her."

"Spies on us."

I breathed the cold water in and out. "My sister has

offered to bear as many of you as she can."

There was a hush, a long, cold silence. The edges of the ambrosia were cooling. Then the ancient spoke again. "No."

"Isn't that what you want? To live?"

"She cannot be trusted! She has ignored us for so long! She is abominable!"

Tongues flickered over my bare feet and arms now. The ancient's teeth grazed my neck as he spoke.

"Maybe she tries to get us to go away for a time only. Maybe bearing just one of us is a trick."

Streams of hissed bubbles—massive agreement—pelted me from the crowd. Eflet did carry a naga soul, then, but these nagas didn't care. Despite the cold, my palms sweated. "What would you have me offer, then?"

"Let us eat her," the ancient said, "and we may leave the roots alone . . . while we devour." His words, the bubbles, felt like they burst halfway into my skull. I clenched my jaw against the pain. Eflet wouldn't make the same sacrifice my mother did.

"You called her untrustworthy. Would you stop attacking now, and wait for her when she might never come?"

"We would let go only once we had her."

More bubbles bombarded me from every direction. I wanted to find the golden vein, disappear. But the nagas were too thick now. One coiled around my ankle, another pawed my cheeks. I would be in shreds before I could reach overhead.

M. K. HUTCHINS

I exhaled slowly. "Is there nothing else I can offer you?"

"No," said the ancient.

The smaller ones writhing around me whispered other things: "Tasty," said one. "Warm," said another as it probed my ear with a forked tongue. "We could make his sister suffer, even if she didn't come," another suggested softly, squeezing my upper arm with a coiled length of body.

"Is eating me really better than the chance of life above Hell?" I thought my chest would explode. Breathing the thick water, treasure or no, felt like drowning.

"We do not trust her," the ancient said, nicking my neck with what I can only assume were his teeth. I tasted it—my own hot, metallic blood. The nagas around me writhed in excitement. Only the core of the ambrosia was left, its edges fading.

"Would you not rather live?"

"We do not trust the Seer!"

Claws pressed against my chest, ready to rip down.

I only had one other idea. I'd been willing to die for this island. Disgracing myself shouldn't seem harder, but my chest was almost too tight to speak. "Then I'll become a hub. I'll only marry someone who agrees to bleed into the water."

The claws paused, curious.

"Will you trust me? I'm no Seer. I haven't neglected you."

Tails flicked, agitated against my arms.

"Perplexing," muttered the ancient one.

I swallowed hard. "I will take a wife. Become a hub. Have children with naga souls."

"Have me?" asked the ancient, each word popping through my head.

"I . . . I can't control that."

"I can. I'm faster than any of the other nagas."

I exhaled. "Yes, then. You will be my firstborn."

The water trembled around him—he was shivering with excitement.

"More, more, more," whimpered the other nagas.

"Raise up others after me," the ancient demanded.

I squeezed my eyes shut, my throat closing up. "Yes." The bubbles twisted free from my mouth.

"And your sister also."

"Yes." The more I spoke, the more the ambrosia faded. My lungs were failing me, slowly collapsing in the bitter cold the nagas brought.

"Others," the ancient demanded. "Others must bleed into our ocean."

Eflet's words echoed in my head: *Others have bargained with nagas. So will we.*

Either Ceibak was real, or it wasn't. Either others in the past had made peace with nagas, or it was all myth. Either I had the power to change our island to a place where no one fought the nagas, where Turtle and fields always thrived, and married men like Gyr earned no scorn—or the notion was nothing but fancy. Either I trusted Eflet, or I didn't.

I swallowed hard. I'd come this far. "If I convince others . . . then you must promise me more. Promise not to attack this island and her people so long as we bear you."

Silence. I struggled to breathe. I was a fool to ask for fables. They didn't want peace; they wanted to kill me.

The ancient one narrowed his eyes. "It is not enough."

My muscles tightened. I wanted a javelin in my hand, for all the good it would do me.

"Another tracks you," the ancient one hissed. "Maybe if we help, you are fast enough to escape. But one day, he will catch you. If you perish a year, or two, or three from now, who will bear us?"

"I'll go to Island Hibu. The man who tracks us lives there. I'll kill him."

"Can't."

"Can't."

"Can't."

The ancient hissed, "He has a treasure of stone skin. Javelins cannot pierce it. Only naga claws can harm him, but he never descends near us."

"Then I will bring him."

"You, a Handler?"

"I also bear the treasures of a Tender."

"Tender."

"Tender."

The bubbles hissed over me, seeming to argue with each other.

The ancient's voice cut them off. "This is sufficient. We will stop gnawing the roots of your island. We will not harm your Handlers. We will escort you to the roots of the other Turtle. Is that not fair, that you will give true life again to those who saved your lives?"

My stomach sank as I realized I'd just agreed to be a self-made hub. But what would that matter, if we turned our island into Ceibak? I always wanted to be like my father—become a Handler, watch over my sister. Now I'd have to be like him in a different way. I'd become the man with the low voice and the patience to tell a little boy his favorite adventure stories over and over again.

"If you fail," the ancient continued, "we return to gnawing your roots, killing your Handlers."

"We are agreed. Let me tell those above, then I will return for your escort."

The nagas floated away. Soon, the water was still except for the ancient naga, breathing next to me. My mouth trembled with the last warm drop of ambrosia.

"Were you one of the ones that devoured her? My mother?" I asked softly.

"No. I do not venture out so far. I heard of it later."

I didn't ask how many other people he had torn apart. I didn't want to know.

"We will fulfill our bargain," he said.

I opened my eyes. His face hung in front of me—two luminous eyes protruding from wrinkled skin over jagged teeth. "I will fulfill my end as well."

He flicked his tail, then gently swam away, serpentine body more fluid than mine could ever be under the surface of Hell.

I kicked up to the golden vein and grabbed it. I tried to work my way back to the High Handler's room. I bobbed up and down in the veins, like a bead in honey. The veins shook, as if people ripped through them—too many, in too many directions. I couldn't figure it out.

Then Avi reached out and pulled me to her. I spilled into her small gray room. Eflet and Gyr sat behind her on her bed, still sipping their infusions.

The last warmth of the ambrosia cooled on my mouth. It was gone. "I . . . succeeded. For now."

Gyr brought me the last of his drink. I gratefully sipped. With my stomach knotted, the sway of the Turtle's swimming made my head spin. "I have to go back, though."

If I told Avi what bargain the nagas extracted from me, would she hate me? Or would she leave the Tree with me?

"Before you do anything, the situation's . . . changed." Worry lines creased Avi's brow.

It couldn't be something small, if her face looked like that. "And?"

"I brought Eflet and Gyr up here for safety. Manoet suggested it, and for once, I couldn't disagree with her. While you were talking, Hibu Handlers invaded our island." Avi sounded choked.

"*What?*" Hibu wasn't supposed to reach us until afternoon. We should have had a few hours more.

Eflet rubbed the bridge of her nose. "It's my fault. I was too busy with other things when we were in the mists of the underside of the Upper Realm, and then watching you bargain, to notice right away."

"Notice what?" I snapped. I still felt shaky from talking with the nagas—and what I'd promised them.

Avi finished. "Their Tenders grew an exceptionally long root, then disguised it by coiling it around other roots. Sometime this morning, probably while we were in Deephell, they shot it at us. While you negotiated, they snagged one of our roots. Our Tenders blocked their root, but not before fifty of their Handlers traveled through the veins and spilled into our Tree."

Fifty. We didn't have that many mucks, half-Handlers, and Handlers combined.

CHAPTER
31

"THE TENDERS ARE trying to contain the invaders . . ." Avi began.

" . . . but we simply don't have enough people," I finished for her.

Avi nodded. "Now that you're back, I'm going, suspension or no suspension, to fight them. Do you want to come?"

"I've got to go back to the nagas." Briefly, I explained that I'd promised the nagas I'd swim to Island Hibu and drag Handler Rydel to Nearhell. I glossed over the bit about getting married after. "If I don't go, we'll be fighting the nagas and Hibu."

Eflet frowned. "I'm not sure you can defeat Rydel. He has so many treasures . . ."

"And I have no choice. Eflet, do you know where he is?"

Grudgingly, she described a system of veins. "At the top of that, the veins stop. I have watched him come in and out of the next veinless room with a council of Handlers. I believe it is his audience chamber. I cannot find Rydel elsewhere on Hibu. That is your best chance."

"Thank you." Time to return to Nearhell. To the nagas. With solid ground beneath me and a warm lattice of veins above, it took more effort than I'd like to admit to stand and put my hand to the wall.

Avi gripped my shoulder. "I'm coming."

"You're injured!"

"And it's very neatly stitched. You said the nagas would escort us, not attack us. Eflet, does Rydel have Tender treasures?"

Eflet shook her head. "No. He's Called many permanent treasures to his grave, but I doubt Tender treasures would have occurred to him, given that usually only women have them."

"Good." Avi turned to me, shoulders set back. "One of us needs to reach him, yank him through a vein, and toss him to the nagas. Wouldn't you rather have another person who could, I don't know, cause a distraction or fight off any other Handlers or Tenders around? If he's as powerful as Eflet says, two of us is better than one."

"You're *injured*."

"Name someone else who can breathe underwater for the trip through Nearhell *and* pull Rydel into a vein if the opportunity appears."

There was no one. Only Avi and I had both Handler and Tender treasures.

"Everyone else is already busy trying to keep Hibu from taking over our island. If I stay here, I'd have to fight while dodging my superiors. I'll do Gunaji more good helping you."

She was right. No one else could be spared to help, and we didn't have time to argue about who should or shouldn't come. She handed me a javelin, keeping one strapped to her own back.

Eflet spoke, eyes closed. "A Tender and a Handler just came out of a vein a few branches down. Young ones. The Handler looks like he's only twelve or so . . . and he's smiling."

"Daef."

"He's climbing up, outside."

I thought about climbing this high up and my head spun. Did someone send him to enforce our suspension?

Avi took my hand. "If he's here to stop us, that will tie up four people who should be fighting."

I ached to see Daef, to bring him with us, but Avi was right. We didn't exactly have time to chat, either. "Let's hurry, then."

"Be careful," Eflet pleaded.

Then Avi pulled us both through the veins—turbulent with what I now knew was the Tenders trying to stop the invasion. We slammed into the unforgiving cold of Nearhell.

A pair of nagas waited for us, long and sleek with small, dark eyes. Avi jerked back, but I squeezed her hand. Small as it was, this appeared to be our escort.

The nagas twitched, nostrils flaring. One wrapped around Avi, flicked a tongue at her wound. I reached for my javelin, but the naga guiltily pulled away. It gestured to its back.

No time to waste fussing. I wrapped my arms around its torso and straddled its back. Avi hesitated, then mounted the other naga the same way.

They shot forward in the water, so much faster than any human could swim. I fumbled to hold on, then caught the feel of it. Light from the roots, then light from the sun overhead on the open sea, flashed over us. The water streamed over my skin. It felt like flying.

And below us followed some hundred nagas, so tight in formation they looked like a single silver fish. I imagined the ancient one kept these nagas back, until he could see I hadn't come with Handlers to fight them.

An hour or so passed before we glided under the shadow of Hibu's Turtle. Our escort rose to surround us and hissed bubbles at the local nagas. Hibu's nagas hissed back. Our nagas shot more bubbles.

I couldn't understand the argument with the ambrosia used up, but apparently we were convincing. Hibu's nagas parted and joined our flanks. A few nagas from both sides drifted from the pack and absent-mindedly gnawed the roots.

I glanced at Avi. Her every muscle looked taut. Her narrowed eyes flickered over all the nagas around us. I probably should have been as vigilant.

Hibu Handlers appeared—five, all close to the root-gnawing nagas. Before I could call out or grab a javelin, three dozen nagas charged them. Nearly as quickly, bones, javelins, and shreds of clothes sank away from their swarm. The water carried a metallic tang. I gagged.

The nagas carrying us swam up to a large root. Avi took my hand, then we both pressed a palm to one of the golden veins.

Eflet's description was perfect. Together, Avi and I felt our way up the thick golden veins. We spilled into a small room. As Eflet had said, the far side held no gold, just a plain door. Handler Rydel should be on the other side. Anxiety and fear flickered through me, but we couldn't turn back.

I unstrapped my javelin. Avi did likewise.

Maybe we'd be lucky and find Handler Rydel alone. Maybe we'd find his full council of Handlers and we'd both be dead in seconds. I told myself it had to be the former. If we failed, the nagas would swarm Island Gunaji and kill Tree and Turtle while our Handlers tried to beat the invasion back.

I wanted to say something profound, but I couldn't think of anything. I met Avi's eye. I nodded. That was enough. We crept to opposite sides of the door. Avi creaked it open.

Leading with my javelin, I stepped into the entry.

This wasn't the council room. A single oil lamp glowed in a niche in the wall, but otherwise, it was an unremarkable square. An antechamber, with another door leading forward.

I signaled Avi to rally forward with me. Useful, those hand signals. We eased the door closed behind us.

Odd. Narrow, deep circles were cut in the floor before both doors. I tapped Avi's shoulder and pointed.

Something shot from the ceiling. I jerked away, farther into the small room. Bars covered the door, each set firmly in one of those holes. I shook them. Hard, thick wood. They didn't budge.

I turned to try the door that would take us forward. Bars covered it as well. I felt out the floor and walls, but the room was smooth except for the lamp niche. The top of the niche held a few small holes, probably for venting the smoke, but I certainly couldn't fit through.

I hoisted Avi on my shoulders and she felt the ceiling one tedious handspan at a time. When she finally jumped down, my shoulders ached.

"Smooth as the floor," she whispered.

"Can you pull out a vein or manipulate the living wood?" I didn't have anything like Avi's practice with either skill.

Avi pressed her hands to the bars, frowned, then tried the floor, walls, and even had me lift her to the ceiling again. "This isn't living wood. This room's been lined with something else. I can't change it."

"Maybe we can peel down to the living wood, then."

We worked at it for what felt like eons. We ended up with a gouged floor and three broken, useless javelins. Avi sunk into a corner, hugged her legs to her chest, and hid her face in her knees.

I banged on the doors with a broken javelin butt. "Hey! I know you're out there!" *Thwack, thwack, thwack.* "Show yourselves!"

"Tenjat, that's only making my head hurt." Her legs muffled her voice. "They would have heard us exploring the cell."

"I have to try *something*."

Avi said what both of us already knew. "We're trapped."

CHAPTER

32

HOW LONG WOULD the nagas wait before they decided we'd failed? Before they streaked back to Island Gunaji and destroyed it? Maybe it didn't matter. Our Handlers couldn't hold off fifty invaders. We'd lost Island Gunaji already; I just refused to admit it.

I slumped against the wall next to Avi. The oil lamp seemed strange, watery, only lighting a portion of the room. The ceiling and far corners lay in shadows.

"At least we perish bravely," I said.

"I wanted to *win*." She shifted closer to me. "Do you think someone will come, or do you think they'll just clean away our corpses once we die of thirst?"

"Cheerful today, aren't you?" I mumbled, but I couldn't

muster actual scorn. Maybe we would die of thirst in here.

"I'd rather die fighting alongside our Handlers, a *whole* javelin in hand." Avi kicked at the splinters and chert dust.

I felt exactly the same way. I had no words to console her.

"Our treasures . . . I thought that was something special," Avi said. "That one day, we'd end up as High Handler and Master Tender. Good, honest ones. The opposite of my hubbish parents."

What a lovely vision—working with her every day to keep the island safe. An impossible vision. "Avi, if we had succeeded, I would have been forced to leave the Tree."

"What do you mean?"

I was suddenly grateful for the poor illumination. Sitting half in shadows made this easier. "The nagas asked for more than Eflet."

Avi stilled.

"I promised I'd marry. That my wife would bear their souls."

She sounded half strangled. "Once we were safe, you could renege."

"I promised."

"It's a stupid promise!"

"If it means the nagas leave us in peace?" What was the shame of having children, if it didn't slow the island? I bit my lip. That wasn't an argument Avi would hear. "I did it for the Tree."

"You belong *in* the Tree. Did they tell you who to marry, too, or were they courteous enough to leave that up to you?"

My throat knotted. "Avi, you're the only one I want to be with."

"Stay in the Tree with me, then." She took my hands, as if we were having a real argument. As if we'd leave this cell alive.

Maybe knowing we wouldn't made me brave enough to say it. "I can't stay in the Tree. But you could come with me. Marry me."

"Tenjat." She twined her fingers through mine. Her voice softened. "You are the last person I could ever damn to the shameful life of a hub."

"I . . . I'm already damned."

Avi cupped my face in both hands. Even in that dim room, she managed to match her mouth to mine. She leaned into me—warm, pure gold. For a moment, I thought she'd changed her mind. That she wanted to be my wife. That my sister's vision of Ceibak would be a paradise, after all, because I wouldn't be there alone.

Then I felt her hot tears on my cheeks. Avi pulled back. "If you must die, die, but don't ask me to be your murderer. I care about you too much, my little muck"—Avi paused to wipe her face — "to be your downfall, your hub-maker."

I held her hand, silent. Avi stared at the ceiling.

I'd learned the word *hub* when I was three. I said it over and over until even toddling Eflet picked it up. Mother shushed me, for all the good it did. Over time, I learned what it meant and swore not to be one. Why did I expect Avi to feel differently than I did a month ago? She didn't trust Eflet. She hadn't spoken with the nagas.

Maybe perishing in this cell wasn't so bad. If we succeeded, I'd only have to say good-bye.

Except Eflet, Gyr, Lyna, and Daef were all on Island Gunaji. I had more than myself to think of. I needed to focus on escaping. I swallowed until I trusted my voice to stay level. "Avi. You claimed my skeleton as a treasure, right?"

"Yes."

"Do you have any guesses what that does?"

"If Jerohn and his codices don't know, why would I?" She leaned her head against the wall. "When I robbed Hell, I told them about the extra bones. We didn't realize it meant a shared cache at the time."

A shared grave, I silently corrected, but I doubted Avi wanted to hear it.

"Handlers Odev and Reliak put me through a number of tests, and Jerohn checked his books. There is such a thing as 'junk' treasure — treasures whose impact is so small it's hard to notice. Jerohn classified this as such."

"Did you ever try to use it? Maybe it's like the copperfoot, where you have to *reach* for it to work."

Avi shrugged. "Nothing happened when I did."

Nothing. That didn't sound promising. Maybe her skeleton—the treasure I claimed—could do more? Just like with the copperfoot, I reached, willing for something to happen.

Avi flinched next to me. "That made my scalp tingle. You tried to use the treasure?"

"You try, now."

Pinpricks rippled across my scalp—I'd never felt that before. "Maybe it didn't work before because I hadn't claimed your skeleton. We needed both pieces."

"I'm glad we've made progress," Avi said, "but making each other's heads feel fuzzy isn't much better than nothing."

That, unfortunately, was an excellent point. Maybe it would make a good substitute for hand signals in Nearhell—we could send the prickles in timed patterns, communicating without the need to look at each other. "Avi, let's try it at the same time."

She nodded. My scalp prickled, then I *reached* as well.

Suddenly, my field of vision shifted. I sat on the other side of Avi. On the opposite side of Avi. We stared at each other.

"Let's try that again." Avi stood and crossed the room, then nodded at me.

And in a moment, *I* stood on the opposite side of the room, looking at Avi, who now stood in the corner where I'd been.

"We can switch places." I felt light-headed, giddy. "No wonder it did nothing before! How could you switch with me before I claimed the treasure too?"

Avi smiled, but it quickly faded. "Tenjat, we're *both* stuck in this cell."

I looked around and remembered where I was. Maybe we did have an amazing treasure, but it couldn't help us escape. Switching places was nothing more than a curiosity, a diversion.

How much time had passed since we traveled up here? Had our naga escort already abandoned us to attack the Tree? How many of our Handlers had died, struggling against the invaders? Maybe I didn't want to know the answer to the last question. Daef was spry, but he wasn't strong. In tight corridors, he'd make a quick casualty.

"Any chance this High Handler Rydel is with the invasion and someone else will kill him for us?" I asked, trying to joke.

Avi shook her head. "Maybe we're thinking about it all wrong. Eflet said this High Handler Rydel tracks you using your kin's blood? There's another way to stop Rydel from finding her."

"I won't kill my own family."

"I meant *rescue* them."

"Oh." This cell had turned me macabre. "We can't reach my father—he's on Island Ita, far from here."

"Then how is Rydel tracking Eflet?"

"My brother Ven, most likely." Little Ven. I swallowed the knot in my throat.

"Would he help us escape?"

"If he was in a position to do so," I said, gesturing at the blank walls, "I think he'd have done it by now."

An odd sweetness filled the room. I frowned. Some kind of white smoke furled from the lamp's air vents. I pointed. "Avi?"

"It smells like herbs." She stood, then swayed and put a hand to her head.

I ran forward and covered the holes with my hands, but I couldn't stop the smoke. It curled between my fingers. It tickled my nose, sweet backed by bitter.

My head swayed. Lilit had once given me something like this. "It's to make us . . . sleep . . ."

I shifted my hands, trying to better cover the holes, and inhaled a whiff of the stuff instead. My fingers tingled numbly. I slumped to the floor.

Someone opened the door we hadn't been through. I tried to stand, but I pitched forward instead. A half-dozen Handlers marched in. They grabbed me and knocked Avi backward. The bars clanged shut after us, trapping Avi behind.

By the time the clean air in this new room cleared my head,

thick ropes bit into my wrists. In shape, the room wasn't unlike High Handler Banoh's audience chamber, but no golden veins touched the walls. Only lamps illuminated it, leaving much in shadow.

A middle-aged man stood in front of me, hands clasped behind his back, radiating a level of self-confidence and dignity I'd only ever seen Eflet achieve. Otherwise, he looked much like a Handler from our island—lean muscles and an immaculate Handler's uniform of a fishskin-tight, gleaming shirt and loose breeches cinched at the knee. "Ah, you must be Tenjat."

"I don't know what you're talking about."

"I apologize; I didn't introduce myself." He nodded politely. "I am High Handler Rydel, commander of Island Ita and all her subordinates. I have many treasures, Tenjat. One of them allows me to Trace kin lines—that's what lets me track your sister. It's clearer when I'm *holding* someone's blood, but with Eflet only an island away, she's easy enough to Trace."

I gritted my teeth and stood stiffly. No veins here to pull him through. Bonds bit my wrists.

"So stern! I'm not your enemy, Tenjat. In fact, we could be good friends. I brought you a gift."

"You can't bribe me, whatever you have or whatever you want."

"Whatever? *Whoever.* I'm sure Ven would be quite heartbroken if you came all this way and refused to visit him."

CHAPTER
33

VEN. LITTLE VEN. He'd be nearing Daef's age now.

"Ah, you are interested in seeing him?"

I quavered. Rydel sounded as polite as anyone I'd met, but I didn't trust the smugness in his eyes. "What do you want? You already know where Eflet is."

"Yes, but it's so tiresome to reach her."

My heart jumped. *Had* our Handlers kept the invaders off? With the nagas only attacking Island Hibu, was Gunaji escaping? How the nagas knew I wasn't dead, I couldn't fathom. But I intended to keep it that way.

Rydel frowned. "So hopeful-looking, Tenjat. Your sister is not safe. I know how fast your island moves. I know how fast we move. We will catch her."

Except Island Gunaji moved *faster* without the nagas, and he moved *slower* with extra nagas here. The thought didn't make me smile. If I failed here, the nagas who'd brought me would return and swarm, making Rydel's words true.

"I'm sure you considered yourself clever, crossing Nearhell with that Tender to bring you up here, but as you see, I planned for such a strike."

I frowned. The Tender that brought me? I remembered what Eflet said. Rydel didn't have Tender treasures himself, likely because it never occurred to him. Why would he suspect I had such treasures? "I want to see my brother."

I was wary of Rydel's offer, but I had to get out of this veinless room. If Rydel didn't know what I could do, why should he be afraid to take me somewhere with veins?

"Ah, I'm glad you've come to see the value of a trade. I only want a piece of information in return. How does one make a Seer? What kind of treasure is required?"

I shifted backward. A pair of guards instantly grabbed my arms and held me fast. "I don't know."

"What a silly thing to say. You obviously care about your sister. Surely you are close. You must know—you are not a child to hide secrets from."

I laughed. It probably wasn't the right thing to do. The guards tightened their grip and Rydel scowled. Maybe everything that had happened recently was getting to me—

Eflet's marriage, negotiating with the nagas, the invasion, Avi kissing me and then telling me she'd never marry me—but I laughed until my ribs hurt. "I didn't know she was a Seer until . . ." I paused. How long ago had that been? ". . . yesterday evening, I think."

"Such insolence. I thought you wanted to be friends." Rydel turned to the guards. "You three, fetch Ven and meet us in the Warbler Room."

"Warbler?" Did they have an aviary in here?

Rydel smiled, all teeth and coldness. Any thought that he might be a kind person vanished. "That," he said, "is where we'll make you sing."

Without fighting, I followed Rydel from the room, two Handler guards escorting me. I couldn't do anything in that veinless hall. Perhaps the Warbler Room would be better.

It almost looked like Lilit's infirmary—clean, neat cabinets; a mortar and pestle on the workbench—except other tools glistened on the walls, each made from polished copper or expertly flaked obsidian. Knives, hooks, pincers, awls. These were not instruments of craftsmanship.

"Tie him," Rydel commanded with a casual wave of his hand. The pair of guards slammed me against the wall and jerked my hands above my head. I tried to yank away, but I couldn't budge the two Handlers. They tied my bonds to a

walk, but carried him across his chest. Ven didn't fight him, though. His face was gaunt, all the babyness of childhood replaced with haunted lines. He stared down at his hands, silent. My throat knotted when I tried to call out his name. To get him to look at me.

Five years. Those five years had been kinder to me than to him, but here he was—alive.

The guard turned, set him on the floor, and lashed his wrists to a low ring. Ven's legs stretched before him, but . . . but how could there be nothing but air beneath his knees? I stared. I watched him shift. But no calves or feet suddenly appeared beneath his truncated limbs.

I pictured that day, six years ago, flying across the ground in our race back to Old Man Tul's. *Oceans*, he loved running.

"Ven . . ." My voice sounded like cracked pottery. "How . . ."

I couldn't force the rest of the question out of my too-tight throat. I ached to run to him, to embrace him. To do something, anything, for this brother we'd left behind.

Ven blinked, confused. His gaze finally settled on me. "T-Tenjat?" Tears spilled across his face. Daef was only a year older, but Ven was impossibly scrawnier. Underfed. "I'm sorry. I'm . . . I'm . . ."

Rydel smiled. "Now, *he* doesn't know how to make a Seer. After we cut off the first leg, he didn't doubt our threats about the second. We've learned everything

Ven can tell us. You, on the other hand . . ."

My entire body stiffened. My muscled filled with cold fire. Rydel. He sounded so *pleased* with himself.

"I'm sorry," Ven spluttered. "Everything I knew . . . I told . . . I'm sorry."

Rydel's grin deepened. He took one step closer to Ven, knife in hand.

I couldn't play Rydel's game, even if it meant feigning indifference toward Ven. I bit my lip hard on the inside. I let my fists unclench. And I didn't look at my battered brother, weeping and mumbling in the corner.

"You'll tell me what you know now," Rydel said.

I knew precious little about Eflet's gift, but Rydel didn't need to hear any of it. I took my anger and shoved it to the pit of my stomach. This man deserved to be devoured by nagas. "I care nothing for my own life."

"Ah, but you care about him, don't you?" Rydel turned the obsidian knife in his hand, golden vein light playing off the black ridges of its flake scars. He stepped closer to Ven. My little brother cringed, pulling himself into a malformed ball.

I wanted to scream and swear, but I forced myself to shrug—awkwardly, with my hands lashed above me. "I haven't seen him in years. Why would I care? If not for his betrayal, I'd still be *free.*"

Ven stared at me, eyes wide and pleading. Quivering like

a half-dead mouse, he whispered, "I missed you."

I bit down harder on my lip, tasted blood, and stared straight ahead. If we survived, I'd take back every word and explain that apathy and anger were the only weapons I had to spare him Rydel's attention.

Rydel turned to the three Handler guards in the room. "Two of you go fetch the Tender."

This time, I let the worry show in my eyes.

I tested the bonds again. I couldn't slip free. But at least I'd gotten Avi out of her impenetrable cell. We'd all be together. We could all escape together.

But I was thinking ahead of myself. To escape, we'd need to be free of our bonds and somehow thrust Rydel to Nearhell. Rydel toyed with the knives while we waited, humming to himself. I stood on tiptoe, trying not to look at Ven. He'd curled himself around the ring he'd been lashed to, as if that chunk of wood could offer him comfort. My calves trembled from the awkward position. I hung for a moment, but the ropes hurt worse than the cramping.

Ven's soft whisper filled the silence of the room. "Eflet hates me too, doesn't she?"

Rydel watched me. I stared straight ahead, blinking regularly, throat knotted. Eflet would always love him. So would I. But I couldn't let Rydel see that.

Ven silently leaned his head against the wall. He looked

more corpse than person, barely breathing, as if the thought of reuniting with his caring sister had been the only thing animating his limbs. I burned to speak the truth, to ease his pain. But any word of comfort would draw Rydel's attention—and his knives.

The guards returned with Avi, her hands likewise bound. The room now held her, myself, Ven, Rydel, and three of his Handler guards. I eyed the ring on the wall within reach of the vein. Maybe they'd put her there. Maybe . . .

But of course they weren't so foolish to put a Tender by a vein. They tied her to the same ring I was on.

"Welcome." Rydel nodded politely at Avi. She spat at his feet. "Tsk, tsk, such manners."

He walked slowly to us, obsidian knife gleaming. And I could do nothing to stop him.

I struggled to find Avi's fingers. I was worse at planning than Daef. No, Avi wouldn't thank me for getting her out of the cell. She'd been tied as tightly as me on the walk here. We found each other's hands and clasped them.

Waiting to be tortured, I no longer worried about being seen as a hub. I memorized the feel of her hands—warm, slender, calloused. I willed time to stop here, Rydel two steps away and Avi next to me.

Would the nagas know we'd failed? Even now, did they head to Island Gunaji to destroy our escape?

I paused as Rydel turned the knife over and considered Avi. "Shall we mar your face first?"

I squeezed her hand as best I could.

Her *slender* hand. My pulse quickened. I reached for our mutual treasure.

In a moment, I hung face-to-face with Rydel, Avi's tighter bonds cutting into my skin. Blood trickled down my arm, but I clenched my teeth and smiled.

Avi slipped out of my bonds and ran to the vein on the opposite wall. Rydel and the other three Handlers were startled, but quickly recovered and charged after. They tackled her — one messy pile of five people.

Avi screamed. Blood blossomed on her shirt. They'd burst her stitches. And they'd wedged her on the floor. Her arms weren't long enough to reach the vein. Rydel raised his knife above her heart . . .

. . . but I reached for the treasure.

Knees and elbows pressed into me, but my larger frame loosed their grip. Rydel's blow sunk into my shoulder, burning. And at the same moment, I reached up and touched the vein.

I dragged all of us — Rydel and his three Handlers — down to Nearhell. Nagas surrounded us. I thought I recognized the one who'd ferried me over, but I didn't stay for pleasantries. The nagas writhed. I touched the vein and yanked myself back to the Warbler Room.

CHAPTER
34

I GRABBED RYDEL'S knife and slashed Avi's bonds, then Ven's. He stared at both of us, wide-eyed. I gave him a grin, then rummaged through the drawers for bandages. "How's your side, Avi?"

"Tenjat, I'm sure *some* Tender noticed what you did. I don't think we have time—"

The door opened. I didn't wait to see who was there. I threw the knife. Someone shouted—it sounded like alarm, not pain. I grabbed Avi's hand, Avi grabbed Ven's, and I touched the vein.

We shot to Nearhell.

The water tasted overwhelmingly sharp. I gagged. I didn't see Rydel or his Handler guards anywhere.

Ven flailed and grabbed at his throat.

He couldn't breathe underwater. I grabbed one arm, Avi the other, and we kicked toward the surface. The nagas seemed to understand our plight. Three of them swam under us, taking us out and up from the Turtle faster than Avi and I ever could.

Under the bright sun, Ven spluttered and coughed, eventually settling into ragged breathing. I laid a hand on his narrow shoulder. "Ven?"

"I'm sorry," he said again. "I didn't mean to tell them about Eflet. I—"

I stopped his stuttering with a tight hug. "Ven, I'm glad they had you in that room today to taunt me. I didn't mean anything I said, but it kept Rydel from hurting you again. I'm glad you're coming home at last. Eflet and I have both missed you too."

I peeled off my shirt and tore it into strips. Most of it I bandaged thickly around Avi, but she knotted a length around my bleeding shoulder. Between the saltwater searing across my cut and the too-bright sun, I felt queasy. I kept my seat well enough, though—the nagas swam much slower on the surface. Even so, Avi seemed to wince with their every stroke.

"Do you think that bandage will keep your mount from

blood-frenzying, if you two swam under the water?" I asked her.

"Maybe. Why?"

"If you can, you should hurry to Lilit."

She frowned, as if about to protest she was fine, or perhaps that I was injured too. Then she glanced between me and Ven. "If my naga starts acting odd, we'll come back up."

Avi pantomimed to her naga what she wanted. She disappeared under the bright water. I watched, but her naga showed no signs of attacking. I'd welcome Lilit's salves right now, but I'd survive, and I wasn't about to leave my brother with only nagas for company.

Ven and I rode silently at first. Then I asked him for news of Father. He spoke slowly, haltingly. "They took him. The week you left."

"Oh. I'd hoped you'd had more time with him."

"Old Man Tul turned him in."

I stared at Ven. I wanted to curse and rant against Tul, but loud words seemed like the wrong thing around Ven right now. "Eflet said he sheltered you."

"Father *asked* Tul to turn him in. It kept the Handlers from finding me." His voice sounded as frail as sun-withered grass.

Both of our parents had sacrificed for their children. I wanted to ask more, I wanted to hear every detail, but pushing Ven seemed selfish. "Do you want to hear about Eflet?"

Ven actually smiled. I was amazed he could manage that much, after what Rydel did to him. The wide ocean stretched in front of us, brilliant blue and glittering like freshly knapped obsidian. Gunaji's Tree cut a shadowy line through the sky. I picked a cheerful story—the time Gyr and I broke Arja's best griddle. In her wrath, Arja declared she wouldn't feed either of us for three days, but Eflet easily snuck cassava cakes around her. Gyr and I had rarely been so full.

"She was always kind like that," Ven said. "Another story?"

I told another, and another. After that third one, his voice softened. "You . . . didn't mention Mother in any of those. Is she . . . still alive?"

My throat tightened. "Mother . . ."

"I wanted to believe Rydel lied." He stared down at the water. "He said he couldn't track her, and that meant . . ."

I nodded.

"Did she go . . . well?" Ven asked.

His eyes were wide with hope and hurt. Mother's screams echoed in my ears. "Mother . . ." I swallowed. She died saving her children. Mother wouldn't think that a bad ending. "Mother died happy."

Hours later, I trudged onto Gunaji's shore, carrying Ven—he was all too light without legs—and found the nearest vein. We appeared in Lilit's infirmary.

Lilit's *busy* infirmary. I'd never seen so many Tenders or Handlers in one spot. Oddly, Eflet was there too. She shouldn't have been able to leave Avi's doorless room. She ignored me to hug Ven. She clung to him. I almost told her she'd crush his lungs, before I saw Ven's face. He beamed.

Tender Avret, a stocky, middle-aged woman, led me away. All the supplies for salving and bandaging wounds were neatly laid out. She was halfway done with my stitches when Eflet took over. I tried not to flinch as she stabbed the thin needle through my skin. "I had a muck escort Ven to the mess. He looked like he could use a meal."

Or a lifetime of meals.

"I also thought you'd want to know the casualties, and Ven didn't need to hear," Eflet said.

I stiffened. "Daef?"

"Is fine. Most of the mucks made it. Jerohn, Gyr, and Enari have been Calling medicines for those who are the worst injured. They've saved a number of them."

"But?"

"Bokan, Indon, and Lasyna died," Eflet said. Two half-Handlers and one Tender. I didn't know any of them well, but I still lowered my head. Eflet ended with, "And there was a Handler Reliak and a muck named Kosel."

Those two names hit me numbly. After all that had happened, I had a hard time digesting Eflet's words. "Kosel?"

"He fought fearlessly, almost recklessly, then bled out while I was trying to put him back together." Eflet shook her head. "Kosel was smiling when he died. Said he'd redeemed himself, that he was a real Handler."

I closed my eyes. If I hadn't opened that chest, if I hadn't shown everyone those red sashes, would he still be alive today?

And Handler Reliak. We weren't exactly close, but he'd been part of the committee that allowed me to call Gunaji home. He seemed a model Handler, and a kind one. Avi would be devastated.

"How . . . why are you here?"

"It's Daef's doing. A Tender felt movements in the veins up by Avi's room—your movement up from Nearhell—and thought you were an invader."

"Avi's the only Tender that can navigate through those tiny veins."

Eflet nodded. "So the Tender took Daef to the window below Avi's, then returned to her post. Daef climbed up."

Just imagining it gave me vertigo. That high up, the Tree swayed. Daef must have climbed like a spider. And what was the Tender thinking, sending Daef alone against invaders? I knew we were outnumbered, but I hadn't envisioned what that meant.

"When he climbed in the window, he leveled a javelin at

us and demanded to know who we were—we didn't look like Hibu Handlers. He knew my name and listened when I explained you'd made a treaty with the nagas. Daef's got a quick head. With the nagas friendly to us, our Tenders had nothing to fear in dragging the invaders to Nearhell.

"Daef climbed back down, convinced his Tender to test his theory, then spread the word. Tenders popped into rooms, grabbed invaders, and pulled them to Nearhell. The nagas did the messy work—and they never so much as scratched our Tenders. I wasn't sure the nagas would be able to tell those Handlers weren't Gunaji, but it worked."

"They could *smell* I was your brother. I'm sure by now they have a good idea of what Gunaji Handlers and Tenders in general smell like."

Eflet smiled. "If they're smart enough for all that, I suppose nagas aren't just monsters."

"You were right," I sighed. "I hope you're not going to gloat."

To her credit, Eflet let the matter drop. "In any case, when all was clear, Daef came with some rope to help me and Gyr down to the next window. I volunteered to assist in the infirmary, so a Tender brought me here."

Daef was one smart kid. "So we've escaped Hibu?"

"Yes. Our nagas already forage for the Turtle."

My gut flipped. I'd succeeded. Our island was safe, and

the nagas . . . the nagas did more than their word. The island's well-being was their well-being now.

Eflet whispered, but pride tinged every word. "You made this possible. With the nagas as allies, we'll always be fast and have plentiful fields. We'll become like Ceibak, where having children is respected as part of our agreement with the nagas."

I'd hated Ceibak my whole life. I hadn't understood what Ceibak meant, because I hadn't listened. When I went to take the test, I was so sure that I could only raise myself and Eflet from shame. Now I'd done something for Gyr, Lyna, and everyone else. Ceibak wasn't a fable, a false paradise. It was going to be home.

"In a generation," Eflet continued, "*Hub* will be a term of respect."

My elation sank. Hub. I'd promised to marry. And Avi wasn't coming with me.

Eflet had barely tied my bandage when Daef ran in. "I'm supposed to bring you to the High Handler!"

How like Daef, to smile even when the world was in chaos.

"I heard you're a hero," I said.

"Something like that." He shrugged, but the grin was anything but humble. I let him lead me through the halls of living wood, some sand-colored, some as deeply hued as

M. K. HUTCHINS

the best loam. Daef rambled about the battle, but most of it drifted past me. We'd won. But I'd lost Avi. Details seemed irrelevant.

He finished his story just outside the mahogany door to the High Handler's audience chamber. "And you! You were on some secret mission, huh? Lucky!"

I smiled weakly.

No Tender stood outside the door today—I imagined the infirmary and attack presented more pressing matters. Daef stood a step back. I entered alone, unescorted.

Only the High Handler sat inside, on one of the chairs sculpted into the circular wall of the room. As far as I could see, he only had a few scrapes and bruises from the battle.

"Manoet?" I asked.

"She's fine—off monitoring the nagas' foraging efforts. They're amazingly proficient."

At least that worked well.

High Handler Banoh crossed the room and bowed. "You and Avi saved this Turtle. Tomorrow, I'm promoting you both to full Handlers."

Finally, Avi was getting the promotion she deserved. A few weeks ago, I would have been thrilled to join her. I always thought I wanted to be a Handler. "I can't accept."

Banoh rose slowly from his bow, frowning.

"I'm leaving the Tree. I'm getting married. That's the

promise I made the nagas." I explained what I'd learned of the nagas and why they'd become so helpful.

Banoh pursed his lips, eyes grave. "Without nagas attacking us, this island will prosper, not just now, but for generations to come. You're a hero, Tenjat. I thank you for your sacrifice in choosing the disgraceful life of a husband."

He spoke with pity, his words giving no hint that he was anything but a respectable High Handler. Maybe it was the long day, but I gritted my teeth. "Hypocrite."

"Excuse me?" The golden vein-light played across his startled face.

"You've *always* wanted a family. You see nothing wrong with it. You're the *High Handler*, a man of *power*. There are good, honest people on this island who don't deserve scorn and broken ribs." I was surprised to find I meant Jesso as much as Gyr. "That scorn isn't necessary now. You could say something, help that scorn disappear."

Banoh shook his head. "I'd be expelled from the Tree if I admit what I am. Wouldn't you stay and remain a Handler, if you could? You're leaving the most critical job on this island for the least important one."

I paused. I'd always dreamed of providing a prosperous life for Eflet and myself, of defending this island, of following in my father's footsteps. Before, that meant being a Handler. Now I could only accomplish all three by becoming a farmer once more.

How odd to realize Banoh was wrong. "Handlers aren't important."

"Excuse me?" Banoh stared at me like I'd taken a blow to the head.

"How long do you think the Tree will rule this island, when we no longer need Handlers to fight the nagas? Who will pay taxes to obsolete warriors?"

Banoh didn't answer.

"People will eventually notice how things have changed. In time, they'll believe that I bargained with the nagas and they'll want to help maintain that bargain. You could make that time a short one." Frustration burned up my chest. Is this how Eflet felt, all those times she'd tried to teach me about Ceibak?

Banoh's eyebrows pinched together. "The Garums' land is empty now. I grant it to you. May those fields prosper under your hand."

"I wasn't threatening you. I'll keep your secret."

"It's a reward for your heroism, not a bribe. Now go."

CHAPTER
36

I STAYED IN the Tree for five days, helping run errands for Lilit, watching over Ven's reintroduction to real food, and helping guard Callers up to the underbelly of the Mortal World to ask for oblations for the recovering Tenders and Handlers. I didn't see Avi. Not once. I think she knew that it would be too hard for both of us.

After those long, hectic days, things quieted enough for me, Eflet, Gyr, and Ven to return to Eflet's house. Watching Ven devour food was my only delight.

The next morning I surveyed the Garums' land. Looters had attacked the three huts bunched together around an open plaza—most of their poles, all of their thatch, and any previous belongings were gone. After the Garums were sold, who would protest such thievery? I drifted from hut to hut. The fields beyond were empty, neglected, populated only by sparse weeds. Broken pottery and bits of cotton string littered the ground, but no cassava.

For a moment, I imagined Avi grinding cassava, Avi making cakes, Avi drawing water and building a fire. That wasn't Avi. She belonged in the coolness of Deephell, brilliantly glowing with a javelin on her back.

Two of the huts were irreparably damaged. I entered the last one and ran my hand over the poles, frowning at their angles, the splintering cracks. My huts had never been fancy, but they were clean and sturdy. I'd need tools, buckets to carry mud for chinking, and a hammer to tear down the other huts. I had none of these, but I knew someone who did.

Dread tightened my throat, but not the usual dread at speaking with Jesso. I'd soon be like him—a married man. I didn't know how to talk to him as an equal. I didn't know how to show how I'd changed. That I didn't resent him anymore.

It was a short walk. When I arrived, he was chatting with one of his adult sons in the clearing while his half-dozen daughters and daughters-in-law cleaned up lunch.

I caught their conversation before they saw me.

". . . really going to let him come back?"

"He's not coming back," Jesso said. "The High Handler has granted him the Garums' land." News traveled fast.

The son slammed his fist onto the rock they sat on. "Why? Was *he* attacked? What harm did the Garums do him?"

"The Garums have their punishment and the Tree gave us the cassava flour and cuttings from their sale. We have no claim on that land."

"So they give it to him instead? A self-made hub?"

Jesso shook his head. "You shouldn't call him such things."

A self-made hub. I felt like my insides were being ground into flour. I stepped into the clearing. "Jesso?"

I recognized the son as Enrat—the one just older than Gyr. As far as I knew, he hadn't married yet. He stood, spat at my feet, and trudged off to his field.

The women glared at me, too, everyone but Reshla, who winked and waved—she'd always been a flirt.

Even Jesso's family found me reprehensible.

"Maybe we should go someplace else to talk, Tenjat," Jesso said. "Walk with me. To your fields?"

I followed. "I suppose Eflet talked with you, then?"

"She was here before lunch, yes." We strolled down the forest path to my new property. Jesso spoke as he always had to me—calm, fatherly.

"Is everyone angry about the land?" Even if my fields were sorry with neglect, everywhere else the island showed signs of recovery, of a well-fed Turtle. Flowers on the chili plants. New glossy leaves bursting from the knobby cassava stems. Abundant clear water in the streams. Island Gunaji would see a decent harvest this season, with some work.

"Oh, mostly Enrat. He failed the tests last week and will probably be courting soon. He'd like a place of his own."

"Oh."

Jesso smiled at me, that fatherly smile I'd always hated so much. "You deserve the land, and you'll need the privacy."

Eflet was wrong—it would take us more than a generation to turn hub into a term of respect. But, because of my bargain, we still had an island *to* change. Enrat could only spit at me because I'd saved him along with everyone else.

Even if it earned me scorn my entire life, I wouldn't change what I'd done.

"How much do you know?" I asked, trying to put the right tone in my voice. I felt like we were already in a secret place, with the thick, humid air and the shade of the forest covering us. Howler monkeys called to each other in the distance.

"Probably more than you do," Jesso said, not unkindly. "Eflet grew to trust me not long after you landed. My masses of children, you see, made me a patient listener. Maybe she knew it's what I needed to hear. I'm not immune to guilt."

She'd told Jesso and not me. I tried to brush that sting aside. "Having an infamous father causes your children grief, you know."

"Yes. But they have each other to help them deal with it,"

Jesso said, eyes soft and thoughtful. "It's better than being alone."

Maybe he was right about that. "I need to borrow tools. To fix the Garums' place."

"You're free to borrow anything I have," Jesso said. "Is it bad?"

He'd see soon enough, so I just shrugged.

"I assume there's no cassava there?"

"No." And I hadn't thought through how to get any. Fixing the huts had seemed the immediate problem, though cassava obviously should have come first. I wasn't thinking straight today.

"I don't have any spare cuttings right now, but I can help you next season. We won't let you starve until then."

I frowned. "I don't want to just take—"

"Help Gyr out with his new fields this season, then. You can pay in advance for next season's cuttings with your labor."

"You know I'd help Gyr anyway if he needed it, whether I had a full field of my own or not."

Jesso grinned. "I seem to recall saying something similar to you about taking in Eflet, regardless of how many jars of flour and beans you brought."

True. I sighed. "Thank you."

"You're welcome."

Slowly, I'd rebuild my new land. Slowly, we'd create Ceibak. I wished I had Eflet's patience, her trust that I

M. K. HUTCHINS

wouldn't be forever hated as a self-made hub. "Lyna . . . did she ever . . ."

"The day after the raid, we had the ceremony, yes. She's over at Bavi's now. Doing well."

"Good." I forced a smile.

Avi or some stranger, then. I should have consented to marry Lyna that day instead of taking the test. I wouldn't have known what I was missing. Memories of Avi . . . that stung more than Enrat's glares. Why did I expect everyone to see this island differently, just because I did?

We reached the Garums' old land—my land. Jesso surveyed the huts. He gave a low whistle. "I think I have all the tools you need. Do you want me to send some of my boys over to help?"

"I'll come ask for help if I need a second pair of hands. I'd enjoy some hard labor right now."

By midafternoon, my angry adrenaline was gone, along with part of one of the ruined huts. I sagged on the platform. The wound on my shoulder burned. I shouldn't have pushed so hard—blood oozed from the stitches.

Not long thereafter, Eflet arrived with a tray of cassava cakes and some clean bandages and salve. I wanted to complain about her spying on me, but I was too grateful for the medicine.

"Ven made the cakes. I've been teaching him."

I hoped that meant he really was settling well into his new life. I munched while Eflet changed my bandage. "Thanks."

"You're a hero, Tenae. People will notice how things have changed."

"Eventually." I tugged my loose farmer's tunic back on. Eflet had spent years trying to teach me, and I had to speak with the nagas face-to-face before I believed her. Trying to convince everyone on the island would be long, thankless work. But at least it was work worth doing. "You've always known you're a Seer?"

"I thought everyone could See until I was about four."

"This does explain why you were such a good tattletale."

Eflet scowled. "I was not."

"Were too."

Eflet shook her head.

I leaned back on my hands, letting the earth and shade cool me. "You've been trying to make Ceibak all along, haven't you? But you needed someone like me—a Handler who could breathe underwater to negotiate with the nagas."

"And a Caller. I didn't know if you'd ever listen to me. Fesi has a Handler's grave." That was Gyr's six-year-old brother. "I've been telling him stories of Ceibak, in case you never listened to me. I'm glad I didn't have to wait another decade for him to grow up."

Even if it took ten years, it wasn't a bad plan. I never thought I'd listen, either. "Eflet, is it safe to tell me what treasure makes a Seer? Why are they so rare?"

"Hm." Eflet considered me with a long look, but I think she felt guilty for keeping so many secrets from me in the past. "It's not the treasure that matters, but the way you're buried. Even Handler Rydel, with all the flutes, drums, and lyres he was buried with, couldn't have Called it."

Eflet picked up a cake and turned it over in her hands. "Usually people are buried on their backs, facing the Heavens. Only the hated are buried facing Hell, and stillborns aren't hated. Or if they are, I suppose they're buried without treasure. I was buried facedown with coins over my eyes."

I frowned, confused, and waited for her to continue.

Eflet tapped the side of her face. "These eyes look up. The golden eyes of my grave look down. Since I look in two opposite directions at once, I See much. If I had no coins, I'd be as blind as Gyr. If I faced upward, I'd only have your kind of sight."

"Do you know why you were buried like that?"

A wind rippled through the scanty weeds of my field, but already, the earth smelled good—rich and loamy and ready for planting. The nagas' foraging was working.

"My father didn't want me. He was poor and thought he already had too many daughters. He offered the midwife extra payment to strangle me when I was born and leave me on the mountain for the wolves. Then I came stillborn. She still wanted her extra payment. While they argued, my mother wrapped me and took me to the forest to bury. She didn't want me eaten."

I winced. "I'm . . . sorry."

"Don't be. I have two mothers that love me."

"Then why did she bury you upside down?"

"She didn't mean to. She stole the two coins meant for the midwife to give me a proper burial. Weak as she was, it took her too long to dig my grave. When she heard my father looking for her, she hastily dropped me in and covered me in dirt. Then she ran the other way so he couldn't find the grave."

Eflet's voice was barely audible above the breeze. "My mother—that mother—regularly descends from the Heavens to search for me around my grave. It took me years of watching and listening to her to piece together my story. All of her other children have reached the Heavens, but she's still waiting for me. She's been waiting for five hundred years."

I had nothing to say to that. Which was perhaps good, or I would have missed Eflet's soft afterthought: "When I'm finally finished here, I cannot wait to be held in her arms for the first time."

I'd had parents before here, too, then. I'd been torn from

life to the surface of Hell. "Do you . . . know what my first parents were like?"

I wanted to think they cared for me.

"As far as I can gather, both you and Avi perished at the same time. A plague decimated your small village. I'd guess that complications from the disease left you both stillborn. Given what you were buried with, Avi came from a wealthier family, but you were both lumped in the same mass grave with three dozen adults and children. You were the only infants, though."

I closed my eyes. How could we be so close in the Upper Realm, meet again here, and then separate?

"Do you want to visit Jesso's tonight? Some of his daughters' friends are coming to prepare for Reshla's wedding. I'll try talking about Ceibak with them. One of them might make a good wife."

"If you want me to talk about what I did with the nagas, I'll be there. Otherwise . . . just pick any woman who'll have me." If it couldn't be Avi, it didn't matter.

Eflet frowned. I sensed a lecture, so I changed the subject. "The ancient naga that I promised to have as my firstborn, does he have some great treasure?"

"His bones are dust, but he should be able to access the essence of the planting stick he was buried with. You'll have to take him past the imps to claim it, when he's old enough."

I supposed anyone who joined with us would need such an escort. At least everything Avi taught me wouldn't go to waste. "What does a planting stick let him do?"

"Grow crops well."

I groaned.

"We'll need that, too. People must eat, even in our new Ceibak."

"Ceibak is real, isn't it?"

"*Was*. Handler Rydel found it and razed it three years ago. We're the only ones left who know how to make peace with nagas. How to live a better life."

"Doesn't Father know?"

Eflet hung her head. "Yes. He and Mother knew everything I've told you."

I glanced at her, but I couldn't read her face. Maybe I didn't want the answer. "What's happening to Father now, with Rydel gone?"

"I can't See Father. He's not anywhere near gold. Maybe Ita's new High Handler will keep him in case they recruit a Handler who can sense bloodlines like Rydel did."

Or they might execute him. Eflet didn't say it out loud. Father was no longer an asset to Ita.

"Why doesn't Island Ita have anyone else with that ability? You said Rydel was a great Caller, that he could change permanent treasures."

"Rydel feared insubordination. He Called treasures sparingly for those he deemed loyal. He kept that one, the key to finding the Seer, to himself."

I knew the answer before I asked, but I asked anyway. "Will we ever be strong enough to take over Island Ita? To rescue Father?"

Surprisingly, Eflet smiled softly. "Maybe one day. Maybe we can raise a fleet. Have other islands join us. I hope many islands will make peace with their nagas and call themselves Ceibak. Perhaps even Island Ita—we may not have to fight them to get Father back."

Eflet had such plans for the future. My old goals of making a life for her and myself seemed small. Almost petty, by comparison. At least if my life didn't have Avi, it would still have purpose.

Eflet squeezed my good shoulder. "Come see Ven. Tell him how much you enjoyed his cakes."

I did. Ven awkwardly hobbled around the hearth on his hands, but he seemed happy to have useful work and to be with his family. I ached for Avi to be part of this picture, but I felt ungrateful for thinking it. I already had Eflet, Gyr, and Ven. Maybe one day, we'd manage to add Father.

Gyr assured me he didn't need any help yet, so I worked slowly on my huts, letting my shoulder heal. After a week,

I'd managed to level the two decrepit ones and had nearly patched up the third for living in. With Eflet's permission, I kept sleeping in their hut. Ven seemed to take comfort from our presence, especially when he woke screaming from a nightmare, sweat filming his scrawny, shaking body. He'd suffered more horrors than I could—or wanted to—imagine.

Just being there seemed like such an insignificant thing, but it was the only thing I could do for him. If I was honest, I didn't want to be alone, either, left to the dark corners of my new hut and memories of Avi.

Midmorning, Daef strolled across my fields. I started, then jogged up to him, grinning. "Daef!"

He didn't smile in turn, but winced and surveyed the land. He seemed to soak in every unlovely detail—the clutter of the demolished huts, the unplanted, torn-up land. "It's true? You're farming?"

"I . . ." My mouth turned to chalk. How to make him understand?

"The High Handler made a speech this morning. About you bargaining with the nagas, saving the island." He bit his lip. "You're not married yet, are you?"

My hut wasn't fit for a wife to move in, though Eflet had a few suggestions of women to propose to. "No."

"You could come back. The Handlers . . . I'm sure they'd understand."

M. K. HUTCHINS

I pursed my lips. I'd already tried to convince Avi that there was no shame in leaving the Tree and failed. But maybe Daef would listen. "This bargain with the nagas—can you see how it changes things? Handlers aren't needed to fight. Being a farmer and a father *helps* Gunaji now. Keeps the nagas our allies."

"Umm." That was all Daef said—Daef who had a thousand words on every topic.

"You're the one who told me that Handlers serve farmers."

He met my eye. "Some of us *still* serve."

The words stung. "Farmers don't need Handlers now. Can't you see that?" I pleaded. "How is farming not better than being a Handler?"

Daef glanced from his clean, fine Handler's clothes, the fishskin shirt gleaming in the morning light, to my well-worn, loose tunic—a spare Jesso had given me. "I'm not sure why you think scraping by for the rest of your life is better than fighting the naga."

"No one needs to fight now and farmers won't be poor forever," I said. "We'll have consistent, bounteous harvests with a healthy Turtle supported by foraging nagas. Even in the last couple weeks, it's started looking better."

Daef shook his head. "I never thought Kosel would be *right*. You're not the first to choose marriage over the Tree."

"Excuse me?"

"Being around Avi rotted your brain. Turned you hubbish."

Daef's tone turned patronizing, like I was too stupid to see the error of my ways.

"Avi's still in the Tree." I tried to keep my voice from betraying any hurt. "This isn't about her."

"Never mind," Daef muttered. "I don't need to know how you became a hub."

The last word felt like a slap. I'd never expected *Daef* to call me that.

But he'd seen less of the bargaining than Avi. Why should he think differently than she did? I inhaled the fresh morning air, trying to push down the knot of frustration growing in my gut.

Time — Daef needed time to see that something important had changed on Island Gunaji and that I wasn't crazy for being part of it. We could continue this conversation on other days. Once he'd gotten used to the idea.

"Do you want to play some Bump?" I asked. "I could fetch my sister — a new opponent. She's better than me. You could meet my brother, Ven, too."

Ven might like having a friend as vivacious as Daef around.

Daef awkwardly scratched his elbow. "No. I can't stay. I'm a half-Handler now. Responsibilities."

"Did something happen in the Tree?" Visions of invaders swarmed through my head.

"Well, High Handler Banoh did more than tell us about

M. K. HUTCHINS

your bargain. He said a bunch of things about Ceibak. About Handlers not being so necessary. Then he told us he was a hub—Avi's father."

The words sank in. Banoh had *listened* to me. Even if Avi and Daef hadn't. "Really?"

"Him and Manoet—that's what he said."

"No, I knew that," I waved a hand. "I just didn't expect . . ." Banoh *did* something.

Daef tilted his head to the side and peered at me. "Oh. Well, the Council of Handlers expelled him. Odev's High Handler now. I think Banoh said he'd go to that infamous Jesso's farm to talk to people."

He'd left the Tree. Banoh, with his reputation and leadership skills, had joined us.

"Anyway, things are a bit hectic in the Tree. But I wanted to see you. See if you really were farming." He sounded disappointed, disillusioned.

"Stay," I said, smiling. Even if he didn't believe me, it was good to see a familiar face from the Tree. "Come play a game or two."

Daef shook his head, already shifting back. No laughter warmed his eyes.

The knot in my gut turned cold. Daef didn't see me as a friend anymore. To him, I was just a hub. A self-made hub.

"I have to go." Daef turned and fled.

~ ~ ~

I strolled to Jesso's, imagining Banoh talking to Jesso's children and maybe a neighbor or two. Water dripped from the trees above me as I walked. This would be one more step toward the Ceibak Eflet envisioned for us. I wanted to be there, to support that step.

Before I reached Jesso's, I heard Banoh's voice.

". . . peace with the nagas. We need not fear being slow when they aid us. Our children will enjoy an always-bounteous island. We have found Ceibak. It is here."

I stepped around a tree and started. Some three hundred people — that I could see — had crammed into the clearing near Jesso's house, trailing back into the forest. Banoh stood on a bench, Manoet next to him, along with four half-Handlers and three full Handlers — Avelo, Torjan, and crotchety old Het. I only spotted one muck, but nearly all the Tenders had come, Lilit included. I tried to count. Twenty of them? At first I thought they were here to make sure Banoh didn't lead a revolt, but then I saw the respect in their eyes.

Banoh hadn't left the Tree by himself.

He spotted me and called me forward. People parted for me. People *smiled* at me. No one said anything about being a self-made hub.

"And here is the man who braved the nagas, who negotiated our peace."

He said a few other things about me, but I had a hard time

listening with my ears burning. With so many looking at me.

But Avi wasn't among them. Neither was Daef.

Banoh announced another meeting in a week, then mentioned the state of my fields. He whispered something to a Handler, who gave instructions to other Handlers and Tenders. The latter navigated the crowds toward my land.

I stood rooted next to Banoh, stunned. When most of the people had cleared away, I found my tongue. "So many from the Tree came with you?"

"Of course. The older Handlers have fought nagas for decades and understand what it means not to fight them. The younger Tenders followed Manoet and Lilit, I think—they trust their wisdom. The older ones feel how effortless it is to draw and filter water now for our island's springs, how easy it is to keep Tree and Turtle healthy. The half-Handlers and mucks are more stubborn, but their government will not last. They do not have the power to enforce it. This"—Banoh gestured at the clearing—"is the capitol of Ceibak."

Eflet had been right.

Lilit interrupted. "Come here, Tenjat. Let's look at that wound."

She dragged me away, sat me on a split-log bench, then rolled up my sleeve. She peered at the wound. "Eflet's done a nice job with this."

"You really left the Tree?" I asked.

"Banoh needs support. I can give him that. I don't have children, but I do have nieces and nephews." She smeared some herb-smelling salve on the wound. It tingled coolly along the cut. "I like the idea of them living on a Turtle with fields that are always rich. I like thinking that if they don't have treasures in Deephell, they needn't feel ashamed."

I peered at her. "You don't feel betrayed? The High Handler was a hub this whole time."

Lilit laughed. "Who do you think found a midwife for Manoet and snuck her into the Tree when the time came? Banoh? Bah!" She shook her head. "He might be good with a javelin, but he hasn't got a drop of medical sense."

Jesso insisted on bringing us a meal. I sat and ate with him, Arja, Banoh, and Manoet. Banoh asked about the neighbors and who else might be receptive to a change in government, then they chatted about the state of farms over the island. With the naga foraging, most farmers would manage a decent harvest despite the season's dreadful start. I nibbled quietly as they talked, soaking in the surreal scene.

Over and over, someone who'd heard about Banoh's departure only recently, or who lived near the fringe of the island, would arrive, and Banoh repeated his speech all over again, often gesturing at me. It wasn't comfortable, but I tried to smile. He even skimmed over my sister's role, preserving her anonymity. People nodded at what he said. A few swore to bring their taxes here and nowhere else. They'd rather support our Tenders and acknowledge Banoh as Island Gunaji's ruler than deal with the Tree.

Banoh briefly mentioned setting up legal committees, like those the Tree had to settle disputes, but made up of both Handlers and farmers. But by then, the sun neared the east and daylight was fading.

As we all stood to leave, a boy about Daef's age jogged up. He wasn't a muck — I wasn't sure whose family he was from. He grinned so wide it had to hurt. "It's done!"

"Good." Banoh jerked his chin at me. "Ujan, take Tenjat to see his fields, if you will."

Done? I hesitated, then followed Ujan. With daylight dimming, I'd need to head to Eflet's afterward — no time for more work today.

I stopped on the edge of my land. Three sturdy huts once again graced the platforms. The weeds had been torn out and the soil cut with turkey droppings. Neat rows of cassava stems stood proudly in the rich ground.

"For our hero!" Ujan wiped his brow. "All of us together can sure work fast, eh?"

I stared at it. "How — all this cassava . . ."

"Oh, everyone donated a few cuttings. Looks pretty good, doesn't it?"

It did. The cassava stems weren't the best, given the hard times the Turtle had just seen, but they still looked hardy. Alive. Banoh had made this—this field—happen in a few words. Perhaps he wasn't High Handler anymore. Perhaps he didn't live in the Tree. But he had the support of so many Handlers and Tenders. He had the love of so many people.

We'd build Ceibak sooner than I thought.

I strode back to Eflet's, half-dazed. The sun cast her hut in brilliant honey-orange. Oddly, Eflet sat on the platform alone, staring at the ground.

Except it wasn't Eflet, I realized as I drew closer. Cropped hair, Handler's clothes.

Avi.

I almost broke into a run, but maybe she'd come for the same reasons Daef did. To check on me, then leave for good.

I walked up, silent, searching for words. Teardrops splattered her hands.

"They expelled me." Avi spoke numbly. She didn't look up. "High Handler Odev cited Jerohn's argument of an unknown, possibly dangerous treasure. But it's because of my father. What he is."

I knelt and took both of her slender, calloused hands in mine. They were cold.

"I—I didn't know where else to turn. I know no one. I thought, maybe . . ."

"Marry me," I begged.

Avi shook her head. "I won't make you a hub."

I echoed Eflet's words. "In a generation, *hub* will be a term of respect."

"Tenjat—"

"Do you think this island is a better place because we no longer fight nagas?"

She jerked her head upright. "Of course!"

"Then why are you afraid to marry?"

Avi's hands tightened into fists around mine. "I've always struggled to be better than my father. Not to make his mistakes."

After seeing what Banoh accomplished today and how well he organized people, aspiring to be like him seemed anything but a mistake. But that wasn't the right thing to tell Avi. I grinned at her. "You have your eye on some other muck, don't you?"

"Tenjat!"

"You know the bargain I made with the nagas. You think it's a good thing. Marriage should be celebrated as keeping our bargain with them—yet you reject me. The only reasonable explanation is that you fancy someone else."

Avi scowled. I couldn't tell if she was trying not to laugh

ring set in the wall, high enough up that I either had to hang by my wrists or stand on tiptoe.

Rydel nodded. "A perfect height for you. Uncomfortable yet?"

I gritted my teeth and ignored him. Behind Rydel, a single gold vein glowed in the wall. Otherwise, the room held none.

"Ah, yes. I thought Eflet might like to watch. Apparently your father knew she could only See near gold. He told Ven as much when we threw them in the same cell. Happily, Ven didn't manage to use that information to warn Eflet. But he did prove most cooperative during his last interrogation."

I tried to shove aside the goad. Ven loved Eflet. He wouldn't betray her. I tugged on the bonds, trying to work myself free.

"Usually I do my work in private, but I'll make an exception for Eflet."

"She won't give herself up. No matter what you do to me."

"We haven't proven that, have we?" Rydel picked up a knife—obsidian—and cradled it. "This is the sharpest substance in the world. Its clean cuts heal nicer than anything else. Perhaps I'll be kind and we'll start with it."

I yanked down on my bonds. It only made my wrists burn.

"How quaint. I'm *sure* you're the first prisoner to try that."

Someone knocked. "Ah. Come in."

A single Handler brought Ven. He didn't even let Ven

or contemplating slugging me. "I don't know how to be a farmer."

"Then I'll teach you. You taught me to be a Handler. It only seems fair."

"I wish you could just be my little muck."

"Times have changed." I stood. "Also, if it's convincing in the least, I have some sizeable fields. I'm probably the richest bachelor on this Turtle."

"Tenjat!" But now she was laughing, smiling.

I kissed her. The tightness in her hands faded.

"Avi, stay with me," I whispered.

She kissed me. I took that as a yes.

Eflet coughed behind us. I jumped. I hadn't heard her step outside her hut. "Aren't you two coming in for dinner? Ven's eager to meet your wife-to-be."

Avi hung her head in shame, but didn't correct Eflet. I squeezed Avi's hand. "I'll bring you a wedding sash. Not red, but yellow—bright as the sun." I nudged Avi's chin upward and smiled at her. Avi managed to smile back. "We have nothing to be ashamed of. We live on Ceibak now."

ACKNOWLEDGMENTS

First, I owe enormous thanks to Stacy Whitman, my editor, for bringing out the best in this story. Without her sharp editorial eye and insightful comments, this would be a very different book.

This novel had a long journey. I revised it on and off again for many years as I developed as a writer. During those years, a variety of people read the manuscript for me; I apologize to anyone I inadvertently forget. Much thanks and appreciation to the Quark Writing Group of yesterdays, as well as Anecka Richins, Eliza Crewe, Kindal and Emily Debenham, Ailsa Lillywhite, Andy Lemmon, Joseph Hutchins, and Michelle Walker. Much thanks to Laura Bingham as well, for kicking me to submit.

Matt Brown first read, critiqued, and approved of this book. Thanks, Matt, for reading so much of what I've written over the years. You're awesome.

To my parents, siblings, cousins, and grandparents—I'm so grateful for your enthusiasm and support. Love you all.

When I started this book, I had no husband or children,

and now find myself with both. They've also been amazing. John, thanks for watching the kids during writing group, smiling at my long-winded rambles, nit-picking my world building, and generally encouraging me when I'm sure everything I've written is horrible. Thanks for being an extraordinary hub.

AUTHOR'S NOTE

Tolkien convinced me that ancient languages are mesmerizing. Accordingly, sometime just before I started high school, I grabbed a copy of *Reading the Maya Glyphs*. I've been fascinated with all things Maya ever since.

In college, I studied archaeology and linguistics. During this time, I excavated in Belize, worked as a research assistant compiling Classic Maya history, received a grant for a paper on Classic Maya interdynastic marriages, and—fun!—learned some flintknapping.

The first time I heard a professor describe the Maya cosmos as a turtle floating on a watery underworld, I knew I wanted to write a story using that element. One turtle became many moving turtle-islands that could compete, war, and trade with each other. The Aztecs saw the world as existing on the back of a crocodile; this also appears in the Maya area, but I stayed with turtles. Crocodiles seemed to promise that someone would get eaten.

Other Maya-inspired tidbits permeate *Drift*. Ceibak comes from two words—*ceiba* and *ahk*. The Maya depict the mythological tree that connects underworld, earth, and sky as a straight-trunked ceiba tree. *Ahk* is the Classic Ch'olti'an word for turtle. Many of the setting details in this novel, including the beautiful turkeys in the jungle, the look of the writing, and the prominence of stone tools, are Maya-inspired.

On the other hand, the numerous floating turtle-islands created a unique environment that resulted in a unique culture—one extremely different than its source of inspiration. *Drift* isn't historical fantasy, or even a fantasy-analog of the Maya. Hoping to avoid confusion, I purposely included divergent details. Most names aren't related to Mayan languages. Gold plays a large role in the plot. I shied slightly away from corn, beans, and squash and turned to cassava. But perhaps that last one isn't much of a deviation; some archaeologists believe that, given the population densities of the Classic Maya, cassava was also an important staple.

Similarly, I looked elsewhere to populate my dangerous oceans. Many cultures use some variation of world turtles. Reading Hindu mythology brought me to the nagas. Stories about nagas abound across many countries—they appear as everything from half-snake, half-human beings, to dragon-like creatures, to a wealthy snake deity of the underworld. Given the breadth of stories about nagas, I felt like including them was the perfect way to nod at other traditions of world turtles.

M. K. HUTCHINS

While studying archaeology, I spent a lot of time looking at, and reading about, grave goods—the stuff people are buried with. Often, these goods are believed to travel with the deceased or bestow some kind of power in the afterlife. Sitting in a class on Early Mesopotamia, something my professor said sparked the idea of an afterlife as active and uncertain as mortality. Why *not* base a magic system around grave goods? I didn't want to write a story about past lives, and so Eflet's secret Ceibak knowledge developed.

Lastly, I bought a book at a sidewalk sale—*Where There is No Doctor* by David Werner. I thought it would be a good reference for writing in settings devoid of modern medicine. Instead, I learned that in many places, children are an economic necessity for the poor, both for the labor they provide and for the care they can give to aging parents. As someone living in the US, I became a little wiser that day. In this novel, I pitted the economic need for children against social stigmas for having them, then let the inherit conflict boil. Jesso emerged as a rich but despised man.

In short, this novel is wholly fantasy, with inspiration from a half-dozen different sources spun together. I love how fantasy novels can show me that the world is an awful, amazing, horrible, wondrous place that I want to keep exploring. A fantasy novel led me to archaeology, and steeping myself in archaeology led to this novel. If reading this has made you curious about the actual Maya, I heartily recommend the books listed below. I should note that this list skews heavily toward the Classic Maya, but Coe's *The Maya* includes some about the modern Maya, as do the extensive footnotes in Christensen's translation of the *Popol Vuh*.

Coe, Michael D. and Mark Van Stone. *Reading the Maya Glyphs*. New York, NY: Thames and Hudson, 2005.

Martin, Simon and Nikolai Grube. *Chronicle of the Maya Kings and Queens*. Second Edition. New York, NY: Thames and Hudson, 2008.

Coe, Michael D. *The Maya*. Eighth Edition. New York, NY: Thames and Hudson, 2011.

Popol Vuh: The Sacred Book of the Maya. Translated from the original Maya text by Allen J. Christenson. New York, NY: O Books, 2003.